LARB

I will not tell a lie. I will not tell a lie.

LIAR

Also by Justine Larbalestier
How to Ditch Your Fairy

I will not tell a lie. I / I will not tell a lie. I will not tell a lie. I will not tell a lie. I will not tell a lie. I will not tell a lie. I will not tell a lie. I will not tell a lie. I will not tell a lie. I will not tell a lie. I will not tell a lie. I will not tell a lie. I will not tell a lie. I will not tell a lie. I will not tell a lie. I will not tell a lie. I will not tell a lie. I will not tell a lie. I will not tell a lie.

LIAR

Justine Larbalestier

BLOOMSBURY

NEW YORK BERLIN LONDON

Published by Bloomsbury U.S.A. Children's Books
175 Fifth Avenue, New York, New York 10010

Library of Congress Cataloging-in-Publication Data
available upon request
ISBN: 978-1-59990-305-7
LCCN: 2009012581

First U.S. Edition 2009
Designed by Danielle Delaney
Typeset by Westchester Book Composition
Printed in the U.S.A. by Quebecor World Fairfield
2 4 6 8 10 9 7 5 3 1

All papers used by Bloomsbury U.S.A. are natural, recyclable products
made from wood grown in well-managed forests. The manufacturing processes
conform to the environmental regulations of the country of origin.

For my father, John Bern

not tell a lie. I will not tell a lie. I will not tell a lie. I will not tell a lie. I
ll a lie. I will not tell a lie. I will not tell a lie. I will not tell a lie. I will
lie. I will not tell a lie. I will not tell a lie. I will not tell a lie. I will not
I will not tell a lie. I will not tell a lie. I will not tell a lie. I will not tell a
not tell a lie. I will not tell a lie. I will not tell a lie. I will not tell a lie. I
ll a lie. I will not tell a lie. I will not tell a lie. I will not tell a lie. I will
lie. I I will not tell a lie. I will not tell a lie. I will not tell a lie. I will not
I will not tell a lie. I will not tell a lie. I will not tell a lie. I will not tell a
not tell a lie. I will not tell a lie. I will not tell a lie. I will not tell a lie. I
l a lie. I will not tell a lie. I will not tell a lie. I will not tell a lie. I will
lie. I will not tell a lie. I will not tell a lie. I will not tell a lie. I will not
I will not tell a lie. I will not tell a lie. I will not tell a lie. I will not tell a
not tell a lie. I will not tell a lie. I will not tell a lie. I will not tell a lie. I

LIAR

lie. I will not tell a lie. I will not tell a lie. I will not
I will not tell a lie. I will not tell a lie. I will not tell
not tell a lie. I will not tell a lie. I will not tell
a lie. I will not tell a lie. I will not tell a
lie. I will not tell a lie. I will not tell a
I will not tell a lie. I will not tell a
not tell a lie. I will not tell a lie
a lie. I will not tell a lie. I
lie. I will not tell a lie.
I will not tell a lie.
not tell a lie. I will
a lie. I will not
lie. I will not
I will not
ot t

PART ONE
Telling the Truth

I will not tell a lie. I will not to

PART ONE

PROMISE

I was born with a light covering of fur.

After three days it had all fallen off, but the damage was done. My mother stopped trusting my father because it was a family condition he had not told her about. One of many omissions and lies.

My father is a liar and so am I.

But I'm going to stop. I *have* to stop.

I will tell you my story and I will tell it straight. No lies, no omissions.

That's my promise.

This time I truly mean it.

———

AFTER

When Zach isn't in school Tuesday morning I am worried. He said he'd call me Monday night. But didn't. Friday night was the last time I saw him. That isn't usual.

Zachary Rubin is my boyfriend. He isn't the best boyfriend in the world, but he usually does what he says he will.

If he was going to skip school he'd have taken me with him. We could've gone running in the park. Or ridden around on the subway all day laughing at the crazies, which is mostly everyone.

Once we walked from the Staten Island Ferry all the way up to Inwood, right next to the big hospital and the bridge that leads to the Bronx. It took us all day. We'd get sidetracked, checking things out, looking around. Enjoying the novelty of walking instead of running.

Broadway was our path north through the island. Zach said it used to be an Indian trail, which made it the oldest street in Manhattan. That's why it twists and turns, sometimes on the diagonal, sometimes straight like an avenue.

Me and Zach had an argument about what the water under the bridge to the Bronx was called. Was it the Hudson or the East River? Or did they meet in the middle under the bridge? Whatever it was called, the water was gray brown and nasty-looking. So it could've been either one.

That was our best day together.

I hope Zach isn't doing anything that cool without me. I'll kill him if he is.

I eat lunch on my own. A cold steak sandwich. The bread is gray and wet, soggy with meat juice. I eat the steak and throw the rest away.

In class I stare at the window, watch the reflection of my classmates superimposed in mottled glass over gray steel bars. I think about what Zach looks like when he smiles at me.

———

AFTER

The second day Zach isn't at school, I wear a mask. I keep it on for three days. I forge a note from my dad to say I have a gruesome rash and the doctor told me to keep it covered. I carry the note with me from class to class. They all buy it.

My dad brought the mask back from Venice. It's black leather painted with silver and unfurls at each corner like a fern. The silver is real.

Under it, my skin itches.

They tell us Zach is dead during third period on Thursday.

Principal Paul Jones comes into our classroom. He

isn't smiling. There are murmurs. I hear Zach's name. I look away.

"I have bad news," the principal says unnecessarily. I can smell the bad news all over him.

Now we all look at him. Everyone is quiet. His eyes are slightly red. I wonder if he is going to all the classes or just us seniors. Surely we would be first. Zach is a senior.

I can hear the minute hand of the clock over the whiteboard. It doesn't tick, it clicks. *Click, click, click, click.* No ticks. No tocks.

There is a fly in the room. The fan slices through the air. A murky sliver of sunlight cuts across the front of the classroom right where the principal is standing. It makes visible the dust in the air, the lines around his eyes, across his forehead, at the corners of his mouth.

Sarah Washington shifts in her chair and its legs squeak painfully loud across the wooden floor. I turn, stare at her. Everyone else does, too. She looks away.

"Zachary Rubin is no longer missing. His body has been found." Principal Paul's lips move into something between a grimace and a snarl.

A sound moves around the classroom. It takes me a moment to realize that half the girls are crying. A few of the boys, too. Sarah Washington is rocking back and forth, her eyes enormous.

Mine are dry. I take off the mask.

BEFORE

The first two days of my freshman year I was a boy.

It started in the first class of my first day of high school. English. The teacher, Indira Gupta, reprimanded me for not paying attention. She called me Mr. Wilkins. No one calls anyone Mr. or Ms. or anything like that at our school. Gupta was pissed. I stopped staring out the window, turned to look at her, wondering if there was another Wilkins in the room.

"Yes, you, Mr. Micah Wilkins. When I am talking I expect your full and undivided attention. To me, not to the traffic outside."

No one giggled or said, "She's a girl."

I'd been mistaken for a boy before. Not often, but enough that I wasn't completely surprised. I have nappy hair. I wear it natural and short, cut close to my scalp. That way I don't have to bother with relaxing or straightening or combing it out. My chest is flat and my hips narrow. I don't wear makeup or jewelry. None of them—neither students nor teachers—had ever seen me before.

"Is that clear?" Gupta said, still glaring at me.

I nodded, and mumbled in as low a voice as I could, "Yes, ma'am." They were the first words I spoke at my new school. This time I wanted to keep a low profile, be invisible, not be the one everyone pointed at when I walked along the corridor: "See that one? That's Micah. She's a liar. No, seriously, she lies about *everything*." I'd never lied about *everything*. Just about my parents (Somali pirates, professional gamblers, drug dealers, spies), where I was from (Liechtenstein, Aruba, Australia, Zimbabwe), what I'd done (grifted, won bravery medals, been kidnapped). Stuff like that.

I'd never lied about what I was before.

Why not be a boy? A quiet sullen boy is hardly weird at all. A boy who runs, doesn't shop, isn't interested in clothes or shows on TV. A boy like that is normal. What could be more invisible than a normal boy?

I would be a better boy than I'd ever been a girl.

At lunch I sat at the same table as three boys I'd seen in class: Tayshawn Williams, Will Daniels, and Zachary Rubin. I'd love to say that one look at Zach and I knew but that would be a lie and I'm not doing that anymore. Remember? He was just another guy, an olive-skinned white boy, looking pale and weedy compared to Tayshawn, whose skin is darker than my dad's.

They nodded. I nodded. They already knew each other. Their conversation was littered with names they all knew, places, teams.

I ate my meatballs and tomato sauce and decided that after school I'd run all the way to Central Park. I'd keep my sweatshirt on. It was baggy.

"You play ball?" Tayshawn asked me.

I nodded because it was safer than asking which kind. Boys always knew stuff like that.

"We got a pickup going after," he said.

I grunted as boyishly as I could. It came out lower than I'd expected, like a wolf had moved into my throat.

"You in?" Zach asked, punching me lightly on the shoulder.

"Sure," I said. "Where?"

"There." He jerked his thumb in the direction of the park next to the school. The one with a gravel basketball court and a stunted baseball diamond, and a merry-go-round too close to be much use when a game was in progress. I'd run past it dozens of times. There was pretty much always a game going on.

The bell rang. Tayshawn stood up and slapped my back. "See you later."

I grinned at how easy it was.

Being a boy was fast becoming my favorite lie.

———

SCHOOL HISTORY

All the white kids sit together. All the white kids with money, I mean.

Our high school is small and progressive and costs money. Not expensive like the uptown schools, but it's not free. Except for the scholarship kids who mostly aren't white. They're here tuition free, only having to pay for their books. They mostly don't go on field trips.

Most of the white kids don't believe in God; most of us black kids do.

I'm undecided, stuck somewhere in between, same way I am with everything: half black, half white; half girl, half boy; coasting on half a scholarship.

I'm half of everything.

———

AFTER

We are all sent to counseling. There are individual sessions and group ones. The group session is first. It's a nightmare.

Jill Wang (yes, really) makes us move the desks and arrange the chairs in a large circle. I've been forced to see Wang before. She is achingly sincere. She believes most everything you tell her. Even my lies.

We sit in the chairs with no desks to hide behind. I wish I were in the library studying.

Brandon Duncan stares at the boobs I barely have.

Sarah Washington turns to look at me, too. Her gaze rests somewhere below my eyes, but not so low as

Brandon's. "Why do you lie all the time?" she asks softly.

"Why do you?" I say, though I've never known her to lie. I say it quiet as her, staring right back, fierce as I can, pushing my gaze through the pores of her dark skin. I imagine I can feel the blood moving in her veins, the sound of breath in her lungs, the movement of the synapses in her brain. She is all buzzes and clicks. "Everyone lies."

"We're here to talk about what's happened, about how we feel," the counselor says. "Is there anything you want to share about—"

"Don't say his name!" Sarah shouts.

Now everyone is staring at her. Her heart pumps faster, pushing the blood through her veins.

"I won't," Jill Wang says. "Not if you don't want me to."

Counselors always say stuff like that. I've seen *lots* of counselors. Psychologists, shrinks, therapists. They're all the same. They're supposed to stop me lying, yet they believe everything I tell them.

"We don't," Sarah mumbles.

"I haven't met most of you before. Tell me about yourselves. Let's go around the circle. Say the first word you can think of to describe yourself." Jill Wang nods at me.

"Fierce," I say.

Sarah shivers.

"Cool," Brandon says. Several people laugh.

"Hot," Tayshawn says. He's the most popular guy in school so there's laughter. But I'm pretty sure he doesn't mean it that way. Not sexy hot. More like prickly hot. Like he needs to loosen his collar. Mine itches at me. The heat is up too high. The steam pipes clank and groan, shouting their own words.

Each student says a word. None of them is right.

The door is behind me, less than six feet away. I imagine vaulting out of the circle, over Sarah in her chair, glaring at her own knees. I can run away.

I will run away.

"Gray," Sarah says, closing the circle of words. A tear eases down her cheek to match it, clings to her chin for less than a second before falling onto the wool cloth of her pants and disappearing.

"Does anyone want to talk about . . ." Jill pauses, swallowing Zach's name. "I hear he was very popular."

"You should ask Micah," Brandon says. "She was his girlfriend."

There's laughter. They are all staring at me now, everyone except Sarah. Her head is bowed further, her breaths shallow as she tries to stop crying. She is close to losing control. I hope she will.

"Very funny," Tayshawn says, glaring at Brandon. I can see he doesn't believe it. Tayshawn is Zach's best friend. Has been since the third grade.

I want to kill Brandon. I know why he told them: to

make trouble. That's what Brandon does. But how did he know?

Everyone is still staring. I hold my chin high and stare back at them. When people look at me my skin crawls. But I never let them see it.

"Do you want to say something, Micah?" Jill Wang asks.

"No," I say.

"She wasn't his girlfriend," Sarah says. "I was."

Tayshawn and Chantal and others agree with her.

"You were his at-school girlfriend," Brandon tells Sarah. "Micah was for after hours."

Sarah goes back to her crying. Tayshawn looks like he might kill Brandon. I'd be happy to help.

Jill Wang looks from Brandon to Sarah to me. I can see her weighing what to say.

"I have a question," Alejandro says.

She nods for him to continue.

"Everyone's talking about grieving and all that shit— sorry, stuff. Whatever. But no one's saying what happened to him. We keep hearing rumors and there are cops and that. But no one's saying what's up. Not really. So is the rumor true? Was he murdered?"

The counselor spreads her hands wide, makes eye contact with all of us, to reassure us that what she is about to say is true. "I know as much as you do. The police are investigating to determine whether a crime has taken place."

Alejandro doesn't say anything else. But he doesn't look satisfied. No one does.

———

AFTER

When the counseling session ends I go into one of the stalls in the bathroom, lock the door, lower the lid, and sit down, thoughts beating loud in my head, drowning the noise of toilets flushing, faucets turning on and off, air dryers louder than a generator, and, more distantly, the sound of steam in the pipes, traffic. I hold my head with my hands to keep it from exploding. My thoughts are all Zach—all about him being dead. No air in his lungs, no blood in his veins.

Or would it still be there? But not moving? Stale air, congealed blood.

Zach is dead.

I will never see him again. Never hear his voice. Never run with him. Never kiss him.

He is gone.

"I know you're in there," Sarah Washington calls, knocking on the stall door. "I saw you come in."

"What do you want?"

"Is it true?" she calls.

I open the door. Sarah steps back from me, her eyes wide—she's afraid of me, I realize—and accidentally sets off one of the dryers. She startles. I go to the sink, squeeze soap out of metal onto my palms, put my hands under the tap and, when no water appears, go to the next sink. This time the sensor works. I wash my hands thoroughly. Under fingernails, between fingers, backs of my hands, wrists. Then rinse until each sud is gone and the slimy feel of soap erased.

Above the sink are windows. Opaque with wire set into the glass, nailed shut, with metal bars on the other side, facing the street. My hands hover over the sink dripping.

"You should be in class," Sarah says.

"So should you."

"Study period. So *is* it true?" She's come to a rest by the door, leaning against it, staring at me. The question is eating at her. She's much prettier than I am. Why would Zach spend time with me?

"Is what true?" I ask. Why is she asking *me* about the truth? She knows I'm a liar. They all do.

"Were you and him . . . ?" She stops, takes a few steps toward me and then away.

"Why don't you ask Brandon?" I ask. "He seems to know everything. Why ask me?"

"Because," she begins, takes another step, and then pauses. "How does Brandon know about you and him? How would Brandon know and me not? Zach was my boyfriend. He told me everything," she says, but her voice falters. No one tells anyone everything.

I stick my hands under the nearest dryer, wincing at the noise and hot air. Back, front, wrists, palms. It's better than listening to Sarah.

"So is it true?" she asks, raising her voice to compete with the roar.

"Why would I tell you?" I say softly. There's no moisture left on my hands, they are starting to roast, but I keep turning them back and forth.

"He was *my* boyfriend," she says. "Everyone knew that. Why would Brandon say that *you* were?"

"Why don't you ask him?"

She shakes her head. "I did. It didn't help. He's still dead." She slumps, wavering between me and the door, her eyes heavy with tears. I wonder how there can be any water left in her. "Brandon loves to make trouble."

I step away from the dryer, ignore the stinging of my hands. "True," I say.

"After-hours girlfriend?" she says, echoing Brandon's tone of voice. "I never even saw him look at you. Not once."

"There you go then."

"He didn't come to school sometimes. And you— you're always skipping class, skipping whole days. Is that where he went? Was he with you?"

"No," I say. "He wasn't my boyfriend."

"I don't believe you. You never tell the truth."

"Then why ask?"

She steps away, leans against the wall again. As though standing is too hard, too much effort. She cries harder. "I want to know what happened to him. His parents won't even let me see his body. How do I know he's dead if they won't let me see?"

I can't imagine her wanting to see a dead body. She won't even cut up rats in biology. "Well, I heard he was shot," I say, even though I haven't heard any such thing. "That can't look good." I try to imagine. But I can only see the whole Zach. Smiling at me, laughing.

"I saw my grandma dead," Sarah says. "She was lying in a coffin, all bundled in white silky fabric. Her hands around this big bunch of white lilies. Open casket, they call it. All I could think of was how much she hated flowers. Cut ones, I mean. Always said they were pointless and a waste. 'What are they gonna do?' she'd ask. 'Rot. That's what. Best leave 'em growing.' That's what happens when you die—you rot."

Sarah doesn't bother to wipe away her tears. "I can't believe he's dead. Everyone liked him. Who would kill him? Who would hate him that much? Do you know?"

I don't, but I want to know. I never saw Zach hurt anyone. Not on purpose. He preferred things to slide by, for everyone to be easy. He didn't like to argue or fight or even mildly disagree. He'd shrug and say, "Sure. Whatever." It wasn't that he was a pushover. He mostly got things to bend his way, but without any obvious effort.

His kisses were sure and easy, too. I put my hand to my mouth, remembering what he tasted like.

"You *were* with him," Sarah says, staring at my mouth. "Weren't you?"

AFTER

The day I find out Zach is dead is the longest day of my life. School has always sucked. Now it's hell.

Everyone is staring at me. Not just Sarah, not just everyone from the counseling session, but every student in the entire school, even the freshmen, the teachers, the administrative staff, the janitors.

It's much worse than when they found out I wasn't really a boy.

Zach is dead.

I cannot make sense of that. How can he be dead? I saw him Friday night. We climbed a tree in Central Park. We kissed. We ran. Principal Paul must have it wrong.

I wish everyone would stop looking at me. They think they know something about me and Zach, that we were—whatever it is that we were—that somehow they have something on me.

They don't.

I keep my head down. Try to block my ears to the

"slut" coughs. Try to focus on my remaining classes. Distract myself studying in the library. Try not to think about Zach. Try not to think about anything other than my studies.

Brandon mouths a word at me as the final bell rings.

Killer.

At least I think that's what it is.

I push my way out of class, down the corridor, down the front steps, quick as I can with backpack slung over shoulder, hands gripping the straps tight, away from school, from people I know. When I turn the corner onto West Broadway I take off.

I run all the way to Central Park and once I get there I run harder and faster, lifting knees high, pumping arms hard. I run distance at a sprint. I pass even the fastest joggers. No one is as fast and fevered as me. I'm going to run all the poison and whispers and grief out of my veins.

I don't go home until I'm run into the ground and taking another step would kill me.

FAMILY HISTORY

You probably think I'm weird with the mask and the sort-of-but-not-really boyfriend who's dead and all the lies.

Past lies, I mean. I haven't lied to you and I won't. Saying that Zach was my boyfriend when he was mostly Sarah's is not a lie. He *was* mine. Like Brandon said— after hours.

You want to know why I used to lie?

Let me tell you about my family:

My parents are still together. Living in the same house. When they aren't arguing, they're doting. I can never decide which is worse.

My dad's name is Isaiah Wilkins. He's black like me. My mom is Maude Bourgault, or was, she's Maude Wilkins now. She's white. Though Dad doesn't believe it. Dad can see the black in anyone even when it isn't there. He tells the world the way he wishes, not the way it is. Dad says Mom's hair is near as nappy as his own and doubts that her full lips came from anywhere white. Mom laughs. How would she know? She's adopted and hated her family. She ran away.

I've never met my mother's family. Just Dad's.

Dad's dad was black, but his mom is white. Grandmother's our whole family. She and Great-Aunt Dorothy, and, when he was alive, Great-Uncle Hilliard. The oldest ones left are Grandmother and Great-Aunt. I call them the Greats.

To say the Wilkins are reclusive would be to understate it. They take keeping to your own a long way past crazy. They stay on their farm. All two hundred acres of it. They are self-sufficient. They don't understand why everyone doesn't do the same thing. Grandmother has never been down to the city.

The Wilkins came to New York State more than a century ago: all the way from Poland or Russia or the Ukraine. One of those. They're from the Carpathian Mountains. Where they lived for generations, going into town as seldom as possible, living far from other families. Mountain people: long-lived, rail-thin, cranky, and taciturn.

They brought that mountain chill all the way to America, to upstate New York, where they live and breed, getting older and crankier and skinnier.

That's my family. All of them *much* weirder than me.

————

BEFORE

At the end of the second day of my freshman year, Sarah Washington found me out.

Nothing dramatic. I didn't slip up and go into the girls' room.

I laughed. Sarah heard me.

"You're not a boy," she said.

We were in the hall. Brandon Duncan slipped—I am

not making this up—on a banana peel. I laughed. Lots of people laughed. But Sarah was walking past me. She heard me laugh, she turned.

"You're not a boy," she said again.

"Huh?" I repeated, continuing toward the exit.

"Boys don't laugh like that," she said, walking beside me, her voice rising.

"He what?" Tayshawn said, sliding across to join us, standing in front of me, blocking my escape. "We played hoops yesterday. He—" He was staring at me now, moving in close. I was forced toward the wall. "She?—shoots like a boy. You are a girl, aren't you? Look at her cheeks. No fluff."

"I'm only fourteen," I squeaked, my voice betraying me.

Now Lucy O'Hara was staring. Will Daniels, too. And Zach. All of them crowded around me.

"You're a girl," Sarah said. "Admit it."

"I'm a boy," I declared, wanting to push through them, to run.

"Let's pull off her clothes," Will said, laughing. "Know for sure that way."

I hugged my schoolbag to my chest.

"Girl!" Tayshawn shouted. "Boy would've guarded his nuts. Hah! You fooled us good, Micah." He nudged Will. "A girl beat you, man. A girl!"

Will looked down, saying nothing, and kicked his shoes into the floor.

I fought an urge to cry. I'd loved playing hoops with them. Tayshawn and Zach were so good. Especially Zach. When you play with the boys and they know you're a girl they either won't pass to you or treat you as if you're too fragile to breathe or they'll try to beat you down. Whatever way it goes it sucks. Playing as a guy had been so great. They'd passed to me, guarded me, blocked my shots, bodychecked me so hard my teeth rattled. But now Will wouldn't look at me. Zach had already gone.

"Freak," Lucy said, walking away. Sarah stared at me a second longer before walking after her.

Then there was me, alone, leaning against the wall, bag still clutched tight, as more and more students flooded by. I waited till they were all gone. Looking back, I saw the banana peel, trampled, broken into bits, but still identifiably a banana peel.

AFTER

I come into the apartment fast as I can, zooming through the kitchen without glancing at Dad, who says hi, looking up at me from his work on the kitchen table.

I lock myself in my room. Collapse on the bed. My eyes are sharp and burning. Without tears.

Slut.

Killer.

Zach is dead.

Through the wall I can hear the *thud thud thud* of the stupid girl next door's music. There's five of them in there. College students, but the loud-music one never seems to go to classes. Never seems to do anything but stay in the apartment and deafen us.

I wish she was dead and Zach was alive.

I hate music. It hurts my ears, my brain. Even the membranes in my nose. Any music. All music. I can't distinguish between hip-hop and hillbilly ramblings, between symphonies and traffic noise. All of it hurts.

The best thing about going up to the Greats is that there is no music there. No noises to make me grind my teeth. Only wind through trees. Foxes burrowing. Deer running. Ice cracking. Mockingbirds singing their never-repeated three-note sequences, each note clear as rainwater. Wood thrushes trilling.

Beautiful sounds.

Zach loved music. He couldn't understand my hate.

Zach is dead.

I wish I had my dad's noise-reduction headphones. He wears them on planes. I like to sneak them from his room, put them on, plugged into nothing, dulling the thud through the walls. If I could, I'd wear them all the time, but I can't afford a set of my own. I'll ask for my birthday or Christmas or something. Not that my parents have much money. The only reason Dad has the headphones is because he had to review them for a magazine and never gave them back.

He gets many things that way.

Someone knocks at the door. Dad probably. Mom's coat wasn't hanging by the door.

"Micah," Dad calls. "Micah! Are you alright?"

I have no idea how to answer him.

Zach is dead.

———

AFTER

The Greats are keener than ever for me to come up to the farm. Dad says they're worried. They think I need fresh air. They want me to be able to run free. I'm wishing Mom and Dad didn't know about Zach.

Ever since Zach went missing the Greats have been calling. This, despite them not even having a phone. They have to ride all the way to the gas station and call from there. Grandmother hates phones. She says they make her ears itch.

It used to be she would only talk to Dad and keep it as short as possible. Barking calls, Dad said. Now she only wants to talk to me.

"Micah?" she says loudly. Then she starts telling me what I should do. Go upstate and spend time with my family. I don't point out that I'm already with my family. Mom and Dad are right here.

She says coming upstate, staying on the farm, running in the forest is the best cure for a broken heart.

I tell her I don't have a broken heart. It's still beating, the blood still moves around my body; it only aches when I remember to breathe.

Grandmother isn't listening. "A broken heart can make you pine away," she says. "Till there's hardly anything left to bury."

I swallow. Zach will be buried. I can't imagine him in a box, six feet under.

"You'll be much happier up here, Micah," she said. "The forest is good for you." I go into my room with the phone against my ear and shut the door.

"I've got Central Park," I say, holding the phone lightly, too tightly. I'm willing it to fly out of my hands. Central Park is where Zach and me truly met. It's our place.

"Too tame for you, my love."

I hate it when she calls me that. It doesn't suit her tongue. My grandmother is not very loving. She orders, she doesn't cajole. Besides, Zach was not at all tame. Neither is Central Park.

"There's so much more for you to learn up here. We miss you, Micah."

I didn't say anything. I never miss them. I miss Zach.

"I wish your uncle Hilliard was still with us. He'd talk sense into you."

The Hilliard I remember was taciturn and gruff. He didn't spend time talking sense into anyone.

"Your aunt wants to talk to you now," she says. I listen to the phone going scratchy. Muffled voices. I put my nose to Zach's sweater, breathe him in. His scent is fading.

"Micah?" Great-Aunt Dorothy shouts at the phone. "That you?"

"Yes."

"We want you to come up. Don't have to stay. Just a week or two. Get away from all the trouble."

"I'm not in any trouble," I say, kicking my desk. The metal clangs.

"Well, I suppose not. But your father thinks you need time away. Death isn't easy. Especially not when you're young."

I sigh, making sure she can hear it. "Then why would it be any easier upstate?"

Zach's still dead no matter where I am.

"You know it is, Micah. We're closer to nature up here. Nature fixes everything." Great-Aunt Dorothy always says that.

Nature also breaks things into a million pieces. Storms destroy, winds erode, and everything rots.

"I have school."

"You're young—that's not so important. Besides, we can help you study if that's what you want."

I'm a senior! My whole future is being decided. How will two high school dropouts help me study? They're crazy if they think I'm going to go live with them. How will they help me prepare for college? They call jeans "dungarees." They don't know anything.

They talk as if I'm not going to college. They don't think I'm smart enough.

I know I am. My favorite teacher, Yayeko Shoji, says so.

"You're much happier up here, Micah."

They always say that, too. But it's not true. They think I am made of country, with forest in my veins. But I'm a city girl: sewers, rats, subways—that's what's in my veins.

SCHOOL HISTORY

Our school is progressive. We call our teachers by their first names. No mister or missus or miz. They're Indira and Yayeko and Lisa. The emphasis is on ideas and learning and encouraging the students to reach "their full potential." Sports are not a big thing. There are teams, but no specialist coaches, just teachers taking it on 'cause they love basketball or football or softball.

Not all our classes have normal names.

We're not channeled toward the SATs.

But we do get into good colleges. Even if we don't test well. They like our "depth and breadth."

And our integration.

We're independent thinkers. We volunteer. We don't discriminate. We recycle and care and argue about politics.

In class, anyway.

Out of class it's the same as any other school. Except with money. And toilets that work and heating that doesn't shut off. We have all the textbooks we need. Computers, too. Bars on every window to keep the badness out.

Real-life forensic scientists come in to talk to our biology class. Real-life writers come to talk to us in English.

Our school looks after us.

———

BEFORE

The first and second week of my freshman year were bad. Really bad. After Sarah Washington and the banana peel, everyone knew who I was: the girl who pretended to be a boy.

So much for being invisible.

I was called into Principal Paul's office and forced to explain.

"My English teacher thought I was a boy," I said. "I thought it would be funny to go along with it."

He said it most decidedly wasn't. Then lectured me about the danger of lies and erosion of trust and blah, blah, blah. I tuned him out, promised to be good, and wrote an essay on Why Lying Is Bad.

"So why's your name Micah then?" Tayshawn asked me. He was the only one who agreed that me pretending to be a boy was funny. He even asked me to play ball with him again. Will was less happy. Zach ignored me. I didn't go. Though I played H-O-R-S-E with Tayshawn a couple of times.

"It's a girl's name, too," I told him. "Just not as often."

"It's as if your parents knew you was going to look like a boy."

"Well." I paused, feeling the rush I always get when I begin to spin out a lie. "You can't tell anyone, okay?"

Tayshawn nodded, bracing himself.

"When I was born they didn't know if I was a girl or a boy."

Tayshawn looked confused. "How'd you mean?"

"They couldn't tell what I was. I was born a hermaphrodite."

"A what?"

"Half boy and half girl. You can look it up."

"No way." His eyes glided down my body, looking for evidence.

I nodded solemnly, figuring out how to play it. "I was a weird-looking baby." (Which is true. I like to thread my lies with truth.) "My parents totally freaked." (Also true.) "You won't tell anyone, right? You promised." In my experience those words are guaranteed to spread what you've said far and wide. I liked the idea of being a hermaphrodite.

"Not anyone. You're safe."

Tayshawn never told a soul. I know because days later there still wasn't a whisper about it. Turned out that he's good that way. Trustworthy.

I figure the rumor finally spread all over school because I told Lucy when she was hassling me in the locker room. I went for the sympathy card: "You keep calling me a freak. Well, guess what? I am!"

She looked more grossed out than sympathetic.

Or it could have been Brandon Duncan, who overheard me telling Chantal, who wanted to know how I managed to fool everyone on account of she wants to be an actress and thought it would be useful to know. She had me show her how to walk like a boy. I taught her how to spit, too.

Or maybe it was all three of them. Most likely. Hardly anyone's as tight-lipped as Tayshawn.

However it spread, it reached Principal Paul, who

contacted my parents, who told him it wasn't true, and there I was in his office again, explaining how I had no idea how the rumor got started and was hurt and upset that anyone would say anything so mean about me. "I'm a girl. Why would I want anyone to think I was some kind of a freak?"

Because I wanted them to pay attention to me.

Something like that.

Mostly it's the joy of convincing people that something that ain't so, is. It's hard to explain. But like I said at the beginning, I've quit the lying game now.

But that's now, back then it was:

"Why did you want everyone to think you were a boy, Micah Wilkins?" Principal Paul looked at me without blinking. I returned the favor.

"You don't know?" He sounded unsurprised. "Perhaps you will find out when you visit the school counselor."

I didn't let him see how much I hated that idea. There have been way too many counselors and shrinks and psychologists in my life. I mean, I know lying is bad, that's why I'm giving it up, but I've never understood why I had to see shrinks about it.

"You've been at this school less than two weeks, Micah Wilkins, and already you have a reputation for telling falsehoods and making mischief. My eye is on you."

I didn't ask him how that affected him seeing anything else.

My second essay for the principal was on the virtues of honesty. I ran out of things to say on the first page.

———

AFTER

At school the word "murder" has seeped into every-thing. We look at each other differently. People stare at me. At Sarah. At Tayshawn. At Brandon. At all the guys on Zach's team. At anyone who has ever hated, or loved, or hung out with him.

We are all made of broken glass. The school grinds along on grief and anger.

I track Brandon down.

He is under the bleachers in the park, smoking. I creep up quiet and stealthy like the Greats taught me.

"Brandon," I say softly in his ear.

"Jesus fucking Christ!" Brandon screams, startling and dropping his cigarette. "What'd you do that for?" he asks, stepping away from me and scrabbling for his ciga-rette. He picks it up and takes a long drag. "Freak."

"I'm not the one under bleachers smoking a cigarette that just fell in a pile of dog shit." Brandon spits the ciga-rette out and looks down at where there isn't any dog shit. I laugh.

"Bitch," he says.

"Why'd you say that about me and him?" I ask, taking a step toward him. He backs away. "It's not true," I say, firm as I can.

He laughs this time. "Sure it is. I saw you and Zach together."

"There was nothing to see."

"Right," he says. "So I hallucinated you running together in Central Park. Him picking you up and swinging you around and then"—Brandon pauses to lean toward me and lick his lips as loudly and grossly as he can—"definitely lots of tongue action."

Now it's me backing away. "Wasn't me," I say, strong as before, but he knows I am lying and I know that he knows.

"Sure it was," he says. "There's no other girl on the planet that looks as much like a boy as you. Maybe Zach was secretly a fag."

"You're a dick, Brandon."

"Whatever." He pulls a pack of cigarettes and a lighter from his pocket, lights one, and deliberately blows the smoke at my face. "Need a new part-time boyfriend, do you? Now the old one's dead. I could volunteer. I don't mind slumming."

"Fuck you," I say, stalking off, annoyed at how defeated I feel.

AFTER

The only teacher who's okay is my biology teacher. Yayeko Shoji doesn't coat things in sugar. She explains what meat is and how it works. How we are all meat. How meat gets into the vegetables we eat. She doesn't modify her words for the vegetarians in the room.

Meat is cells.

Meat is flesh.

Meat is muscle.

Meat is 5 percent fat.

Meat is 20 percent protein.

Meat is 75 percent water.

Zach was meat. Meat decays.

"Yayeko," I ask, "how long before a body begins to rot?"

I can hear the sudden intake of air.

"Gross, Micah," Brandon says.

"Do you have to answer that?" Sarah asks, her eyes filling with water again.

"Decay, decomposition, are natural processes," Yayeko explains. "The same basic things happen when anything dies: a flower, an ant, a dog, a human, anything."

"But do we have to talk about it *now*?" Sarah asks, speaking more firmly than I've ever heard her before. Especially to a teacher.

Now is especially when I want to know. Now, with Zach in the morgue.

"I understand that you're all upset, but for some people understanding the processes involved can help with grief," Yayeko says, and I find myself nodding. I am desperate to understand. "We are all of us subject to the same laws of nature."

"And of God," Sarah says.

"The first thing that happens after death," Yayeko says, "is that blood and oxygen stop flowing through the body. Gravity causes the body's blood to drain from capillaries in the upper parts and to pool in the lower blood vessels. So that parts of the body seem pale—those upper surfaces—and parts seem dark."

"What if you're already pale?" Tayshawn wants to know. The class laughs but I'm not sure he meant to be funny.

"Pale is a relative term, Tayshawn," Yayeko says. "The lower parts of your body become darker than the upper parts."

"What do you mean upper part, then?" he continues. "Like your head?"

"It depends on how the body is positioned. If it's lying supine—on its back—then the blood pools there. In the heels and calves and buttocks, the back, the back of the neck, the head. The face will be pale."

Tayshawn nods to show he understands now. I wonder how they found Zach. Which parts of him were pale, which dark?

"Next, the cells cease aerobic respiration so they can't

maintain normal muscle biochemistry. Which means what?"

Only two hands go up. Mine and Lucy O'Hara's.

"Lucy?"

"They stop making energy."

"Out of what?"

"Glucose," Lucy says. "Oxygen."

"Yes." Yayeko continues, "And when that stops, calcium ions leak into muscle cells, preventing muscle relaxation, which causes rigor mortis."

"When the body goes all hard?" Tayshawn asks. There are more giggles, but he ignores them.

"Yes," Yayeko says. "The cells begin to die and can't fight off the bacteria, which causes the body to decompose and the muscles to become soft again. As soon as the body dies, flies are attracted to it. They start to lay eggs in open wounds and orifices. The eggs turn into maggots—"

"No," Sarah says, holding her hand over her mouth and running from the room. Two girls get up and follow her. I'm also imagining maggots eating Zach. Maggots in his eyes, maggots between his toes, maggots all over him. Wriggling, feeding, tearing into his body. I have to concentrate to keep from joining the other girls in the bathroom.

On the way out of class Brandon hisses at me. "You're not normal," he says.

Tell me something I don't know.

AFTER

"I bet you killed him," Brandon says on the way out of biology. "You probably got your dad to make him disappear."

"I heard it was you," I tell him. "That you read somewhere if you kill and eat the brains of people who are better than you then you get to be like them."

"That makes *you* safe," Brandon says. "And everyone else in this school."

I laugh and almost tell him touché. He walks away. I follow. "How come you're always hissing at me on the way in and out of class?"

"Are you kidding? I can't have anyone see me voluntarily talking to a murdering freak like you. I wish you'd go back to wearing that mask. That way none of us has to see your freaky face."

"Shut up, Brandon, or I'll have my dad take care of you." Briefly I imagine what it would be like to have such a dad. Ready at a moment to kill all my enemies.

Brandon's eyes flick at me as if he's trying to assess whether what I said could be true, but doesn't want to contaminate his eyeballs by actually looking at me. "Like your dad took care of Zach?"

I want to hurt Brandon. Slap his face, kick his nuts, spit in his eyes. "You'll never be as good as him. No matter how hard you try." It's true, but that doesn't make it sound any less lame.

Brandon laughs and moves away from me as quick as he can. He knows he's won.

———

HISTORY OF ME

Sometimes I am still for hours.

It's like I'm waiting. Watching. Biding my time. When I'm ready, I'll leap.

Sometimes my whole life feels like that.

I never said that to Zach but I think he would have understood.

There's a lot I didn't tell Zach that I should have.

Sometimes thinking about him stills me, shuts everything else down.

Other times I have trouble sitting still.

I pace.

Mom hates it. Dad looks at me nervously.

When I pace, the apartment is so small I don't understand how the four of us can fit in it.

Four? you ask.

Yes.

Four.

Me, Mom, Dad, Jordan.

My brother. My younger brother. My ten-year-old brother, Jordan.

He has the opposite effect on me. He is the opposite of Zach.

———

BEFORE

My next big lie of freshman year, after passing first as a boy and then as a hermaphrodite, was getting them to believe that my father was an arms dealer.

I still can't believe anyone bought it.

It started when Dad came to pick me up in a long black limousine. Not just long, but ridiculously long. Almost as long as the block. He was reviewing a new luxury limousine company and had to test all their services, including the champagne and flowers and their promise to drive you wherever and whenever.

So he picked me up from school, wearing the tuxedo he was married in, looking like James Bond. The chauffeur was at once respectful and jokey with him. They "hey man'd" and "brother'd" each other. Discovered they were both named Isaiah and made jokes about their super-strict religious parents. (Parents Dad does not have. The Greats never go to church.)

"Who's that?" Chantal asked me as Dad waved. I could see Sarah and Zach looking at my dad and then back at me.

"My dad," I said.

She looked at me sideways as if she could see the truth better from that angle. "No way," she said.

I smiled.

"He's so cool. What's he do?"

"Stuff," I said.

"What kind of stuff?" Chantal asked, watching Dad walk toward us.

"I gotta go," I said, and walked up to Dad. He kissed my cheek.

"Hurry up," he told me, sweeping me into the limo. I was relieved to see the brat wasn't already in there. I enjoyed Chantal and the others watching us.

"Who else are we picking up?"

"No one," he said. "I thought we'd cruise for a bit."

"And help the planet warm up some more. Climate change not quick enough for you, Dad?"

"I don't see you getting out and walking."

"Can't," I said. "They's watching."

"*Are* watching," he corrected. "This is Isaiah. Yes, same name as me. He had a shot at the world middleweight title. Back in the early nineties. Isn't that right, Isaiah?"

We both climbed up closer to Isaiah. Dad repeated the stuff about Isaiah and boxing.

"It is," Isaiah said, nodding. "You must be Micah. Your dad says you're a handful. That right?"

"Nope," I said. "It's my brother who's the bad one."

"They're both bad seeds," Dad said, patting my head 'cause he knows I hate it.

"Dad!" I protested.

"I am cursed," he told Isaiah, who nodded back at him.

"Who'd have children? Other than the two of us," Isaiah said, laughing. "Mine are more than a handful. But none of them in jail yet. That's the blessing I'm counting."

Then they started talking boxing. Dad told Isaiah about his career as a lightweight. Lightweight was right, but only if you left out the boxing part. Dad liked to say that he was "averse to violence." As far as I knew he'd never hit anyone. Not even me. Though, trust me, he'd wanted to.

"I got out before it was too late," Isaiah said. "Wanted to keep a few of my original smarts." He tapped his left temple to demonstrate there was still something in there. "I can add up and read and I know who the president is. That's a lot better than some of the brothers I went through with."

Dad nodded wisely.

"Dad got out after his nose was smashed up," I said, and Isaiah peered at Dad's nose in the rearview mirror. The crooked lump in the middle came courtesy of his oldest cousin, Cal, up on the farm. Or, at least, that was the story I'd heard most often.

Dad nodded again. "'Course," he said, "I was never going to be a contender. Nose was broke in my fifth bout."

"You did right," Isaiah said. "Look at you now! Riding around in a limousine."

Dad laughed. "Just reviewing it."

"Good enough," Isaiah said.

Next morning at school without saying anything directly I let it be known that my dad was a man to be reckoned with. By the end of the day it was Micah's dad, the arms dealer.

I neither confirmed nor denied.

AFTER

The police interview all the seniors. The art room becomes the inquisition room. I am one of the first they call. I wonder why. I am a Wilkins so it can't be alphabetical.

When the officer says my name I stand up and walk slowly out of English. Everyone looks at me. The teacher, too. I lift my chin a little higher, threading my way through the desks, trying to close my ears to the whispers, but my hearing is too good.

They talk about me and Zach. Disbelief echoes around the room and follows me out into the hall. How could he? With *her*?

I hate English. Even when no one is whispering about me.

The police officer smiles at me. "I'm Officer Lewis."

"Micah," I say, even though she already knows that

since she asked for me by name. I wonder if she heard the whispers.

"The art room is this way," she tells me, making it even. I told her something she knew, now she's telling me something I know.

She's shorter than me. She looks young. Like she could still be in high school. Her uniform is neat and she has a gun in a leather holster on her side. I wonder if she's ever fired it.

"Don't worry," she says. "One of your teachers, Ms. Yayeko Shoji, will be there. We just want to ask a few questions. You might be able to help us find out what happened to Zachary."

"Do you have any ideas at all?" I ask her. "Was he really murdered? Everyone's saying so."

"I'm sorry, I can't answer that. The investigation is ongoing," she says, still smiling. "Was he a good friend of yours? It's hard when someone you care about dies."

"No," I say, feeling weightless for a moment. I skid on a tile. The officer puts her arm out to steady me. "Slippery," I say. "He wasn't a friend of mine. It's weird. You know . . . someone you've seen around."

She pats my shoulder. "I understand," she says.

I hope she doesn't, and follow her along the empty hall into the art room.

AFTER

"This is Micah Wilkins," Officer Lewis says.

Two men nod. One of them, tall and thin, is leaning up against the wall. His elbow rests against someone's painting of a cow exploding. At least, that's what it looks like. The other man is sitting in a chair that's too small for him. It looks as if it might collapse under his weight. He's much fatter and more gray than the man standing. Neither of them wears a uniform and if they have guns I can't see them.

Officer Lewis gestures to the chair next to Yayeko Shoji, who turns and nods at me. Under the table she squeezes my hand briefly. For a moment I think I might cry.

Officer Lewis stands by the door. I am perched on the edge of my seat, toes flexed. I haven't been in the art room since the tenth grade. I hated it then; I hate it now. The smells of paint, paint remover, clay, glue, chalk, pencil, dust are overwhelming.

I sneeze. Yayeko blesses me.

Why is the art room never clean? I look around at the messy paintings, the sculptures, the cabinets and desks and chairs in every imaginable color.

"Micah," the older-looking man says, turning from his notes to me and then back to his notes. "Micah Wilkins. I'm Detective Rodriguez."

"Hello," I say. I wonder if they picked the art room

on purpose, hoping that ugly art will make us want to confess.

The other man looks down at me, bares his teeth, and says, "Detective Stein."

I smile but it's a little smile. I glance at Yayeko; she nods.

"We're going to ask you a few questions. That alright with you, Micah?" Detective Rodriguez asks.

"Okay," I say. It's not okay. I don't want to answer questions. I don't want to talk about Zach. I want to run.

"Anything you can think of, even if it seems kind of irrelevant to you," Rodriguez continues. "It might help us with the case. We need you to think hard. Tell us everything you can remember."

"Okay," I say again.

"Did you know Zachary Rubin well?"

I shake my head.

"Did you know him at all?"

"We were in some of the same classes."

"Which ones?"

"Biology," I say, glancing at Yayeko. She smiles. "English, math, Dangerous Words."

"Dangerous Words?" Detective Stein asks.

"It's a class about censorship."

"Interesting," he says, but I can tell he means weird.

"When was the last time you saw him?" Rodriguez asks.

"Friday, I guess. In class." Friday night sneaking around in Central Park. "The Dangerous Words class."

"Did you notice anything about him? Did he seem different?"

"Different?" I ask.

The man nods.

"I didn't really look at him," I say. "He's—he was— popular. I'm not. I stay out of his way. I don't think he's ever said a word to me in school. Or me to him."

"I thought," says Detective Stein, looking down at me, "that this school wasn't like that. Isn't this one of those alternative schools where everyone's happy and no one gets beat up at recess?"

"Does that question have anything to do with your investigation?" Yayeko asks.

"I was just wondering, Ms. Shoji," Stein says. "I didn't think a hippie school would have popular kids."

"Wherever there are people," Yayeko observes, "there are hierarchies."

"True enough," Stein says. "And Zachary Rubin was high in this school's hierarchy? Is that right, Micah?"

"Very," I say. "With students. With teachers. He was good at everything. Especially hoops."

"Hoops?" Stein says with a smirk to his voice. "I thought schools like this didn't have much of an athletics program."

"We don't," Yayeko says. "Not compared to more

traditional schools. But some of our students are very athletically gifted."

"Like Zachary?" Stein asks.

"Like Zach," Yayeko confirms.

"Was he ever mean to you, Micah? Popular kids often are."

"No."

"Where are you in the school hierarchy?"

"Not very high." I prefer being invisible. Not that I am anymore. Thanks to Brandon.

"Micah is one of my star students. She's popular with me," Yayeko says, and I wish she hadn't. Detective Stein smirks some more.

"Do you think other students resented Zachary's popularity?" Detective Rodriguez asks.

"I don't know," I say. "Probably." Brandon Duncan certainly does. Did.

"You say Zachary was popular," Rodriguez says. "Did you like him?"

"Sure," I say. "I certainly didn't *not* like him, you know? He seemed like a nice guy. He never did anything mean to me. Or anyone else that I saw."

"But some other students have?" Stein asks.

"Have what?" I ask.

"Been mean to you."

"I can take care of myself," I say, crossing my arms. I bet Detective Stein was as unpopular as me. More even.

I bet being back in high school makes him tense. Even a "hippie" one like this.

"I'm sure you can," Stein says. "And which students have forced you to take care of yourself?"

"No one in particular. I mostly get left alone."

Stein stares at me. I can tell he doesn't believe it.

"Well, if you think of anything that might help our investigation," Rodriguez says, glancing up at Stein and then back to me, "you let us know."

I nod. "I will."

"You can go back to class now."

I don't. I go into the bathroom and hide in one of the stalls until the bell for next period. I don't want to hear any whispering for a while.

BEFORE

It's true that Zach never spoke to me in school. He didn't look at me either. Not before, anyway. After, he would sometimes catch my eye when he was sure no one else was looking at him or at me. Easy to find a moment when there were no eyes on me, difficult to find one for himself.

We met for the first time in Central Park. Under a

bridge hung with icicles. Winter of our junior year. Middle of the day. A weekday. A school day.

I say "we met" even though we'd been in school together since we were freshmen. We exchanged a few words during the one game of hoops. But we'd been in classes ever since without so much as saying hi, how you doin'. He spoke to the cool kids. I spoke to no one, not even my teachers—except Yayeko—if I could avoid it.

Under the bridge he spoke to me.

"Micah, isn't it?"

I was staring up at the icicles. It was warmer that day and they were dripping. I wondered how long before they fell, which one would be first.

"You like icicles, huh?"

I turned to look at him. I knew who he was from his voice. I am better at voices than faces. His was deep. The kind you want to hear sing or read a sermon. So that you can float away on the words blurred together. It was too deep a voice for a sixteen-year-old boy. It was deeper than my dad's.

This time, I really looked at him. I never had before. I have learned to let my gaze slide over the surface of people without retaining anything or resting anywhere. That way no one calls me "freak."

I saw that he was beautiful. Not weedy like he'd been in our freshman year, though still lean. Taller, too. Much taller. I guess we both were.

"I'm Zach," he said, even though he knew I knew that. "I like them, too. Icicles, I mean. Only good thing about winter."

We stared at each other. I saw how smooth his skin was, how fine the pores. Then we looked up at the icicles. Fifteen of them. Each one dripping.

"You think they're going to last the day?"

"No," I said. Surprised that I could find my tongue. "It's too warm." Why was he talking to me?

He took a step closer. "We're in biology together, aren't we?"

I nodded.

"That Yayeko is weird, don't you think? Smart though. She's probably the smartest teacher we got."

I nodded again. No boy had ever stood this close to me before.

"I like those classes," he said, moving even closer. He didn't mention that if we were in school where we were supposed to be, Yayeko Shoji's class would be starting soon. "Cells and glycolysis and fast-twitch muscles. I play ball better from learning all that stuff, you know?"

I nodded. I wasn't sure I could speak with his breath misting so near my own. But it was true. Yayeko taught us about life, broke it into its components, so that our movements through space made sense. When I ran I thought about the movements of my muscles and joints, the glucose and oxygen making energy together.

He brushed his lips gently along my cheek.

I didn't move. The shock of it froze me. Why had he done that? He'd never looked at me that way. He'd never really looked at me any kind of way.

His lips were dry and warm. No other part of us touched. Blood moved faster through my veins and capillaries. Without willing them to, my lips parted slightly. An "oh" escaped from me.

"Biology is probably my favorite class," he said, letting his lips slide toward my ear, gently pressing his teeth into my lobe.

"Mine too," I said, glad to be able to speak again. Because it was true: biology is the *only* class I like.

The smell of him was curling into my nose and mouth. Sweat, meat, soap, and something else I didn't have a word for. My pulse beat faster. I felt it in my throat. The skin all over my body tightened.

Why was he kissing me? How many other girls had he kissed like this?

"No one else notices. But I seen how pretty you are," he said. "You got the biggest eyes."

He kissed the corner of each and the tip of my nose with his dry, soft lips.

Something crashed beside us.

We turned.

The largest of the icicles lay shattered into hundreds of slivers of ice. I bent and picked up one of the largest pieces. Cold, and the broken edge sharp like a knife.

———

FAMILY HISTORY

Dad grew up with two crazy white ladies who worried about the family illness, how to increase apple and hay yields, how to keep the farm animals living longer, and whether their children were running too wild or just wild enough.

Grandmother had the one child. Great-Aunt Dorothy and Great-Uncle Hilliard had six. If he hadn't died it would probably have been more. Four of them with the family illness. Because of that they homeschooled all of them. Not Dad, who didn't have the illness. He went to a boarding school in Connecticut on a scholarship, where he was one of only five black students. None of whom he liked. He kept to himself, proving himself to be more of a Wilkins than he cared to admit. He studied French and everything he could about France, especially Marseille. Because all he knew about his father was that he was a French sailor from Marseille.

Dad went to France when he was eighteen. Worked his way over as a merchant marine, which he hated. He didn't find his father. But he did find lots of pretty French girls. Including my mom. He brought her home, though not all the way upstate. He stopped in the city and stayed there.

Mom's never gone back to France. When I ask her if she misses it, she laughs.

Here, she is a schoolteacher. Teaching French, while Dad writes. He's a professional liar, Mom says. Even his journalism is lies. Travel writing. Appraisals of hotels, spas, and resorts. If they pay him enough he'll say whatever anyone wants him to say.

He's away a lot. When he's away they don't fight so much.

I never tell anyone about my family. Especially not counselors like Jill Wang.

I never talk about the family illness and how Dad passed it on to me.

———

AFTER

Sarah is following me home from school. She thinks she's being stealthy.

She's managed to stay a block behind me since we left school. But the blocks between school and my home aren't that crowded even after school on a weekday. So at every corner, as I turn, I glance back and see her. Finally I'm around a corner waiting.

Sarah turns and there I am staring at her.

"Oh," she says, taking several steps back, looking away. "Oh."

"Hmmm," I say.

"I," she begins, looking at me briefly, slipping her hands under the straps of her backpack, resting her left foot on the curb.

"You," I say, mocking her. She blushes and looks down.

"I was . . ."

To increase Sarah's discomfort I continue to stare at her.

"I was going to . . . ," Sarah says. "I was just . . ."

Sarah hasn't found the rest of her sentence yet, so I give it to her: "You were just following me?"

"Yes," she says, incurably honest. "I wanted to see where you live."

"Why?" I ask. She's still not looking at me.

"I heard that he'd come visit you." She slides her right hand out from under the backpack strap, wipes it on her skirt, and then slips it under again. "I wanted to see."

"To see what? Him with me? He's dead, remember?

Sarah shakes her head, her heavy loose curls swaying. She's still looking down.

"What did you want to see, Sarah? The outside of my apartment building? The inside? My bedroom?"

She looks up. Her eyes are wide and wet. "Yes," she says. "No. Maybe. I don't know. I didn't think it all the way through."

"Come on," I say, turning on my heel. I am tempted to run flat out and leave her in my wake. Instead I march fast up Second Avenue. She has to scurry to keep pace.

———

AFTER

"Your desk is so big," Sarah Washington says, looking around. "It's bigger than your bed."

It's not that the desk is big, more that the room is small. In any other city in America it would be a closet, not a bedroom. The desk, the chair, the bed, the crate beside it are the only furniture. I sit down on the bed, cross my legs underneath me. I prefer to sit on the floor, but Sarah is standing on the only floor space.

She picks up the silver packet of tiny pills by my bed, holds them in her hand and stares at them, then holds the packet out to me. Her eyes are too wet. A tear leaks out and then another. I wonder what it's like crying so easily.

"You were sleeping with him, weren't you?"

"They're for my skin," I tell her.

"Your skin?" She drops them back on the crate as if they might contaminate her. "You take birth control pills for your *skin*?"

I nod. It's odd how often telling the truth feels like lying and lying like the truth. "I have acne. When I take those pills I don't have acne. You can look it up."

"So you never slept with him?" she asks, emphasizing each word.

I hadn't said that. "No," I answer.

"Then why do you have his sweater?" she asks, much louder this time. She squeezes past my bed to where it hangs on the back of my desk chair. She holds it to her nose. She can smell him, too. Her eyes leak more water. She better not cry on the sweater.

"I was cold." I am never cold.

I only let Sarah into my room to stop her from bothering me. She's one of those people who cannot let things be. I thought about hiding the sweater. I thought, too, about wearing the sweater. But I don't want to lose his smell.

"Put it down," I tell her.

She does. I can smell salty fear on her. She is afraid of me. She is afraid of everything.

"I don't have anything of his," she says. "Not one thing."

"What about the chain around your neck?" It's thin and gold. It would be easy to break. "Or that ring on your finger. He gave you those."

"He bought them. They don't . . ." Sarah trails off, glances at the sweater again. "They weren't ever *his*."

She means that they don't smell like Zach. Sweat doesn't soak into metal. Jewelry doesn't have the fragrance of where it's been; only of what it is. Besides, he never wore them. He bought them for her to wear. He never bought anything for me. I think about telling Sarah this, but it will only confirm that me and Zach were together.

"When was the last time you saw him?" she asks, sliding away from the sweater, her back against my desk.

"Why is everyone asking me about that?" I know why. Ever since Brandon told about Zach and me, everyone has been staring, whispering. But I want to hear her say it, to admit that she suspects me of killing him, too.

I miss Zach so much. The thought of him makes my breath hurt. I'm afraid I'll choke. His death, his absence makes everything tighten, thicken, break.

"We're all trying to figure out what happened. Who did this to him. Why." She doesn't look at me directly. Her hand reaches toward his sweater again. She stops herself before she touches it.

"Who killed him, you mean?" It's what everyone's saying: Zach was murdered. But no one knows who or how or why. The why is huge. Zach is a good guy. Was. I cannot imagine a reason to kill him.

"Last time I saw him was Saturday night," Sarah says. Her voice wilts on "Saturday."

"Me, too," I say, though I didn't. I don't know why I say it. Those two words mean I'm admitting to seeing Zach. To being his—his whatever I was.

"You're lying. I was with him Saturday. We were at Chantal's party. You weren't invited."

As if I would want to go. So much noise. Not just the music, but their voices all loud and raucous from drinking. I never drink. None of the Wilkins do.

"The party didn't go all night," I say. "He saw me after." I cross my legs the other way, stretch out my spine.

"At 5:00 a.m.?" she asks. "When he was so drunk Chantal's older brother ended up helping him get a taxi home?"

"He wasn't that drunk. I climbed in through his window."

"Through the window? Of a seventh-floor apartment?"

I nod. I've climbed into higher windows. "I went up the fire escape. His bedroom's right next to it." Not true. The kitchen is. I have to climb across ledges to get to Zach's room. Sarah's not the kind of person who'd notice where the fire escape is. "He always leaves the window open a crack. He used to anyway. He was snoring. I crawled in next to him. He woke up." I can see it clearly though I know it didn't happen. Not that night.

"I thought you said you never slept with him?" She's

crying again. It amazes me she can do that even through her questions and her anger.

"I didn't. There are other things you can do." Sleep for instance. He *had* been drunk. He'd woken up, grunted "Micah," then rolled over, and gone back to snoring. Or at least that's what would have happened if I'd been there that night. It had gone that way before.

Sarah takes a long look at me, without any fear for a moment. "You," she says, at last, "are nasty. I don't believe a word you've said. Can you even describe his bedroom?"

"Lots of trophies."

"What jock boy's bedroom *doesn't* have lots of trophies?" She shifts against my desk. It's hard and metal, even with the cloth draped over it. She can't be comfortable. "What color are the walls?"

"At night? Dark."

"Very funny. What's the rest of the house look like?" She's sneering.

"I told you. I get in through his window."

"What's—?"

"Why am I answering your questions?" I want her to go. I want her to stop interrogating me. I want her to leave me alone.

"Why won't you tell the truth?" she asks, glaring at me.

"Why won't you?" I ask, even though she is an incorrigible truth teller. I glare right back.

"You're not even pretty!" Sarah shouts, pushing off from the desk, past the bed, opening the door. "You look like a boy. An ugly boy! What did he even see in you?"

She slams the door behind her.

So she doesn't hear me say that I have no idea.

HISTORY OF ME

"Did you take your pill?" is the first thing my parents ask me each morning. Well, mostly my dad.

It annoys me. It annoys me a lot.

Especially when Jordan echoes their question. It's too icky to have your ten-year-old brother ask you that. It doesn't matter that I don't take the pill for that reason. It's still not something he should be thinking about.

It's not something I want to think about.

I hate the whole thing: menstruation, pills, blood.

So. Much. Blood.

I don't take the pill just for my skin, it's to fix my periods, too.

They used to be awful. Lie-in-bed-sobbing-with-pain awful and an ocean of blood: instant anemia once a month. The first time I got my period I thought I was going to die. The pain was so bad. The bleeding wouldn't stop.

My doctor cured it by making me take a birth control pill every single day. No fake sugar pills—I take the real ones every single day of my life. Now I never get my period. I never have that awful pain. My blood stays in my body, keeping me upright.

My mom freaked out a bit. She was worried that it wasn't natural. She thought having your period was what makes you a woman.

I wish I was a man.

I asked my doctor to explain how it worked, but what he told me about cycles, and uterine lining, and elevated risk didn't make any sense, so I asked Yayeko Shoji. She's a biologist, I figured she would know.

She did.

She told me that women used to have so many babies they hardly menstruated at all. But now women have only one or two or no babies, and they have them when they're already old, which means they have too many periods. All that bleeding puts a strain on their wombs.

I try to imagine being a woman in the olden days, being pregnant over and over again, having a dozen children. But I can't imagine being pregnant even once.

Yayeko says that taking the pill to stop bleeding is more natural than bleeding all the time. She does the same thing. She hasn't had a period in two years.

Yayeko talked to my mom, explained it to her, and

Mom felt better about it, but she still wasn't happy. "You are my daughter," she said. "It is difficult to be happy for you to take these *très* adult pills."

Dad didn't have to be persuaded; he's against anyone suffering when they don't have to. Especially him.

For the price of remembering to take one little pill every morning of my life I get good skin, no blood, no pain, and, according to Yayeko, less chance of cancer. It's a fair bargain.

I *really* don't understand why my parents don't trust me to take a pill every morning. I'm the one it hurts if I forget. I'm the one with incentives. Strong incentives. But, no, every morning it's the same question: "Did you take your pill?"

"Yes, Dad, I took it. Okay? Like I did yesterday and the day before. I'll take it tomorrow and the day after that and so on, forever."

I take the pill and I don't complain about their nagging. Well, not as often as I could.

———

BEFORE

That first time, after that first kiss, after the icicle fell and I picked up a broken shard, felt it cold and knife-sharp in my fingers—after that—I dropped the ice and ran.

That's what I'd been doing before I paused under the bridge to look at the icicles, before Zach Rubin saw me— I'd been running.

That's what I liked to do in Central Park: run and run and run and run as hard and fast as I could.

Zach took off after me. He caught me, breathing hard to keep pace. I ran harder. He accelerated, too, but was struggling. "Wait up," he gasped.

I slowed.

"You're so fast," he gasped, matching my stride. "I'm fast. But you're faster."

"Yes," I said. I'm faster than anyone I've ever run against. Too fast, my dad says.

To really show Zach, I took off, ran as hard as I could. All the way up and over Heartbreak Hill. Then I stopped at the first empty bench and waited for him.

He got there at last, dripping with sweat, collapsing beside me.

"How?" he panted. "You're not even on the track team." The school's track team is as crappy as all our other teams. "I run. I run all the time. How can you be so fast?" He wiped the sweat from his face with the sleeve of his sweater. It was synthetic and not very absorbent. "Do you train out of school?"

I shook my head. "I just run."

"I heard a rumor," Zach said, more evenly, his breath starting to catch up with his words, "that you were born a boy. I don't think you look like a boy. But you sure as hell run like one. You should be going to the Olympics. You're crazy fast!"

I laughed. Crazy fast. That's how it felt sometimes. Good crazy. There's nothing I love more than running.

"Do you ever compete?"

"We just did!" I was still laughing.

"*Real* competing," Zach said. "Races. Medals. Ribbons. All that stuff."

I shook my head. "Too much fuss. Too many rules." I wished he would kiss me again. I wondered if I should kiss him.

"Who *are* you?" Zach said. He straightened up, wiped his face again. "You're not even sweating."

"I run a lot," I said. "The more I run, the less I sweat."

I leaned forward, wiped the sweat between his upper lip and nose, and then I kissed him.

___

AFTER

Climbing someone else's fire escape is as easy as climbing your own. They're all basically the same: the only differences lie in how recently painted they are, how bad the rust, how loose the bolts holding them to the brick-work, how much laundry hangs from them, how many potted plants.

The higher you climb, the more likely a window will be open. Most often not directly by the fire escape, un-less they've left one open for you on purpose. Like Zach used to do for me. When he was still alive and waiting for me.

This time the kitchen window is firmly closed and the grate pulled across and locked. I crouch on the es-cape, looking in. Even with no lights on, through a dirty window and the gaps in the grate, I can see that it's a mess. There are things all over the floor, the kitchen ta-ble is piled high with stuff, the sink full of dishes. I don't think they've cleaned anything since Zach disappeared.

I bet it smells worse than it looks. Even through a closed window I can tell. The place is thick with grief and dust. And emptiness. The kitchen is the heart of Zach's home but there's no one in it.

I swing to the outside of the escape, then step across to the first windowsill. Zach's brother's room. Mostly a storage room now that he's in college. Or has that changed? Has he come home to be with his parents? Wher-ever he is, there's no light on in the room. No sounds of movement.

One foot on the staircase, the other on the sill, I lean forward and grip the bricks with my fingertips, transferring the weight from my right foot to my left. I crouch down to try the window.

Locked.

I wipe my fingers on my pants and step across to the next windowsill. I don't look down. Not for fear of falling but because in the dark my balance has to stay on the horizontal, not vertical axis. I need my eyes focused on here, not there.

The bathroom window is also dark. It's open a crack, but it's too small and too high for me to get through. No one in there either. I step to the sill in front of Zach's room. The window's a fraction open, barely enough for me to slip my fingers under. I ease it open, swinging my right leg, then my left, then the rest of me through, dropping to the floor on a pile of Zach's clothes.

I wipe my grimy hands on my pants. Bird shit, too, I'm fairly sure. I can smell the phosphate. Though not as strongly as I can smell Zach.

Even without turning on the lights I can smell that they haven't changed a thing. Haven't stripped the bed or changed his sheets. Haven't moved anything. It's like Zach is still here. I'm almost afraid to breathe for fear of replacing his breath with mine.

My eyes adjust, my ears, too. I can hear traffic from the street below. A helicopter overhead. Someone shouting in the apartment next door. But there's no one but me in this one.

The pile of clothes extends into the middle of the floor. From the smell they are gym clothes: salty and rank and Zach.

I step past the bed, not looking at it because I don't want to think about what's there, what's not there, what was there. I knock over water bottles. They're all at least half full. Water trickles across the floor. I bend down and start righting them, my eyes on them, not the bed.

My eyes sting. I swallow. I'm here for a reason, I remind myself, but I can't bring myself to stand up.

The desk is cluttered with notes and books. I should look at those. My throat feels tight. I haven't been in this room since before Zach disappeared. I swallow again, stand up, close my eyes, willing them dry. I concentrate on the smells. On the Zach funk. Zach stink. Zach sweat, Zach dirty socks, Zach meatiness. I cringe from the word. Meat is what Zach is now. Meat is a word for a person once they're dead.

I'm not entirely sure why I'm here. I was sure when I started climbing the fire escape. I try to recapture that certainty.

Was I hoping to find him?

He's not here. There's only the smell of him, his sloughed-off skin and hair cells, clothes that were once pressed against him, bottles he's drunk from.

A hundred signs of what he used to be, how he used to be, but not him.

Not Zach.

I open my eyes, move to his desk, treading carefully over the clothes.

I turn the desk lamp on and blink at the brightness. For a moment black spots play across my eyes and then I'm looking at a pile of books. The nearest one has a plain red cover with the word TRAINING printed in caps in black marker. Zach's handwriting. His training log. All the guys on the team have to keep one. It's a record of their progress, what they've eaten, how many calories, how much they weigh, how many extra hours training they've done, how many games won, by how much, and all his own stats.

I pick it up, turn the first page, it probably won't tell me much. It occurs to me that the cops must have seen it. Seen this room. Have they taken things away, examined them? The thought appalls me but I'm not sure why.

I point the lamp toward the floor next to the desk and sit there, with my back to the bed. I turn the pages, trying not to think of it in Zach's hands, him scrawling these numbers and words. It's exactly like any other training log. Calories, pounds, reps, points, wins, losses. His weight stays steady. He increases his calories. His weight doesn't budge. He writes his frustration at his lack of bulk: *Shit. Still 170. 171. 172. 169. 170. Shit.*

The pages are all the same. Calories up. Weight steady

or down. Wins and losses. Points and rebounds and steals. Starting. Not starting.

A punishing inconstant heart.

More than thirty pages in. It's scrawled on the left-hand side.

I don't know what that means. It's not anything Zach would say. It's not even something he would think. I never heard him say those words. Well, "heart" maybe, possibly "punishing," but definitely not "inconstant." That word seems so old-fashioned. Who would say that? Or write it?

I peer closer. It's definitely not his handwriting. Too spiky.

I think about tearing the page out. Comparing it to Sarah's handwriting. She's poetic and overwrought. It's like something she might say.

Does Sarah think Zach had a mean heart? That she does? Is it a message for me?

I keep turning the pages, but those are the only words that aren't about his weight and the games he's played.

I search the rest of the room, but I don't know what I'm looking for, so I don't find it.

I take one of his dirty jerseys. The number 12 on the back. It reeks of him. I plan never to wash it.

———

AFTER

The rumor that Erin Moncaster is missing rustles through the school. From student to student, classroom to classroom. The teachers, too.

I'm not sure who Erin is. I don't recognize her name.

I hear about it in English, struggling to read a poem about an icebox. Chantal whispers to Sarah.

"No," Sarah says.

First Zach, now Erin. Is she dead? Did they know each other?

She a freshman, he a senior. It seems unlikely. They look at me. I can hear them thinking how unlikely Zach being with me was. So why not Erin? It couldn't be a coincidence. Two kids from the same school going missing so close together. How often does that happen?

Does someone out there hate this school? Will it happen again?

I can smell the fear. Chantal already carries pepper spray. By the end of the day other girls are saying they will, too. That or a loud whistle. The boys talk about knives.

I'm not afraid. I sit in Dangerous Words, failing to learn about some code our teacher, Lisa Aden, seems to think we should know. Rules for Hollywood in the olden days. Who cares?

I won't be arming myself. The Greats say you should

never carry a weapon if you don't know how to use it. I know how to hunt with a knife. Grandmother's taught me how to use a slingshot and bows and arrows. Neither of them are as effective as traps. But there's a world of difference between killing a rabbit, or even a deer, and defending yourself against a person. Besides, I can't imagine anyone attacking me. I'm too fast.

"Micah?" Lisa says loudly.

I look up. "Sorry," I say.

"Do you know the answer?"

"Um."

"Do you know the question?"

"I'm sorry," I say. "I was thinking about Erin Moncaster."

She nods. "Many of us are. But we have to go on with this class. My question was, What are some of the words that are generally acceptable to use now that were forbidden by the Production Code?"

"Um," I say again. I have no idea. I try to think of a word that might have been bad in the olden days but isn't so much now. "Damn?" I ask.

"Sort of," Lisa says, and begins to explain. I tune out.

I'm trying to remember which one was Erin. Was she black or white? Kind of a white-sounding name. I don't pay attention to the freshmen except to be glad that I'm not one. A few more months and I'll be out of here; they have years to wait.

I'll be honest: I don't really care about Erin. Maybe that's why I'm not afraid? Erin isn't Zach. Her going missing isn't going to bring him back. Part of me is mad that people are talking about her. As if she's as important as Zach. As if they've forgotten him.

I hate them. By the end of a day filled with talk and speculation, not to mention rumors that she and Zach were together, I start to hate Erin, too.

Zach hasn't even been buried yet.

BEFORE

I only did the DNA testing because the results went to our homes, not to the school. Because Yayeko promised that we didn't have to share the results with the class if we didn't want to. I probably shouldn't have done it. I was curious.

But when the results came, I hid them in a drawer unopened. I didn't want to see the proof of the family illness in black and white. I certainly wasn't going to share the results with my biology class.

But I was there for the day everyone—except me—shared their results.

No one was 100 percent anything.

I could have told them that without the expensive testing.

The whole class buzzed with it. Calling out their results. Laughing. Only a few of us sat quiet. Me, one. Zach, another. He was in back. I was toward the front. But I could hear his quiet.

Brandon didn't believe it. Or said he didn't. But his 11 percent African made him happy. He started joking about basketball. As if a drop of African DNA would suddenly give him a crossover dribble.

"Oh, please," Tayshawn said, looking at Brandon as if he were something foul stuck to the bottom of his shoe.

"Eleven percent!" Brandon said.

"Which makes you 89 percent dickhead," Tayshawn said.

Everyone laughed. Brandon started to respond but Tayshawn was louder. "Says here I'm 23 percent white. That mean I'm gonna be a stockbroker who can't dance? Please."

Brandon laughed like it didn't bother him. But it did. The look he gave Tayshawn was savage.

"What do you think these numbers mean?" Yayeko Shoji said into the brief silence.

No one put a hand up.

I knew what it meant: that no one is exactly what they think they are. We all have every kind of DNA floating in us: black, white, Asian, Native American, human, monkey, reptile, junk DNA, all sorts of genes that do not express.

I have the family illness. My brother doesn't, nor my father. But who knows what will happen if Jordan has kids? His genes are as tainted as mine.

"You think these numbers are meaningful?" Yayeko looked around the room, making eye contact with each of us.

"Well," Lucy said tentatively, "I guess not. Because even though it says here 10 percent Asian and 3 percent African, when I fill in the next form that asks for race I'll still write 'white.'"

There were murmurs of agreement around the classroom.

"There's no space on those forms for percentages," Tayshawn said. "You only get to be one thing."

Yayeko nodded. "Indeed. Additionally, these tests are not currently reliable."

The murmurs got louder. Brandon squawked. "Why'd we do it then?"

Yayeko held up her hand. "The test's ability to identify your DNA is dependent on what DNA is available to the company."

She turned to the board and started drawing a DNA spiral. The light caught particles of chalk floating in the air. I could smell it, taste it on the tip of my tongue.

"This test was done," Yayeko said, "by comparing your DNA"—she pointed to the spiral she'd drawn—"with the DNA in that particular company's database.

What percentage of the world's DNA do you think they're likely to have? Five percent? Ten? Fifteen?"

Brandon looked at Will. No one said anything. I couldn't imagine it would be a very big percentage. The world is so big. There are so many people in it.

"Less than 1 percent," Yayeko said at last. "Considerably less. So they have a very small database of DNA. A database that does not contain the DNA of everyone in the world."

She waited a moment as we digested that. I was wondering how they could tell us anything at all about ourselves if they had so little data. I still wasn't going to open my results.

"They take their DNA from 'pure' sources—African, European, and Asian groups where there's been relatively little marrying into different groups. But there are very few 'pure' people left in the world. Many people argue that these tests work from a faulty premise."

The class was silent. What was Yayeko saying? That the test couldn't tell us anything? That there was no such thing as race? I looked around the room and saw lots of frowning faces. All except Brandon, who was doodling on his hand.

"The company looks for markers in our DNA that they have identified as African or Asian or European or Native American. But with so little of the world's DNA mapped, the odds that they are correctly identifying the markers in your DNA are not high. Say they identify one of your markers as African. It may be that they are identifying your unmapped marker from another part of the world with their mapped marker from somewhere in Africa."

"Does that mean if the test says you've got no African DNA, it's wrong?" Sondra asked. She's very light-skinned. Lighter than Chantal even, several shades lighter than me. White people usually think she's white, despite her relaxed curls and full lips. She'd been still since reading her results. Like me and Zach she hadn't said a word.

"Definitely," Yayeko said firmly. "If we did the test with a different company using a different database your results would change. Biologically speaking, the so-called races have more similarities than they have differences. There is only one race: the human race. Sickle-cell anemia is sometimes called a black disease because it is more common in people of African descent, but it is also relatively common in those of Mediterranean, Middle Eastern, and Indian descent. We are one race.

"Right now, what you know about your ancestry and cultural heritage is likely to be more true than anything a test like this can tell you. That may change if we ever get to the point where all the world's DNA is mapped. But right now, you are what you think you are."

I thought about my family and found myself nodding.

Sondra was, too. I've seen her parents. Unlike mine they're both black. I wondered what my DNA test looked like, but I still didn't open the envelope that night.

———

FAMILY HISTORY

Jordan and me?

We hate each other. He thinks I should be locked in a cage; I think he should never have been born.

You think I exaggerate? That siblings often say they hate each other, but don't mean it?

You're wrong. We hate each other. Like Cain and Abel. Siblings fight and kill each other all the time. I read about brothers who fought on opposite sides of the Civil War. Fought and killed each other.

Jordan's worse than that. It's not that we believe different things, it's that he doesn't smell right. There's something wrong with Jordan. I think he's a bad seed, but Mom and Dad won't believe me. He steals from me. Sneaks into my room and takes things. I told him I'd kill him next time he did it.

So he took Zach's sweater.

———

AFTER

I love my mom more than my dad, though sometimes the fractured un-American way she talks is embarrassing. She doesn't nag me the way he does. She doesn't always take Jordan's side.

At breakfast Dad starts in again about my going upstate. We're all squeezed into our tiny kitchen, around the table that's not a whole lot bigger than a school desk. There's barely enough room for our plates. Our bikes are hanging upside down over our heads 'cause there's nowhere else to put them. If I get up too quickly I forget they're there and bash my head. Unfortunately Jordan's still too short to get clobbered. He'll grow.

If I stretch out my right arm, reach past Jordan, I can almost touch the fridge. When we sit at the kitchen table you can no longer open the pantry door. My feet are tucked up under my chair because the food processor, coffeemaker, and toaster live under the table.

"I hate the Greats," I tell Dad, shoving bacon into my mouth. "Don't," I snap at Jordan, who's just elbowed me in the process of twisting to pick up the toast he dropped. "Brat."

"Leave it, Jordan," Mom says. "I will clean after. You do not want to be late for school."

"Yes I do!" Jordan says, sticking his tongue out at me.

"*I* do not want you to be late for school. Stop with these wriggles! Eat your breakfast. You have ten years, not two!"

"No, you don't, Micah," Dad says, ignoring Jordan and Mom. "You always have a wonderful time up there."

"No, I don't. I always run away and hide so I don't have to be anywhere near them. Or my stupid cousins." I'm keeping my elbows firmly by my side so I don't whack into the wall or Jordan's sticky mouth. Not that I object to hurting him, but I don't want slimy syrup all over my elbow.

"Jordan! Stop!" Mom takes the maple syrup away.

"But I don't like bacon without sweet."

"Your bacon, it *drowns*! You have ten minutes to finish. We must go. *Vite!*" Mom walks Jordan to his school on her way to the posh one where she teaches French. Every school day she battles to get him out the door.

"I think it would be good for you to get away, Micah. With everything that's been going on. Fresh air—"

"You mean with . . ." I falter. "With him being dead?"

Dad nods. "Yes. Zach was your friend. You're taking it hard."

"She mourns, Isaiah," Mom says. "We must allow her this."

"Zach's a fart!" Jordan says. I am tempted to strangle

him right there at the kitchen table. I would love to watch his head fall into his syrup-drowned bacon.

"Quiet, Jordan. You must act your age," Mom says, squeezing out of her seat, avoiding the bicycles, putting her plate in the sink, and the maple syrup in the fridge.

"There's much more space upstate," Dad says.

"There's more space in a coffin than there is here!" I imagine Zach stuck in one. The bacon loses flavor. I'm chewing dust.

Dad turns to Mom. "She belongs there."

I force myself to eat the rest of my bacon.

"She should be put to sleep," Jordan says.

"Quiet," Mom tells him.

"You should be flushed down the toilet," I say, without even looking at him. "With the alligators."

"Mom!" Jordan wails.

"Quiet, please. You know she doesn't mean it."

Dad looks at me. He knows that I do.

"You do not have to go where you don't want," Mom says, her back against the kitchen sink. "But perhaps you could think about it. Things have been so . . ." Sometimes she struggles to find the right English word. "So . . ." She pauses again and notices Jordan pulling his bacon to pieces and then pushing it through the lake of syrup. "Stop, Jordan! Either you eat or you don't." She turns her attention back to me. "Foul. Things have been so foul. Perhaps it would help to get away? It does not have to be with the Greats."

"Where else would she go?" Dad says. "Are you proposing we send her to Club Med?"

"Well, couldn't you take her along on your next assignment?"

Dad and I look at each other. "No!" we say at the exact same time.

Mom starts laughing. "You two could not be more alike."

Dad is wearing the same scowl I can feel on my own face. The sight of it makes me scrunch my forehead even more.

Mom leans forward over Jordan's head, ducking to avoid the bicycles, and kisses my cheek. "You do not have to go anywhere you do not want."

"Did you take your pill?" Dad asks.

I don't bother answering.

AFTER

"I don't think he loved me," Sarah tells me.

I am sitting alone. She slides in next to me as if we're friends. How can she have forgotten how much we're not? Why is she talking to me about whether Zach loved her?

"Did you?" she asks.

"Did I what?" I don't want her to sit next to me. I want to eat my lunch alone, undisturbed, unobserved. Ever since Zach disappeared—no, ever since Brandon blabbed—people have been watching me, talking about me. But me and Sarah sitting together for lunch? That's too weird. Everyone in the cafeteria is watching, leaning forward, trying to overhear.

"Did you love him?" she asks, lowering her voice.

I roll my eyes so I don't have to say out loud how stupid I think her question is. "He's dead, Sarah," I say quietly. "Thinking about him, talking about him all the time, that's not going to make him come back to life. You do know that, right?"

She flinches but her eyes don't fill with tears. "I just asked you if you loved him. Why's that such a hard question to answer?"

I sigh. "It doesn't matter. He's dead."

"You're scared of answering," Sarah says. "That means you loved him."

"If you say so. I suppose you think you loved him." I don't want to talk about Zach with her. I don't want to talk about Zach with anyone. Saying his name hurts, thinking it . . . I realize then that neither of us has been saying his name. We say "he" or "him" or "his" but never "Zach."

"Of course," Sarah says.

"We weren't together, Sarah. Brandon was lying. And I've been messing with you. We'd run together sometimes. There wasn't anything else to it."

"You have his sweater."

"I was cold. He loaned it to me." I wasn't cold. My head was in his lap. He was stroking the tiny curls on my scalp. All I could smell was him. I said I liked his sweater. He took it off, gave it to me. It stank of him. Zach reek. I love that sweater.

"I'm not stupid," Sarah says, and I don't laugh. "You think you're so good at hiding things but I can read you. I know you were together. You can't keep the way you think about him off your face. I know you loved him. You did, didn't you?"

I shrug. Sarah starts to cry again. Quietly, but it doesn't matter. Everyone is staring. They can see. I wish I could cry.

"Why are you so cynical?" It's not an angry question. I think she really wants to know.

"Trying to be like my dad," I tell her, which isn't even close to true. But she's seen my arms-dealing daddy so she probably believes he's all tough and cynical and worldly-wise. Dad isn't cynical at all. Not really. He's chock-full of hope and optimism.

I suspect my cynicism comes from pretending to be what I'm not; covering myself in lies makes me cynical. I know I'm not trustworthy. How likely is it that the world is true if I'm not?

But my dad lies as much as I do and he's not cynical.

"Do you think he loved you?" Sarah asks, wiping her eyes discreetly. I wonder who she thinks she's fooling.

"Who? My dad?" I ask, even though I know exactly who she means. "Of course he does. He's my dad."

"No, Zach. Do you think Zach loved you?"

I have a strong urge to punch Sarah in the face.

She said his name.

Instead, I turn to my cold BLT, peeling away the damp bread, pushing the wilted lettuce aside. The bacon is burned. I have to chew hard to get it small enough to swallow.

"As much as he loved any of his running partners, I suppose," I say at last, hoping that I never have to speak to Sarah again. But June is so far away.

———

FAMILY HISTORY

The family illness isn't just acne and excessive blood. There's more to it than that—yet another reason I take the pill every single day of my life.

Remember the fur I was born with? The light coat of hair all over my body?

It came back.

Along with the usual puberty horror, I got hair in all the wrong places.

No, you don't understand. In the *wrong* places.

Like my face and back and stomach.

My *face*.

Yeah.

So the pill. It keeps the hair away, as well as my period, and acne, too.

Without it, I'm a freak.

Though, according to the kids at school, even with it my freakishness is not well disguised. But there's no pill for that.

I blame my family for contaminating me with their weirdness and their tainted hairy genes. The family illness, they call it. If I were from a different family—a normal family—I wouldn't have it.

To my grandmother's credit, she did try to dilute the family disease. Instead of marrying her cousin Hilliard, she left the farm to find a father for her baby. Grandmother was convinced that too much cousin-marrying was responsible for the family illness. She was going to have a child whose father was as unrelated to her as she could find.

Grandmother went to San Francisco and got pregnant

by a black sailor. She said they spent a week together and that he loved to gamble. He was from Marseille, she said. His English wasn't very good. That was all she could remember. She was relieved that Dad hadn't inherited the gambling love.

Or the family illness.

That was left for me.

———

BEFORE

One time I was walking along Broadway playing dodge the crowd. Which is me testing myself, moving as fast as I can, weaving through them all without accelerating into a run, and without touching anyone or having them touch me. Any time I make contact I have to go back to the beginning of the block.

It's a game.

I'm really good at it. When I play it I don't think about anything else. Not Zach, not anyone.

I only ever play it on crowded streets and avenues. Broadway works. But Fifth Avenue's okay as well. Times Square is the best.

This time it was Broadway. A Sunday.

I was weaving, concentrating on the muscles of my

body, on the air around me. It was like those few inches of air above my skin were part of me, too. An extra layer. Antennas. Me, stretching into space.

When I spread like that I can go for miles and miles untouched and clear.

I could feel everyone as they moved through air, feel them and their clothes and their bags, swinging arms, hands clutching cell phones, sodas, other hands, closed umbrellas for the rain that wouldn't come even though my nostrils prickled with the smell of it.

Then there was someone looking at me as I slid past them. Looking straight at me. A stare more direct than my mother's. Like how the Greats stare.

I twitched and stopped and turned to look back at the person with the staring eyes.

Two people walked into me. They swore. I said sorry.

It was a white boy. Same age as me, I thought. Maybe younger. He was smaller than me, skinny.

He was standing and staring at me standing and staring.

Then he took off the way I would. And there was me, too befuddled to follow. How did he do that? How did he see me first?

———

AFTER

I force myself to go to school.

I regret it almost immediately. The first words I hear as I walk up the front steps: "I heard they were killed with an axe."

The school is floating on rumors about what happened to Zach and Erin Moncaster. He's dead, so she must be, too.

An axe murderer did it.

A serial killer.

Her father's religious. He caught Erin and Zach together. If Zach went with that Micah girl he'd go with anyone.

Her boyfriend did it.

This, despite Zach and Erin not knowing each other. Despite no one knowing if she has a boyfriend. Or a religious father.

They were both locked in a basement. The serial killer tortured them and then dumped the bodies in Times Square. Or was it Rockefeller Center? Only Erin hasn't been found yet. And no one at school knows where Zach's body was found.

Maybe she's still in the basement. So are Zach's ears. The killer kept souvenirs.

The worst rumors are the ones about me. Some are saying that I killed him. That I killed them both. Everyone talks about me. Even the teachers. They stare. Some are not talking to me. Cutting past me on line. Averting their eyes, whispering: *We know she's a liar. A slut. Killing's what comes next.*

Liar. Slut. Bitch. Murderer.

Always whispering.

It doesn't matter that there are also whispers about Brandon. (Though not nearly so many.) And Sarah and Tayshawn. Were they sleeping together? Did Zach find out and Tayshawn accidentally kill him? But that doesn't explain Erin. Maybe Brandon killed her? A copycat killing and now he's waiting till he gets someone alone to do it again.

Doesn't matter that none of this stuff is true. The less we know, the more ferocious the talk gets.

All we have is a dead boy, a missing girl, and rumors.

How can they say those things about Sarah and Tayshawn? They're the most popular kids in school. Yet now, while they grieve, they have to deal with these stupid rumors?

The school is nastily off-kilter. Everyone's gone nuts.

Teachers stutter-step their way through their lesson plans. Students keep drifting back to talk of Zach, of Erin. (Of me. Of Tayshawn. Of Sarah. Of Brandon.) They try to talk about school, games, TV, their boyfriend/girlfriend, regular gossip. But they can't stay there. Zach. Erin. They have to talk about it, speculate, imagine, scare themselves so bad that no one's walking or riding the subway home alone anymore. Despite the crazy traffic some parents are sending their children to and from school in cars.

All of them worry about who'll be next. I'm hoping Brandon. But right now they can all go to hell as far as I'm concerned. Especially the ones calling me *Liar. Slut. Bitch. Killer.*

I can't imagine this ever ending.

I will always be at school. Skin tight, head high, acting like I don't care. Avoiding everyone. Avoiding everything. Only when I'm running in the park does my head stop throbbing.

It will be like this for the rest of the year. I bet they'll still be talking next year, too, when there'll be a new set of seniors and we'll all be off to wherever it is we go next.

I'm hoping hell for most of them.

I'm not sure where I'm going. I've filled out applications, sent them off, but I'm not optimistic. CUNY is my best chance. Though I'm not sure we can afford even that. Part of me would be happy to wind up somewhere no one's heard of Zach or what happened to him. Somewhere far from the city.

Wherever I go, I doubt I'll be with anyone from here. Sarah will be at some Ivy League school: Harvard or Yale or Princeton. Or at the very least, Vassar. Tayshawn will be at MIT. Brandon will be in jail. I'll never see any of them again.

I'm glad.

I think.

I don't want to talk about Zach. But how will it feel not to be able to?

I try to imagine myself at college. I fail. I want to keep studying biology but I'm not sure why. If all else fails then I guess I can work up on the farm.

A fine way to spend the rest of my life.

———

AFTER

At the second group counseling session Jill Wang asks us to tell her what we think about Zach.

"Are we going to talk about Erin, too?" Kayla asks.

Everyone starts talking at once. I close my eyes and wish I could shut my ears.

"Why would we talk about Erin?" Brandon shouts over the top of everyone else. "She's a freshman. Do you even know who she is?" I dislike agreeing with Brandon, but he's right. Looking around the room, I can see others agree.

"As a matter of fact, yes, I do," Kayla yells back. "Her sister and me have been friends for years. I've known Erin since she was a baby."

"Well, I haven't," Brandon says.

"Just because you—"

"Erin's disappearance," Jill Wang interrupts, raising her voice, letting us know that she's the boss, "is disturbing. We most definitely can talk about it—"

"Yeah, like, who's next?"

"You really think that?" Tayshawn says. "She could have run away. I heard she was fighting with her mom and dad a lot. Maybe it's got nothing to do with Zach."

"Erin's a good girl," Kayla says.

"Sure," Tayshawn says. "I'm just saying it doesn't seem like the two things are connected. He's Hispanic, she's white. He's a senior, she's a freshman. He was on a scholarship, she's from money. They don't even live in the same part of the city." Tayshawn talks as if he didn't know Zach, as if they weren't best friends.

"He *was* Hispanic," Brandon says. "He *was* a senior."

"We know he's dead," Sarah says. "You don't have to go on about it."

"Isn't that what we're here for?" Brandon asks, sneering. "To go on about it?"

Jill Wang holds her hands up, palms out, reassuring us, but all I can see are the calluses where her fingers join her palm. I wonder how she got them. "We are here," she says loudly and clearly, "to try to cope with what happened. A senior, Zachary Rubin, who you all knew and many of you cared about, is dead. We all have a lot to say and a lot we don't know how to say. That's why I'd like us to do this exercise. What did you think of Zach? What did he mean to you? Sarah?" she asks, lowering her voice. "Do you want to go first?"

"No," Sarah says. "Yes." She pauses to look anywhere but at our faces. "He was gentle," she says, and Brandon snickers so loud it ricochets around the room.

"That's enough, Brandon," Jill Wang says. She's giving Brandon her evil eye.

"I meant," Sarah says, "that he's—he was—a gentle person. Kind. He never said anything mean about anyone."

That's true, too. He was both kinds of gentle.

"Thank you, Sarah. Brandon, since you're so eager to speak, what did you think of Zachary Rubin?"

Brandon shrugged. "He was alright. I didn't have nothing against him."

"*Anything* against him," she corrects. I don't think counselors are supposed to do that. Her dislike of Brandon is leaking out. Happens to all of us.

"Not that neither," he says, grinning at his own wit.

"Do we have to say different things?" Lucy asks. "Because I was going to say he was kind but Sarah already said that."

"You can say whatever you want."

I want to say that this is bullshit and everyone should shut the fuck up, but I suspect that's not what the counselor had in mind.

"He was kind, then," Lucy says. "And funny. He made me laugh. I liked him."

He wasn't kind. Gentle, but not kind. They are confusing his easiness with kindness. A kind person goes out of their way to do right by people. Zach wasn't like that. He wanted smoothness. A life without agitation.

"All the girls *liked* him," Brandon says, then he lowers his voice to a whisper. "But you were no chance, Luce. He liked dark girls. *Really* dark girls." He smirks at Sarah. "Micah was barely dark enough."

"It's no longer your turn, Brandon," Jill Wang says.

I wonder if she heard all that he said. Sarah did. She's glaring at Brandon like she wants to smack him. I'd like to kill him.

I'm next. The counselor looks at me and nods.

"I don't know," I say. "I pass."

"You can't think of anything you'd like to say?" Jill asks. "Even something small? The exercise works much better if we all contribute."

I can think of many things I want to say: the taste of his mouth. The smell of him after he ran. How it felt to run my fingers along his flank. Sarah is staring at me.

"Micah?" Jill Wang prompts.

"Like Lucy said. He was funny."

"Andrew?"

He shrugs. "I didn't know the guy. I don't even know why I have to come here."

"You were all in the same year as Zachary. Such a

violent, unexpected death is shocking whether you knew him well or not."

"I guess," Andrew says, sounding bored, not shocked. "I try not to think about it, you know? Zach was okay, I guess."

"I can tell you one thing," Alejandro says. "No one but teachers called him Zachary. To everyone else he was Zach or the Z-Man."

"Z-Man?" Brandon laughs. "How lame is that? Who called him that?"

"Me," Tayshawn says. "The other guys on the team. It was respect. You wouldn't understand."

"I thought he was cute," Chantal says, smiling at Sarah. "I was kind of jealous of Sarah. You know, 'cause she was dating the cutest guy in school. Sorry, Sarah."

Sarah gives a tight smile in return. Everyone else is looking at me.

Lucy nods. "Lots of us thought he was cute. We're all sorry."

Sorry about what? That Zach's dead or that they didn't get to date him before he died? I never heard Lucy say anything about Zach before he died. She'd always been pining after Tayshawn. Did being dead make Zach cuter?

They continue to go around the circle. Each person says something meaningless. By the end of the session none of us knows a single thing about Zach that we didn't already know.

He's still dead, and we don't know how, or who made him that way.

———

FAMILY HISTORY

One time, I almost killed Jordan. I can't remember what he'd done. It could have been the time he told about my sneaking out at night down the fire escape. Or the time he drew all over my favorite running shoes. Telling, stealing, destroying—that's Jordan's standard m.o.

But one day the heinous thing he'd done pushed me over the edge. I stood looking at the broken fragments, or the ashes, or whatever it was, and glowered over him, clenching my fists, ready to throw him against the wall, smash his skull in. Have the shards of it pierce his brain. Watch the blood sprout from his nose. His eyes flutter, all whites, jaw loose, tongue lolls. Him falling, shuddering, stilling.

I could see from his eyes that he knew I was ready to do it. He was frozen and trembling. He didn't scream or cry. Or he knew it wouldn't make any difference. Even if Mom and Dad were home, which they weren't, they wouldn't get to us in time. They wouldn't stop it. Who knew if they could? I'd been stronger than them for years.

I drew back my right arm, ready to smash his nose across his face, drive him into the brick wall.

But I didn't.

I drew back from my rage. I didn't tear him apart limb from limb.

I wouldn't get away with it. Even with Mom and Dad away—the walls between apartments are not thick: if he'd screamed someone would have heard him.

I went into my room, shut the door, sat on the floor with my back against my metal desk, and decided to poison him instead.

I didn't want Mom or Dad to suspect.

He was still little back then. Four or five. Stupid enough to drink Drāno. I decided to put it in his path. Tell him not to drink it. Then walk away.

I didn't do that either.

Not for Jordan's sake, but for my mom's. Killing him would hurt her.

And me, too. If I was busted. Sitting down, thinking it through meant that I would never do it.

I had to hope for an accident.

BEFORE

Me and Zach, we were put on library duty together.

That's another thing about our school: you have to contribute, give back to your community. Community starts with the school, which is very clever 'cause that means we students save the school money by doing their work for them. Mostly you volunteer for tasks. I always volunteer to pick up the trash in the park and on the sidewalk outside the school. Anything that gets me outdoors.

But they also like to stretch you. Get you to do stuff you would never do otherwise. Like for me and Zach— neither of us readers—they make us work in the library. Shelving and all that.

That first time it was me, Zach, Chantal, and Brandon. A quartet of nonreaders stuck together. At any other school that would be no big deal, but our school is full of readers. Didn't surprise me that Brandon doesn't read, he can barely talk—but Chantal wanted to be an actor. I always thought actors read a lot. It's their job, isn't it? Reading words, memorizing them, saying them out loud.

Not Chantal.

I don't read, but I do like libraries. I like order, and libraries are all about order. Every book has a place. It's quiet, too: no music.

I watched Zach at the other end, framed between shelves, gathering up books left on desks, on couches, on the floor. Brandon helping. Though not really. He kept trying to talk. Zach would say "yes" or "no" or grunt. He likes quiet. He likes that I talk as little as he does.

My job was to scan the shelves for books in the wrong place. Of which there were many. I was doing fiction. Chantal, nonfiction. I looked for numbers where there should be letters; she looked for letters where there should be numbers.

"My cart's full," she called out to me. "Time for you to shelve them."

Mine wasn't, but it wasn't far off. I wheeled it over to her. Hers was less full than mine. This meant she wanted to talk. Chantal is so afraid of silence she will even talk to pariahs like me.

We swapped carts. I pushed hers in the direction of fiction.

"Did you hear that Zach and Sarah split up?" Chantal asked, to stop me from going back to fiction.

I hadn't. I hoped it wasn't true. I looked over at him. He didn't look any different. Maybe it wasn't true. I looked at Chantal. She nodded. "Happened yesterday."

We were both staring at Zach. I was willing it not to be true. Him and Sarah being together was what made me and Zach possible.

"They'll be back together in seconds," Chantal said.

I hoped she was right.

"Pity. He's gorgeous. But those two can't live without each other."

Zach was on the ground reaching for a book under the couch. Tables and chairs obstructed my view, but I could see his legs, calf muscles clenching and unclenching, and the top of his head. Brandon was telling him something. I heard the words "class" and "shit" and "no." Brandon liked to talk, I decided, as bad as Chantal.

"He's cute, isn't he?" Chantal said.

"Brandon?" I asked.

She laughed. "No! Zach. I'd date him in a heartbeat. Wouldn't you?"

I wouldn't. I liked our secret. If he and Sarah really were broken up that meant our secret would be broken, too. I couldn't think of anything worse than Chantal and Brandon and the whole school knowing about us.

———

AFTER

Halfway to school I turn around and head home. I was planning to go, but as I'm crossing Broadway I lose heart. The strength that's been holding me together slides away. I can't take another day of being stared at. Of listening to rumors and innuendo. Of Sarah interrogating me. Of classes that I cannot follow. Of Zach everywhere and yet nowhere.

Of stupid talk about Erin.

I'm not sure I can ever go back to school.

Dad is flying out this morning on assignment to Jamaica to stay in Ian Fleming's house. It's 8:15. His flight is at 9:00. Even with his love of close calls he should be gone by now.

I don't remember the last time I was alone in the apartment.

Every step I take toward home is lighter than the one before it.

I turn the corner and there's Dad getting into a cab.

I step back.

Just like Dad to be crazy late. How's he going to make it? Well, if—really, when—he misses the plane, surely they'll put him on a later one. It should still be ages before he turns up. But I want to throttle him. It feels like he did it on purpose to thwart me.

Once I'm sure the cab is gone, I climb the stairs to our apartment. The only time I like it is when it's empty. Especially after Dad has gone on one of his trips. He says he can't pack unless the apartment is neat, so he cleans and polishes and tidies. That's how he likes things: clean, shining, orderly. As unlike the farm as possible.

It is the only thing we have in common.

I walk in and shut the door behind me. Lock it. The stupid girl next door has her music up loud.

I go directly to the brat's room. It's not clean or orderly. There are dolls and trucks everywhere. Though the brat calls them action figures. It drives him crazy when I call them dolls. So I do. It's what they are. Fake people that you can dress and play with and accessorize. What else would you call them?

I start with the toy boxes, going through each one. Then his chest of drawers.

And there it is, in the second drawer, underneath his pajamas.

Zach's sweater. I hug it. Press it to my nose.

It doesn't smell like Zach anymore. It smells like the brat.

Doesn't matter that I also have Zach's jersey, which reeks of him; I stole that. The sweater, Zach gave me. It's a direct connection between us.

I'm going to kill the idiot boy.

I take the sweater into my room and put it in the one place I know the brat will never go, even if he's stupid enough to brave my room again. I push back the cloth over my metal desk, lift up the lid, and put it inside.

———

AFTER

When Brandon follows me after school he is much more stealthy than Sarah. Which isn't hard. For a while I don't notice him because I am lost in playing dodge the crowd, floating in the movement of air currents. Me and my backpack in space, weaving around everyone, listening to the rhythms of feet on sidewalk. Forgetting anything that isn't weaving and dodging. For whole seconds at a time I am not thinking about Zach.

Part of me must sense Brandon following because I am jangled. I am off my game. I keep misjudging the distances—narrowly, the merest touch—the corner of someone's coat grazing my backpack, the clip of the back of a heel. Stupid. Annoying. Back I go to the start of the block.

It isn't till we're in Central Park that I spot him. If you can call it that. He wants me to see him.

I'm going through one of the stretch routines Zach taught me. My heel resting on a low fence, I lean forward till I feel it along my hamstrings. My skin prickles, not from the stretch, from something else. I look up.

A couple are making out on a blanket under an elm tree. There's a family with four kids and one mother picnicking on a much larger blanket. The kids are laughing. The oldest, with braids, is tickling the youngest; the mother is moving the cake out of the way of the toddler's flailing feet.

Then there's Brandon sitting on the grass, staring at me, smirking. He stands up, walks toward me, sits on the fence.

"Stretching, huh," he says, as if there's something sinister about it.

"What do you want?" I say, and immediately wish I hadn't. I should ignore him. He wants to get me riled. But I want to know why he's here. He doesn't like me. I don't like him. We have nothing to say to each other.

Half a dozen runners stride past. I watch them go. They're wearing the same shorts and T-shirts. Yellow and green. I wonder what kind of team they are because they're not runners. Their technique is all wrong. Barely lifted knees, arms swinging all over the place, heels pounding flat-footed.

Zach taught me to run more on my toes. To strike only lightly on my heel and have full flexion through the foot. It made me even faster.

I resume my stretch. Brandon pulls out a pack of cigarettes, lights one, inhales, blows smoke at me.

I lean deeper into my hamstring stretch. I'm thinking about how much stronger I am than Brandon. I doubt he realizes that. Boys never do. He should be scared of me. Because I *really* don't like him and I'll hurt him if I have to.

A single runner pads past. A real one this time. I don't have to turn; I can tell from their stride: no drag, no pounding of heels.

"You do this a lot, don't you?" he says. "Especially here."

I switch legs, ignoring the foul smoke, ignoring Brandon.

" 'Cause I heard they found the body in Central Park. Not far from here actually—and I thought, shit, Micah's always here. What are the odds? Specially with her and Zach being so . . ." He pauses, takes a long drag on his cigarette, blows the smoke in my direction.

I have to stop myself from looking up. From telling him that Central Park is not exactly unpopulated. Hundreds, no, thousands of people are here all the time. Night and day. Is he blind? Does he not notice the kids on blades who just floated by? All the runners? What about the family on the blanket and the couple making out not six feet from where he was sitting on the grass? There's hardly an empty patch in Central Park this time of year. Even in winter there are people out in it, tromping through snow, past leafless trees, seeking a respite from concrete and steel.

I want to ask Brandon how he knows where Zach was found. Was it really here? Where exactly? What else does Brandon know? But if he knows, then someone else at school does, too. Maybe I can find out without asking Brandon a thing.

I take off at top speed, knowing he couldn't keep pace even if I went at a slow trot.

———

FAMILY HISTORY

I wouldn't mind going upstate so much if my family went with me. Well, okay, they take me up—Mom and Dad and idiot brother—but they don't stay. Just me. Sometimes I'm afraid they won't return. I'll be stuck there forever.

My parents have excuses for not staying but it feels like they want to be rid of me.

Dad says he can't work there. Not without electricity. His laptop has at most four hours of life. He has to go into town to work. Mom hates it. "I can never get clean," she says. "The water is so cold."

Jordan would stay but the Greats don't want him. He doesn't say anything in front of me but I know he's jealous. I've heard him whining to my parents about wanting to play in the woods. "Why doesn't Grandmother like me?" he asks. Because you're a sniveling useless brat, I want to tell him. But I'm not supposed to have heard. Our apartment's so small that we always pretend we can't hear the things we're not supposed to. It's a good rule.

I'm happy the Greats don't want Jordan, but I wish my parents would stay.

The Greats have a thing about the oldest child.

Which is me.

The Greats teach me woodcraft—tracking, hunting, skinning, how to find my way in the forest, how to find food, make shelter. It's more work than school. But if the world ends we'll be ready. That's the idea: survivalism.

Some of their neighbors are that way. They have basements full of canned food, dried beans and fruits, secret wells, bows and arrows.

The other neighbors are sheep farmers who think the survivalists and the Greats are crazy. But then they're always complaining about coyote taking their sheep. Coyote bigger and tougher than any coyote previously known to the universe, Grandmother says. "I've never seen one," she always says. "Man with coyote-skin jacket, maybe. What would Hilliard have said about that?"

I never saw any coyote either. Not on our property. Black bears occasionally, but never coyote.

Or deer. Not like on some of the neighbors' places, where there's more deer than flies. Though we have more raccoons and foxes, and our forest is much more foresty. Without all the deer chomping away, herbs and shrubs and saplings have a much better chance. We have taller, stronger, healthier trees and birds and insects everywhere you look. In spring there are more kinds of flowers than

I can name. Their fragrances float on air, making breathing a pleasure.

It's beautiful. I can admit that.

While I hate music, I like birdsong. Their bells and flutes don't hurt my head.

The Greats aren't happy when I call them survivalists. They didn't know the word when I first brought it up. When I described it to them they sneered. They hate their neighbors. But what they say sounds the same as all the crazy survivalist sites about hunting and tracking and building your own shelters and knowing what's edible and what's not. How to survive when the end-times come.

Grandmother doesn't talk about end-times, though she does say that the world is off-kilter. Everything, she says, is hotter and colder and more extreme than it used to be. She prides herself on having stuck to horse and buggy. On growing her own food. On needing hardly anything from outside.

The Greats think I'm like them.

I'm not. I'm a city girl. I like electricity and running water. I don't want to know how to ride a horse, how to slaughter a calf, how to set a trap, or any of the other things they teach me.

I do not belong there.

Though sometimes it *is* fun.

Because of Hilliard.

Now I must confess to a lie. Everything I've told you

so far has been completely true except for the tiny matter of Great-Uncle Hilliard. Hilliard's alive.

But it's not my lie, it's the family's. Hilliard's in hiding on the farm. I don't know what it was he did or who he's hiding from, but to everyone other than us Wilkins, Hilliard's dead. Grandmother and Great-Aunt hiss at me if I slip up and talk about him in the present tense. Idiot Jordan doesn't know. Only Dad and me.

I love Hilliard.

He taught me how to track and, when I was little, how to run. We run in the forest together. He's not as fast as me—he's old, after all, but it's still fun. He may not be fast but he's better at running through the woods. I still stumble, sometimes I fall. Hilliard knows the woods: every old stump, every tree root, every shrub. He never even gets spiderwebs in his face.

When something warm and breathing and edible is near he goes stiller than a rock. Sees it long before it sees him.

I wonder how it would have been if Grandmother had married Hilliard. If Hilliard was my grandfather. If I'd grown up in the woods. If there was no city in me at all.

I'd never have met Zach.

Would that have been better or worse?

I think some—maybe most—of what Zach liked about me was the country parts, not the city. When I showed him how to find food in Central Park. How to hide. Really hide. Showed him red-headed woodpeckers and chipmunks, too. He hadn't thought there was any wildlife in the city—not anything that wasn't a rat or a pigeon.

He thought I was wild.

He liked the wild in me.

———

BEFORE

I didn't do it to show off.

We were running, Zach and me, slow, four or so miles in, halfway up Heartbreak Hill, when I smelled fox. I knew they were there. I'd caught their scent before. But not this strong. They were close.

"Want to see some foxes?" I asked Zach, slowing my pace to barely running at all.

"Foxes?" he asked, looking at me odd. "What do you mean 'foxes'? Hot girls I didn't notice? Other than you, I mean." He stopped, looked around.

"No, foxes. Actual foxes."

"Does it mean something I don't know about? 'Cause you can't mean the red animals with the big tails, right?"

I laughed. He was balanced on one leg, staring at me as if I was about to do something weird.

"Yes, doof. Foxes. The animals." I wrinkled my nose, brought my hands up to my face. "Red. Tricky. Eat rabbits. Foxes, you know?"

"Okay. Foxes. The animals. What about them?"

"Do you want to see some?"

"Here?" Zach looked around. "In Central Park?" A Mercedes drove by. Four bikes with riders tricked out in dazzling fluorescent zipped past.

"Yes, here. C'mon," I said, taking off at a slow trot. "Follow me!" I breathed deep, sucking in fox scent, weeding out all other odors. Mine. Zach's. Car fumes. Rubber. Urine. Rain getting ready to fall. I left the path and headed deeper into the park.

Zach followed.

When we came to the den, I led us upwind and crouched down on rocks behind bushes.

"Now what?" Zach asked.

"Now we wait."

"But I don't see anything."

I pointed at the brush a little downhill from us. "In there is a fox den."

"That's just bushes."

"And a fox den." I couldn't believe he didn't see the trampled grass. Or smell the sharp meat-eater odor. "See those white and brown things lying there?" I pointed.

Zach nodded.

"Bones."

"Fox bones?" Zach asked.

"No, bones of stuff they've eaten. Probably chipmunk or rabbit. Though mostly they get into the trash cans and eat our leftovers."

"You're really serious? That there are foxes in there?"

"Yes! Shhh, now. Wait. You'll see."

Zach blew air through his teeth but he hunkered down lower, his thigh brushing mine.

When the first fox emerged it was dusk. Its snout was in the air, orange and white, black tip glistening, tongue hanging out.

"No shit," Zach whispered. "A fox!"

———

AFTER

"When we interviewed you last Tuesday," Detective Stein says, "you said you'd never spoken to Zach."

"Yes," I say, because that's what I'd said. I don't like them calling him "Zach." They didn't know him. They should call him "Zachary" like all the other clueless adults.

This is a house visit. Even though we live in an apartment. A *tiny* apartment. We are in the kitchen. My dad leans against the fridge next to Detective Rodriguez, who's leaning against the sink. They are mere inches from where me and Mom are seated side by side on the other side of the kitchen table from Detective Stein. I hope one of the bicycles falls on him.

Mom has offered both of the detectives coffee and tea and juice and water. They've rejected everything. She offers Rodriguez the seat next to Stein. He says no, he prefers to stand. At the last interview he sat and Stein leaned.

I figure they reject all forms of hospitality to make it clear that they don't trust me and thus, by extension, my parents. It feels petty. I wish I could ask them questions. Where did they find Zach? Who killed him? Why?

"Now, we hear that Zach's your boyfriend," Stein says.

I look down at my hands. I want them to think that I am shy and afraid of them. Not that I am pissed that I have to talk to them. Mom takes my left hand in hers and squeezes it. Like Yayeko did at the first interview.

"Is that correct?" Rodriguez asks.

"What?" I ask. Maybe if they think I'm stupid they'll leave me alone.

"Is it true that Zachary Rubin was your boyfriend?"

"He was Sarah Washington's boyfriend."

Stein shifts in his seat and accidentally kicks the toaster under the table. There is a loud clang that echoes around the tiny kitchen.

"And also your boyfriend," Detective Stein says, as if he hasn't just hurt his toes. "Or was every student who told me that lying?"

He leans across the table. I can smell his breath. He's a smoker. He's tried to cover it up with something peppermint flavored, but the nicotine is stronger. Three of his fingers are stained yellow. "I hear that it's *you* who tells lies. Is that true?"

The unanswerable question. So I don't. I stare at my fingers interlaced with Mom's. My nails need trimming. Mom squeezes my hand a little tighter.

"You're a liar, aren't you, Micah?" Stein hisses at me.

"Is your rudeness necessary, officer?" my father asks in his calm tone of voice, which means he's really angry.

"Detective," Stein and Rodriguez say at the same time.

"Detectives, I'd appreciate it if you didn't yell at my daughter. We agreed to this interview because we want to assist with your investigation. I don't want to call my lawyer, but I will."

As far as I know Dad doesn't have a lawyer.

"Sorry, Mr. Wilkins," Stein says, not sounding even slightly apologetic. "We're trying to get to the truth."

"We're very sorry, ma'am, sir," Detective Rodriguez says, looking first at my mom and then my dad, and sounding more sincere. "But we have to ask these questions. We can also conduct this interview at the station.

We don't want to insist on that, but this is a criminal investigation."

Dad opens his mouth to object and Stein talks across him. "Was he your boyfriend, Micah?"

"No," I say. We never used that word. Well, okay, sometimes I did, but in my thoughts, not out loud. Zach never called me anything but Micah. I glance at Dad, who gives me half a smile, but he is not happy. Mom's squeezing my hand again. I'm glad for the comfort of it, but I don't think it will continue after this interview.

"He wasn't your boyfriend?"

"No." I think about telling them that it's a lie Brandon has been telling. He says he saw us kissing in Central Park. We never kissed, I could tell them. He's such a liar. It is dawning on me that I am a suspect. Not just at school but with the police.

"Did you see him outside school?" Stein's cheeks are red. He looks like he wants to shake me. I glance at Rodriguez. He's harder to read, but he doesn't seem kind.

They really believe I could have killed Zach. I move my head—something that's half nod and half shake. They take it as a yes.

"Why didn't you tell us last time that you knew him outside of school?" Stein asks.

"It was a secret. I promised I wouldn't tell anyone."

"I'm sure," Detective Rodriguez says, "that Zach wouldn't have meant the police."

Well, he's dead, isn't he? None of his wishes mean anything now. My promises are as dead as he is. I still don't want to talk about him. Not with them.

Detective Stein is leaning across the kitchen table, staring at me. It's creepy. I wish the table was wider. I wish the kitchen was bigger, too. Or that there was a living room. Instead of it being Mom and Dad's bedroom and where we watch TV.

"What did you do together outside of school?" Stein asks, in a tone of voice that implies we must have been doing something he didn't approve of.

I look at my mom. She squeezes my hand tighter. Dad nods and smiles.

"We ran," I say. "Training. I like to run."

"She's very fast," my dad says, sounding proud.

"Where did you run?" Rodriguez asks.

"Central Park mostly."

"When did you last see him?"

"Friday night."

"You ran at night?" Rodriguez says, as if that's unusual.

"Lots of people do," Dad says, in a tone that says he thinks Rodriguez is stupid and from the sticks. It's one of Dad's favorite tones. Stein briefly transfers his glare from me to Dad. But then he's back to glaring at me. I want to tell him he's not getting to me but that would probably prove to him that he is.

"So you ran together? You didn't chat or go get a malted?" Stein asks.

"We ran," I say. I wonder what a malted is. I know it doesn't matter. I don't want to think about them believing I killed Zach.

"What time did you stop running that night?"

"I'm not sure," I say. "Maybe 9:00 or 9:30?"

"Was it any different from your normal running sessions?" Rodriguez asks.

"No," I say. "We stretched. We practiced sprints. Then we did distance. A bit more than ten miles."

"Ten miles?" Stein asks. "What time did you start?"

"Must've been by 8:30."

"You started your ten-mile run at 8:30 and were done by 9:30? What? You're running six-minute miles?" he asks. He thinks I'm lying. I never lie about running.

Six minutes? I am tempted to tell him that I go sub-five all the time. But Dad hates it when I show off. Besides, if they know how fast I run maybe that will make them suspect me more. "We were running for a long time," I say.

"I told you she's good, didn't I?" Dad says.

"We were building up to twenty-six," I add.

"That's the length of a marathon," Dad explains, to show them how stupid he thinks they are. "Twenty-six miles, 385 yards." He is not helping me.

"When you were done training that night," Rodriguez says, "what did you do?"

"Went home."

"Did you go home together?"

"No," I say, even though we did. "He lives—lived—in Inwood and I'm all the way down here."

"And that's the last time you saw him?" Rodriguez asks.

"Yes."

"Did he seem upset?" Rodriguez asks, trying to sound concerned.

"No."

"Did he say he was going to meet with anyone?"

"No. He said he was going home." Didn't just say it. I ran with him every step of the way from the park to Inwood.

"Did he ever tell you he was afraid of anyone?" Stein wants to know.

"No. Never. I don't think he was afraid of anything."

"Or anyone?"

I shake my head. He wasn't even afraid of me, which made him different from almost everyone else at school. Most of them are too scared to look me in the eye. It's like they think my lies are contagious. Or that looking at me will turn them into as big a weirdo as I am.

"What was his frame of mind when you last saw him?" Rodriguez asks.

Frame of mind? I want to mock him, but he is a

policeman who thinks I might have killed Zach. "He was tired. Beat. But he seemed happy. I didn't think it would be the last time I'd ever see him." I have to concentrate to keep my voice steady. I can't cry in front of them.

"Was it the last time?"

"Yes," I said. "Like I told you."

"We have an account from another student who says you saw him late Saturday night. Or rather, early Sunday morning."

Sarah. Had to be. Why had I lied to her about that? Because I wanted her to feel bad, wanted her to think I was the last one who kissed him, not her.

"No. You can ask Mom and Dad. I was here all of that Saturday. Sunday, too."

Rodriguez turned to Dad.

"Yes," Dad says. Mom nods. "Micah was grounded that weekend."

"Why?" Rodriguez asks.

Dad pauses. Mom and Dad look at each other. "No," my mom says. "It is not for us to say."

They grounded me because they caught me kissing Zach. One of their many rules for me is no dating until after high school. There'll be no such rule for Jordan; he doesn't have the family illness.

"It is a private matter. For the family only," Mom says.

Stein and Rodriguez don't look convinced or

impressed. "We can continue this at the station. Sounds like we might have to interview all three of you."

"Fine," Dad says. "Micah stole money from my wallet and then lied when I asked her about it."

Great, I think, now Dad's lying about my lying and calling me a thief. That will really help. Mom shoots him a soul-chilling glare. "Isaiah," she mutters.

"How do you know she did it?"

"I saw her," Dad says. "We wanted to see what she would say when we said the money was missing."

"So you both agree that your daughter is a liar?"

Well, they walked into that one.

"Sometimes," Dad says, as if it's no big deal. "Aren't most kids? We're trying to teach her better. Hence the grounding."

"Have you been telling us the truth today, Micah?" Stein asks.

"Yes, sir," I say. "I have."

"Because if we find out you've been lying, the consequences will be much worse than being grounded for the weekend. Do you understand?"

I nod. "Yes, I understand."

Rodriguez coughs. "I suspect we'll be talking to you again," he says. "In the meantime, if you think of anything else—no matter how small—let us know." Rodriguez leans over to hand me his card. I put it on the table, staring at it. Maybe they don't suspect me after all?

Stein stands up and bangs his head on Dad's bicycle. He swears.

Dad looks down and Mom bites her lip. Rodriguez smiles briefly. I'm the only one who's not tempted to laugh.

———

AFTER

"I'm sick," I tell my dad, who's slipped into my room to see why I haven't gotten up yet. I've been holding an ice pack in my hands and overheating my face by holding it too close to the radiator. The sheets and comforter are pulled up to my chin. I'm hot and cold and sweaty.

I can't face school. I bet they all know that the cops were here. The rumors about me and Zach and what I did to him are getting out of control. Today I can't deal with the whispers.

"Sweetheart," Dad says, sitting down on the bed, "I know it's all been a shock. You need to take time off. Go upstate."

I have an urge to tell him how bad it is at school. To beg him to let me finish the school year at home. Stay in my room and send in my assignments. But I'm afraid he'll pack me off to the Greats. No finishing the school year, no college. Just the farm for the rest of my life.

Faking sick is my compromise. I want to have a legitimate absence from school. Maybe I can fake a serious illness long enough not to have to go back and yet still finish the school year.

"Dad," I say, weakly, worried I'm trying too hard. It's hard to fake regular sick when you've almost never had a cold or flu. Only the family illness. "I'm really sick."

He puts his hand on my forehead. "You do feel a bit hot. Is your throat sore?"

I nod. It feels like it's full of razor blades, but not the way he means.

"Give me your hand."

I do.

"Cold! Clammy, too. That can't be good. Maybe I should take you to a doctor?"

I look at him. Dad knows how I feel about doctors. There have been way too many in my life.

"Okay, not a doctor. But if you're still like this when your mom gets home you might have to. I'll get you some water. What do you want for breakfast? Scrambled eggs okay?"

I nod. For once I'm glad he works from home.

He stands up. "Did you take your pill?"

I don't groan, just nod weakly. When he closes the

door behind him, I pull the covers up over my head, close my eyes, and fall asleep.

Sometimes I can be very still.

———

BEFORE

"Why'd you tell that lie about being born messed up?" Zach asked me, his mouth tickling my ear.

We were at his place, curled together on his bed. His parents were out of town visiting family. The window was wide-open and we could hear all the traffic noises from the street seven stories below. Sometimes even snatches of conversation from people walking by. I hear people talking all the time at my place, but I figured that was 'cause we're only on the fourth floor. Seven stories ought to bring some quiet with it. Especially here in Inwood, so much less congested than downtown.

"C'mon, Micah, why'd you lie like that?"

"Wasn't a lie," I told him, turning so that our faces were barely an inch apart. "I was born messed up." I was tempted to tell him about the hair. I was tempted to tell him the truth.

Zach leaned up on his elbow, looked at me straight. His eyebrows unmoving. His mouth still, like he didn't approve, but wasn't going to show it.

I leaned up, too. "My parents don't like to admit that I was born funny. *They're* the liars, not me."

"Born with boy parts and girl parts?" He stared at me, trying to read my face. "You know that's gross, right? If I believed you there's no way—"

"Really?" I asked, shocked. "It would change how you think about me?"

I don't know why I was surprised. I was brought up my whole life on the belief that telling people the truth leads to disaster. I've done it, too. Told the truth and watched everyone freak out.

"Are you kidding me?" Zach said, moving a little farther away from me. "Bad enough that you're a liar without thinking about you being all messed up down there." He shuddered.

"Fine," I said. "Think what you want to think."

"I think that you're a mess. But not *that* kind of a mess. I like you. But I wish you wouldn't lie to me. You don't have to. You can tell me true things. You can tell me nothing at all. But I don't like you lying."

"You want me to tell you a true thing? Okay, and I never told anyone this before." I truly hadn't. I could feel myself holding my breath, getting ready to let it out. But Zach laughed.

"Never told anyone before? Tayshawn said that's what you said when you told him about being a girl *and* a boy."

"Tayshawn told you that?" I asked, leaning against

the wall, making myself smaller. Talking was making Zach not want to touch me. I wanted us to stop talking and start kissing.

"Tayshawn's my boy. You told him you'd never told anyone before, but then you went and told Chantal and Brandon and I don't know who else."

"Well, they were giving me grief for pretending I was a boy. I wanted to shut them up."

Zach didn't say anything but I could tell that he didn't believe me. Fair enough. It was a lie: I told them for the attention, for the pleasure of fooling them, for the look of shock on their faces.

Zach put his thumb to my mouth like he didn't want to hear it. My lips felt warm and tingling.

"How long you been lying for?" he asked. "Tayshawn thinks you don't know how to tell the truth. Why is that?"

"How come you and Tayshawn talk about me?" I asked. I didn't want to answer his questions. "I thought we were a secret!"

"We're guys, we don't *talk* about nothing. Not like girls do. I never told him about you and me. We're a secret. It was before, when everyone was talking about you."

"Great."

Zach laughed. "Well, you pass for a boy, you lie inside out—people talk." He held my face in both hands and then kissed me, a short closed-mouth kiss. Not the kind of kiss I was longing for. "How long you been lying?"

"All my life," I said, because he wanted honesty.

That's the truth. I don't know if Zach believed me, but I hope you do. Because you're the only one I've never lied to.

"What?" Zach asked, pulling his hands away. "When you were a baby in your crib sucking on your pacifier you were telling lies?"

"Okay, so maybe I haven't been lying *always*. But from the time I started talking. I learned it from my parents. Well, my dad mostly. My mom's lies are white ones. 'You look fine.' 'Oh, is that what time it is?' You know."

"Regular lies."

I agreed. "What about you? What kind of lies do you tell?"

"Regular ones. And as few as possible. I don't like 'em."

"Why not?"

He shrugged. "It's not right."

"What do you tell Sarah when you're with me?"

"White lies. The kind that don't harm anyone. But your lies are crazy. Why would you pretend you was a boy? That you were born messed up? Why do you lie all the time?"

"If you've got a big secret it's best to paper it over with lots of little ones."

"So what's your big secret, huh?"

The moment had passed. I wasn't going to tell him about the family illness. "I can't tell you."

"I'll tickle it out of you," he said, going for my armpits.

"No!" I yelled, trying to roll away, but I was against the wall. "You will not!"

I grabbed for his wrists. He twisted away. He was on top of me and then I was on top of him and we were going around and around and there was less tickling and yelling and mouths were close and hearts were beating faster and I forgot what he was asking. Lost it in the taste of his mouth. The feel of his tongue and lips against mine.

"Micah," Zach breathed, "I don't care what you are."

I did.

Do.

HISTORY OF ME

You're wondering if we slept together, aren't you?

I know you are. It's what everyone wants to know. Did they?

Then there's me telling you about us *in bed together*.

With no mention of whether our clothes are on or off. And we're doing what?

Talking.

You don't believe that's all we did, do you? Not with all that tickling and kissing and stuff. You want to know what else we did together. How far it went. First base? Second? Third? All the way home?

You know I'm on the pill so it's not like I'd get pregnant. You know I'm old enough. It wouldn't make me a slut, would it? He was my only one. But then there's Sarah—Zach's *real* girlfriend. She's allowed to think that I'm a slut, isn't she? I mean, it's her boyfriend we're talking about. If she's allowed, then everyone else can think it, too. Sleeping with someone else's boy is the definition of slut.

Except that, as it happens—and not that this is any of your business—we weren't.

We didn't.

It was kissing and holding and hugging. *Lots* of kissing. But we never took our clothes off. Never got past that very first base. He didn't touch mine; my fingers got nowhere near his.

See?

I am a good girl after all.

I didn't kill him either.

AFTER

For the first time in my life I want to be up at the farm, out of school, and out of the city. I want to go running with Hilliard. Have him show me some new tricks.

I know that after a few days up there I'll be longing to be back home, but right this instant it's what I want.

School is too much.

But I make myself go anyway.

A day in bed was more than I could stand. Dad worrying over me was too much. Everything is too much.

In the hall, Tayshawn nods at me. I nod back. He's always been nice to me. I don't know why. I've heard that the police have been interviewing him at home, too.

No one else greets me. They stare. They talk about me, but not to me.

I eat my lunch in Yayeko Shoji's room. She's not one of the popular teachers. It's not one of the popular rooms. I can sit in bio, eat, look at the diagrams and posters on the wall, think about evolution and fast-twitch muscles, entropy, death, and decay.

Zach.

All right, the biology room is not such a good idea. But what *doesn't* remind me of Zach? Of what happened to him. What place in this school, this city, is safe for me now?

Nowhere.

There are seven more months of school left. I don't think I'm going to make it.

But if I go upstate now I might not ever finish school.

Worse, if I go upstate now I'll miss the funeral.

———

AFTER

I haven't been entirely honest. I mean, I have been about the facts. About Zach and the police. How awful it was at school, at home. My family history. My illness. How I showed Zach foxes. How everyone suspects me, if not of killing Zach, then of something.

I haven't made myself out to be better than I am. Or worse.

But I haven't been entirely honest about my insides. How it is in my head and my heart and my veins.

Let me come clean:

This is what it felt like when the principal strode into the room to tell us that Zach was dead:

Sharp and cold and wrong.

Like the world had ended.

I thought I knew what the principal was going to say. I thought I knew that Zach was dead. Zach had been missing since Saturday. If he'd been found alive he would have texted me. The principal didn't drop in on class-rooms, not unless something was seriously wrong.

But I'd been hoping. I'd been praying that I was wrong, that Principal Paul was going to say something else. That Zach had been found and was coming back to school. He could have lost his cell phone. He could be in the hospital with a broken leg. Hurt but nothing serious.

I sat there staring at the principal, thinking about everything Zach had ever said to me. That he needed me. That he depended on me. That the smell of me could keep him going all day.

Or did I say that to him?

Him being dead confuses things.

I know he told me that what we had wasn't love. It was something stronger. Me and him weren't like him and Sarah, or him and anyone else. Or any two people together ever.

Zach said that.

Then he went away. He didn't come back.

I thought he would. I was sure he would. Even now, I'm waiting for him.

I wore the mask to keep my face unmoving and un-seen. To keep everything inside where it belonged.

When the words were leaving Principal Paul's mouth—in that moment—I wanted to leap at him. Hold his mouth shut. Or tear out his throat.

Keep the words in.

Because maybe then Zach would be alive.

And I wouldn't be so alone.

BEFORE

One of the true things I told the police was that Danger-ous Words was the last class I had with Zach before he disappeared that weekend—before he was murdered. It's not nearly as good as bio but it's the only other class I don't actively hate. Partly because Lisa Aden is a blusher and partly because she's pretty smart and sometimes it's kind of interesting hearing about what gets banned, how the meanings of words have changed, censorship. All that stuff.

We need signed permission from our parents to take it. Because in Dangerous Words we're allowed to use any dirty words we want. But none of us does. It doesn't feel like we really can. It feels like a trick.

The only time we say dirty words in that room is when we're reading out loud. Some of the assigned books have them. But it feels awkward and forced and we stum-ble over the same words that, outside the classroom, flow from our mouths easy as lies.

Most of our mouths. I've never heard Sarah swear.

No one said any of the words we were supposedly allowed to say. Not until the teacher, Lisa Aden, invited a guest the Friday before Zach was killed. A writer. A foreign writer, from England or something. I wasn't paying attention when he was introduced or when he started talking. I didn't listen to a thing until he picked up a piece of chalk and wrote all the worst words on the board. One by one. Then everyone was paying attention to the chalk in his hands and the words he made.

He wrote each word up on the board, then he said each as if it weren't any different from saying "yes" or "no" or "pie" or "sky." After each word he wrote a date. Really old dates. Every single word was hundreds of years old. From the 1300s or 1400s or 1500s. I tried to imagine people in the olden days saying them, but I couldn't.

"These dates, of course," he said, "refer to the earliest written records, but it's very likely the words themselves are much older. Much. But they were not written down. This is often true of taboo words. Until very recently written language has tended to be more formal than spoken."

He stopped and looked at us like we were supposed to say something. I noticed Lisa Aden had changed color. Even whiter than usual, except for her cheeks, where all the blood in her body seemed to have gathered.

"Of course, some of these words weren't always taboo. And the way we use them now is not necessarily the same as how they were originally used. Words change. I'm sure your teacher has mentioned how the word 'girl' originally meant a child of either sex."

She hadn't.

"This is my favorite." He tapped the worst word on the board and underlined it. The red in Lisa's cheeks spread. "Here in America it's probably the most shocking. But back home, where I come from, there's little force behind it. In fact, it usually gets used as a synonym for 'lad' or 'bloke.'"

"What's a bloke?" Zach asked. His voice buzzed in my ears even though he was at the back of the room.

"A guy. A fella. A man."

"So you wouldn't say, 'those guys over there'?" Zach asked. I didn't turn to look at him. "You'd say, 'those—'"

"Yes." The writer nodded.

Lisa Aden was starting to sweat. I could smell it on her.

"What if they're your friends?" Zach wanted to know. "Or you weren't mad at them?"

"Wouldn't matter," the writer said, and I wondered what kind of books he wrote. Probably not travel guides. My dad never even said "shit," let alone wrote it. "Angry has nothing to do with it. Friends, enemies, acquaintances. They're all—"

"Um," Lisa Aden said, then faltered.

"What about girls? Women?" Kayla wanted to know.

"Just men. If you say it of a woman it means the same thing it means here. So you don't. Unless you're really angry."

Zach looked fascinated.

"So, um, that word doesn't mean the same thing here that it does where you're from?" Aaron Ling asked.

"That's right."

"Like the way English people don't use 'erasers'?" Aaron Ling asked. "Or say 'lift' instead of 'elevator' or 'flat' for 'apartment'?"

The writer nodded.

"Can you tell us a little about how you came to write a book about taboo words?" Lisa Aden asked.

The writer laughed. "Well, you could say it was a lifelong interest."

Half the class laughed, too.

"This is my first book about language. Before that I mostly wrote true crime, which grew out of covering the crime beat in Glasgow. The kind of people I write about, they're not clergymen, you know? Not even close. Rough as guts, more like. I got interested in the words they used so often, and so, er, colorfully. Then I started looking stuff up and before I knew it I was writing a book about so-called bad language."

"So what's the worst swear word where you come from?" Zach asked.

"You know, that's a hard question to answer. The more research I've done on this, the more it seems to be that it's not the words so much as the force behind them. I think people get too caught up in whether a word is or isn't offensive and lose sight of what's actually being said. I mean, is it more offensive for someone to advocate the killing of Arabs or the killing of 'fucking Arabs'? Either way, that's racism, pure and simple."

There was a moment of quiet.

"Do your books ever get banned?" Kayla wanted to know.

"Not that I know of. I don't think books about language or true crime attract the book banners. Not sure why. Isn't it mostly books for teenagers and children that get banned? Like that one about the two boy penguins who fall in love?"

The class laughed again. I wondered if that was a real book or if he was making it up.

"What do you think?" Lisa interjected, addressing the class. "What is it about writing for teenagers that leads to so much censorship?"

I knew the answer to that one but I didn't raise my hand. It's because grown-ups don't remember what it was like when they were teenagers. Not really. They remember something out of a Disney movie and that's where they want to keep us. They don't like the idea of our hormones, or that we can smell sex on one another. That we walk down halls thick with a million different pheromones. We see each other, catch a glance, the faintest edge of one, that sends a shiver through our bodies all the way to the parts of us our parents wish didn't exist.

Like the glance me and Zach exchanged just then. I shifted in my seat. All nerve endings buzzing. Making me itch. Making me have to run. Run far and fast and wide. With Zach beside me, matching me stride for stride.

Not long after the class ended that's what we did. Ran and ran and ran.

But after that night I never saw him again.

FAMILY HISTORY

When Mom and Dad told me I was going to have a baby sister or brother I wasn't upset. I wasn't happy either. I didn't really think about it much, to be honest. I had other problems: dealing with doctors, school.

I was seven years old and covered in hair. There were lots and lots of doctors. I was pulled in and out of different schools. Each one worse than the one before. When the medication wasn't working I wore pants and long-sleeved shirts. (We'd tried waxing, electrolysis, laser. The hair always came back within a day or two.) Sometimes I had to wear scarves and gloves as well. Even when it was ninety degrees. The other kids thought I was weirdo religious or covered in a dreaded skin disease. They weren't far off. They didn't want to go near me.

The growing bump in my mom's stomach wasn't much on my radar.

I was shocked when Jordan was born. Us racing to the hospital. Dad yelling at the taxi driver. Then hours and hours waiting with Mom's friend Liz, who insisted that she hold my hand, before I was finally led in to see my dad tired and sweaty and beaming, and Mom, even tireder, holding a tiny blue bundle.

"Hallo, my darling," Mom said. "You must meet with your brother."

I looked up at Liz, who smiled at me. Dad nodded. "Check him out, Micah. Your brother, Jordan."

"Do I have to?"

Mom laughed. A tiny laugh. She looked ready to sleep for a month.

Liz gave me a little push and I took a step closer to the bed.

I took another step and put my hands on the edge of it, standing on tiptoe to peer at the baby.

It was hate at first sight.

Jordan was grayish blue and uglier than sin. His hair pointed in all the wrong directions, but at least it was only on his head. No family illness for this Wilkins child. His eyes were puffy little slits. "Why's he that weird color?" I asked.

Dad reached down and took the bundle from Mom. "You want to hold him, Micah?"

I shook my head.

"You won't drop him. See?" he said, demonstrating. "It's easy. You make sure you have one hand under his head and one under his body. Isn't he tiny?" Dad passed the bundle into my arms. I got a whiff of something not right that made the hair on my arms stand on end. Not poop or anything like that. A wrongness. The blue baby didn't smell right.

I held him, making sure my hands were where Dad said, though now I wish I'd dropped him. He opened his little beady eyes to look at me. *I don't like you*, I could almost hear him thinking. I didn't like him either. Right away he started screaming.

It's been like that ever since.

AFTER

The funeral goes on forever. I'm uncomfortable and irritable and not just because it's so hot. Nothing anyone says about Zach bears much resemblance to the Zach I knew.

Everyone is lying.

Everyone is creating an ideal Zach with their words.

A Zach in their own image.

It's a Catholic church. I've never been in one before. Light comes in colored by the stained glass windows.

At first I stand at the back, not sure where to sit. I watch people filing in. Most of them people I've never seen before. Do they know who Zach is? Was?

There's organ music. Heavy and somber like an old horror movie. It hurts my head. There's incense, too, as heavy and dense as the music. It doesn't do much for my head either.

His parents walk by. They've shrunk, fallen in on themselves. Grief makes gravity even stronger. His older brother's face is blank. Looking at them makes my eyes sting. They sit at the front near the flowers and the coffin. I've been trying not to look at it, but there it is, dark wood with golden handles. The shape and size are wrong. It doesn't seem long enough. Zach was tall.

Almost all the seniors walk past, teachers, too. The guys wear suits; the girls, black dresses. They don't look like themselves. I'm in the same black-dress disguise. The ones who notice me look away, disgusted. Only Yayeko and Sarah say hi. I lose track of Yayeko. Sarah sits down in front with Zach's family.

Detectives Stein and Rodriguez walk past me. For a moment I am afraid that they will arrest me. They don't nod. I'm not sure they see me.

The church is approaching full. While there's still somewhere to sit, I slide onto the edge of a pew two rows from the back. I don't recognize any of the people near me. That's a good thing. None of them will whisper and point. The dress I'm wearing itches.

I wonder why I'm here. Zach knew I liked him. It doesn't matter what any of these other people think of me, or of me and him.

I wonder what Zach would think.

But Zach doesn't. Not anymore. He's going into the ground. Or into the flames. I'm not sure which.

I try to remember the last time we saw each other. Once again. I try to pull together every detail. What he looked like. What he wore. I don't really remember. The details are blurring. It hasn't been that long and already I'm forgetting things.

The preacher drones a welcome and starts talking about Zach as if he knew him. But I can tell from what he's saying that he didn't. It's easy to block the preacher out. An older man stands up a few rows in front of me and moves up to the podium.

"Scoot over."

I look up.

Tayshawn. Wearing a suit. I almost laugh even though

he looks good. I've never seen Tayshawn in jeans before, let alone jacket and tie. He's always wearing a tracksuit or shorts and jersey so that he can transition into playing ball at a second's notice. He's not nearly as good as Zach but he loves the game way more.

There isn't a lot of scooting space. I turn to my neighbor, a fat old white lady in a black cotton dress. I wonder how she knew Zach. She glares at me, but turns to her neighbor, and they make more wooden pew emerge. Tayshawn squeezes himself onto the last few inches, trying not to press into me, as I try not to touch my neighbor.

"I hate funerals," he whispers to me.

I nod. Though it's my first one. They can't all be like this.

"Some of us are going to hang out after. Drink and stuff. At Will's place. You wanna come?"

I don't drink—one of the many things doctors have forbidden me—but I don't tell him that.

"Not sure," I whisper back. The woman beside me shifts her body in an I-disapprove-of-you-whispering-at-a-funeral way. I lower my voice. "I don't think I'm welcome." Not here. Not at Will's place.

Tayshawn looks at me. I can see him thinking about lying, then deciding not to. "I guess not," he says. He smiles at me. "So you know—I don't believe any of that shit about you."

"Thanks," I say. I mean it.

"Hush," the lady next to me hisses. "A young boy died."

I almost tell her that he had a name and if she actually knew him she wouldn't be calling him "a young boy." I want to tell her that Zach was my—my what? What noun comes after "my"? Running partner? Friend? Best friend? No, that's Tayshawn's. Boyfriend belongs to Sarah.

"You wanna go?" Tayshawn asks. "I really hate these things."

I look at him, at the cranky lady next to me, at the old guy leaning into the podium, talking about Zach's unfulfilled potential, his brilliance on the court. Must be his coach, I guess.

"Sure," I say.

Better to be anywhere than here.

AFTER

Sarah is sitting on the church steps. She does not look all right but Tayshawn asks her if she is anyway.

"No," she says, looking up at us. "But I'm not going to be sick if that's what you mean. It was too much in there."

She's also wearing a black dress. It makes her look

older. Mine is my mom's. I wonder if hers is too. Her eye makeup is smeared from crying.

Tayshawn shifts his weight from one leg to the other and back again. I clasp my hands and stretch my arms out behind my back.

"Where you two going?" Sarah asks.

"Dunno," Tayshawn says. "Away. I don't like funerals."

"Who does?" Sarah asks. "I can't go back in there."

Tayshawn nods. I bite my lip, wonder what to say.

"Can I come with you guys?" she asks.

"Sure," Tayshawn says. "We wasn't going to do anything much." He shrugs.

The plan was getting out of there. I haven't thought beyond that. I think about the time Zach and me walked the whole length of the island. We started down at Battery Park and wound up here in Inwood. Well, not this here, this church, but farther up, on Broadway, at the bridge to the Bronx.

"Micah?" Sarah asks.

"Yeah?"

"You don't mind if I come along?"

"No," I say, realizing that I don't. She knew Zach better than I ever did. Tayshawn has been best friends with Zach since the third grade. They are the two people who knew him best. They are who I want to be with. "Sure," I say.

"We could walk," Tayshawn says. "Down to the park."

Sarah nods, standing up slowly. She has a tiny black sparkly purse looped over her shoulder. "You live around here, too, don't you?"

"Yeah," Tayshawn says. "This is the neighborhood. Me and Zach, we used to, you know. . . ."

For a moment the weight of Zach's death is too much. I feel my throat and chest tighten.

"I could show you. I guess."

Sarah blinks back more tears. "Please," she says.

FAMILY HISTORY

One time when Dad was blue he told me that his father wasn't French after all.

Mom was with the brat at soccer and Dad was sitting at the kitchen table trying to work. When his writing didn't go well, he got sad.

I'd gone into the kitchen to get some juice. I was thinking about going for a run. Dad looked up and I knew immediately he was going to unload.

"I went all the way to Marseille," he told me, without any word of greeting. "I was trying to find him. I knocked on the door of every black family in the city, which is way more than you'd think."

Okay, I thought. He's talking about his dad. I wondered how he knew he'd knocked on all their doors.

"My mother lied to me," he said. "Again."

I leaned against the sink. "Maybe he moved?"

"Ha!" Dad looked at me like I was being crazy. "I found a letter. Upstate. It was in English, not French—*American* English. Addressed to 'My darlin Hope.' Your grandmother's name is Hope," he told me unnecessarily. "The letter was asking after their child—after *me*. It was all about how much my dad missed my mom. How much he wanted to hold the baby—to hold *me*!" Dad's eyes are welling. "It was signed, 'All Yers Always.' There was no other name unless my dad's name was Always or Yers Always. There's no way a Frenchman wrote it."

"Oh," I said.

"I waved the letter in Mom's face. You know what she did?"

He was looking at me. I shook my head.

"She told me not to be so melodramatic. She told me to act my age. I was twenty-two! I *was* acting my age."

"Did Grandmother say why she lied to you?"

"She said, 'You had a good time in France, didn't you, Isaiah? Found yourself a good wife.' She wouldn't tell me who my father is. She said I didn't need to know. That it's better to keep the past muddy. That's her all over, isn't it? I don't think my past could be muddier.

"I still haven't gotten anything out of her. She's back

to acting like my dad was French. So I do the same. Push the truth out of the way. Go on acting like the lie is true. Don't tell your mom. She doesn't know."

He grinned, gave me a wide-open smile that made his eyes crinkle. Dad's teeth were shiny white. "Just another family secret to add to the pile. This one's between you and me. Like Hilliard."

"Right," I said. Dad opened up his laptop. I got myself a glass of orange juice. The end of our father-daughter bonding.

Is it any surprise that I turned out the way I did, with so many family lies?

I'm at least a third-generation liar. Though I bet it goes back earlier. If I could get Grandmother or Great-Aunt Dorothy to talk about it. I wouldn't bother asking Hilliard. I don't think I've ever heard him say a whole sentence.

I wonder if there is a lying gene. If so it runs strong in my family. Which makes me wonder about Dad's story. Was there a letter? Is anything he said true? The only story I've ever had out of the Greats is the one about the French sailor. Maybe Dad lied to me about the letter? Maybe he lied about having gone to France?

No, that has to be true because my mother really is French. Marseille is where they met. Sometimes I think she's the only part of the story that's true. I stick to the French sailor story because I've heard it so many times before. Because Dad only told me about the letter once. I have no idea which version is true. Maybe neither is.

"Keep the past muddy." I believe my grandmother would say that. It was something the whole family lived by. Dad, too, whether he admitted it or not.

It leaves me feeling unanchored.

Telling you the truth is my attempt to anchor myself. It's all I've got.

———

BEFORE

The next time I saw the white boy was in Central Park.

Me and Zach were running. Lockstep. Not talking. Just breathing. My thoughts weren't anywhere but in the feel of my feet hitting the ground, my elbows at my side, the breath in and out. Zach beside me: feet to ground in unison. Breath in and out at the same time.

The boy came from the other direction. Running toward us in jeans and a T-shirt and beat-up pair of boots. Not regular running-in-Central-Park clothes. And so skinny the clothes flopped around him, engulfed him, slowed him down, almost tripped him. He was still fast though. Even with his elbows askew and his heels hitting the ground.

Zach nudged me. But I'd already seen. Already recognized. The boy was looking at me, too. I didn't have words for the expression. Intense. Almost like he hated me.

Then he was past us.

"Ha," Zach said. "Freak."

I didn't say anything. I couldn't help thinking that Zach thought the same of me. Or used to. I imagined him in school, watching me walk past, then turning to Tayshawn to spit out the word: freak.

I had more in common with that boy than I did with Zach, running with his high-knee lift and elbows tucked tight at ninety degrees. No one ever called Zach a freak.

———

AFTER

This is how it feels now.

Blankness.
Numbness.
Nothing.

Without Zach I'm nothing. I'm not even half of anything, not even the in between I was before. Not girl, not boy, not black, not white.

It's all gone.

I'm gone.

———

AFTER

Tayshawn shows us the court where he and Zach first played ball together, the court where they first dunked, the spot in the park where they first got drunk together. He shares a whole series of firsts.

It feels as if Tayshawn's telling us that Zach was his. That we could never know him the way he did.

I don't care. I know he belongs to them more than he did to me. Sarah's been with him—on and off—since freshman year, and Tayshawn and Zach go back to the third grade. I shouldn't be here.

He takes us to a little cave deep in Inwood. Their firsts here were playing truth or dare with neighborhood girls and smoking pot.

It's dank and musty. My nose wrinkles. There are lots of cigarette butts, empty beer bottles.

"Classy," Sarah says.

Tayshawn laughs. "You're probably the only one of his girls he never took here."

Sarah stiffens. I don't. I'm not even offended that Tayshawn clearly doesn't think of me as one of Zach's girls.

He sits down a little bit in from the cave's mouth, where it's still light enough that we can see each other but not so far forward that people walking by on the path below would know we're there. Sarah crouches next to him, unwilling to get her dress dirty. She clutches her purse. I sit cross-legged on Tayshawn's other side, letting the skirt of Mom's dress pool in my lap.

"I'm honored," Sarah says. "Clearly he only brought his trashy girls here."

"You should be."

"He never showed me this place," I say, though we'd run past it. Sarah looks at me quickly and then away and I regret saying it, asserting that I was one of his girls, too. I don't know either of them. Not really. I'm only here because I miss Zach.

"You and him . . . ," Tayshawn begins, staring at me.

Sarah nods. "How'd you two . . . ?"

Neither of them can say what they want to say. The frame of their question is broken.

"It just happened," I say.

I've been asked this question so often but finally I want to answer.

"I guess. We were both in the park. Central Park, I mean. Not here. We said, you know, 'Hey, how you doing?' We'd seen each other in class. Never spoken though. So we got talking. Turned out we both loved running so we started running together."

"You really ran together?" Sarah asks. "You're not lying? I never saw you run."

"I'm not lying. I like running. We ran together. It wasn't the same as you and him, Sarah. Honest. He wasn't my boyfriend."

"What was he then?" she asks. "For you."

Tayshawn holds up his hand. "None of our business, right?"

"I'm not sure," I say. "I guess it is your business, isn't it? You were his best friend. You were his girlfriend. The two people who knew him best."

"I don't think I knew him that well," Sarah says. "I didn't know about you."

"Like I knew!" Tayshawn says. "But I thought something was up, you know? Been a few months. He wasn't hanging around as much. I noticed. Asked him about it. But he was all, 'What do you mean? Nothing going on.' Made me think there was. Now I know."

"I didn't even suspect," Sarah says. "I had not clue one."

"We mostly ran." I uncross my legs, pull the dress over my knees and hug them, resting my chin. I haven't talked about this with anyone but the cops.

"But you didn't only run," Sarah says.

"Zach's fast. How'd you keep up?"

"I'm fast, too," I say, relieved at Tayshawn's interruption. He looks skeptical. So does Sarah. "We ran in the park. Sometimes we'd run up there all the way from school."

"What else d'you do?" Sarah asks. "I mean, me and Zach, we talked about stuff, hung out with friends, went to movies. Stuff like that." Her eyes fill with water but she doesn't start crying. I know how she feels. This talk of Zach is making the rawness inside me swell.

"That all?" Tayshawn asks. "'Cause, you know, talking and going to the movies, that is not the main thing I do with my girl." I wonder who his girl is. She's not anyone at school.

"You want all the details? Pervert!" Sarah laughs. "Sure. We made out. He was my boyfriend. He tell you about that stuff?"

Tayshawn smiles but he's not saying anything.

"He did, didn't he? Shit. And everyone says girls are blabbermouths!"

"He never said a word about Micah." Tayshawn is having fun. He winks at me.

"Great," Sarah says. "He keeps her sex life private but not mine."

I don't say anything for the moment, but then I think, why not? We're all being honest, aren't we? "He was too ashamed. Why would he tell anyone about me? You saw what everyone said when they found out. First they didn't believe it. Then they acted like they felt sick. 'Cause Zach and *me*? No way!"

"I believed it right away," Sarah said. "I heard it and I knew."

"Really?" I ask. "I thought you said I was too ugly for him. I'm like an ugly boy, you said."

"Harsh," Tayshawn says.

"I was mad," Sarah says. "I'm still mad." She's not looking at me.

"It's what everyone was thinking," I say. "Is thinking."

"Not me," Tayshawn said. "I don't think you're ugly. I mean, you're not beautiful or anything, but ugly? Nope."

"Thanks," I say, smiling. It feels strange on my face. The muscles almost don't know what to do. Sarah and Tayshawn laugh. "It's not me not being pretty. I know that. It's what a freak I am. I mean, look at me, look at you. You wear makeup and walk and talk right. Anything I say, people stare. You got your hair all pretty and relaxed and long. I'm cropped short."

"I wish I could do that," Sarah says. But I know she's lying. She's proud of her hair. "You got any idea how long this takes?"

I do. I can't imagine spending that many hours every morning combing my hair out. But I like the way it looks on her just as much as she does. Loose curls that tumble to halfway down her back.

"What do you think happened to him?" Tayshawn asks.

I don't know what to say. I've thought about it. I've wondered. But I know so little.

FAMILY HISTORY

I remember my first visit to the Greats. I was very small. Too small for coherent sentences, but already walking around.

My father hadn't been speaking to them since his first baby—me—was born. He wasn't answering their calls and returned letters unopened. That was until my mother wore down his resistance and made him take me up to see them for the first time. She didn't join us.

I remember being in the front seat, even though I should have been in back in the car seat. I remember wriggling out of the straps that held me to the seat, so I could crawl in front and see over the dashboard and out the windows to the trees bending in over the car as it went up the bumpy road. I remember green leaves as far as I could see, the sunshine blurring blades and veins and stems together, so that all those branches and leaves swaying in the wind became a green, almost golden, glow.

It must have been summer.

I remember laughing at the sparkling gold green light and my dad shushing me and cajoling me to sit down again but I wouldn't: I wanted to see.

Then we were almost at the house.

Dad stopped the car. We got out and Dad pulled me up onto his hip so I could see as good as he could from almost as high. We pushed through trees until we were at the house that was right in the center of them. Trees leaned in so close they were almost pushing in through the windows. The only clear space was the veranda that wrapped around the house.

Five adults were sitting in rocking chairs. There were children in their laps and at their feet. A few as little or littler than me, but mostly bigger. They were tugging and nipping at one another.

The adults stood up when they saw us, but they probably heard us before then. All the Wilkins have good ears. Even Dad.

I don't remember which adults it was, probably Grandmother and Great-Aunt and Hilliard, maybe two of Dad's cousins. Mine were the children on the floor. They were who I was looking at. They weren't like the children from day care.

One of them hissed at me.

Like a monkey on a nature show. I pressed in closer to my dad, rested my head against his shoulder.

"It's okay, sweetie," Dad said. "They're your kin."

I'd never heard him use that word before. Even little as I was I didn't trust it. *Kin.* It sounded dangerous.

BEFORE

"Do you love me?" Zach asked, panting between each word. We were going up Heartbreak Hill. Zach always liked to talk during the hardest part of the run.

"That's not a question boys ask." I was not panting nearly so hard as Zach.

"How do you know? I'm your first."

"Just do."

Zach's expression said he didn't believe me.

"Do you love me?" I asked.

Zach slowed way down. "That's definitely a question girls ask." The sweat dripped into his eyes.

"I know. So, do you?"

"I never answer."

"Never?" How was that fair?

"Nope," he said, slowing even more. "This hill gets bigger every time we climb it, don't you think?"

I didn't, but I grunted in a way that could be a yes or a no. "So what do you say when they ask you?" I wondered how many theys we were talking about.

"I say . . . Can we stop for a second? Need breath for this." He staggered to a stop, bent down, and put his hands on his knees, took long gasping breaths.

I halted beside him, standing on my toes to stretch a little, before letting my heels touch the ground for the first time in many miles. My calves clenched and then unclenched, thanking me for the consideration.

"Thanks. Damn, girl. I wish you'd sweat more."

"I'm sweating." Though not nearly as much as him. "I can't help it if you're not as fit as me."

"Well, I'm not whatever it is you are. So, you know, I pant and sweat."

"And bitch and moan."

He grinned. " 'Cause I'm regular people."

I punched him.

"Shit, girl." He rubbed his arm.

"You're so regular," I said, "you'll probably get a ball scholarship to college. I heard there are scouts watching every time you play. Then there's you not even going to a high school with a real team."

Zach shrugged. "I'd rather get a scholarship for my brains. But we'll see. Imagine if they saw you run! Wouldn't be a college in the country that wasn't throwing money your way."

"Shut up. Tell me what you tell all your girls."

"Well, you know, *that*. I said it to you, didn't I? How sweet you are." He touched my cheek with his fingers. I rolled my eyes. I wondered if he said it to Sarah, too. "How about that," he said. "You do sweat!"

"Everyone sweats. But you haven't answered my question. When they ask you if you love them," I said, "how do you answer?"

"I say"—he leaned into my ear and started whispering—" 'you're so sweet. Just the way you look and taste.

Well . . .' And then, like I can't control myself, I kiss them—"

He leaned in, I leaned away.

"Don't be that way."

"What's with the 'them,' anyway?" I asked, moving still farther away. "I thought you were only dating Sarah."

He laughed. "There've been others."

"I'm sure." I was. Girls often looked at Zach. I didn't think he was that good-looking. His skin was clear and his eyes bright, but his nose was kind of big and some of his teeth crooked. He wasn't straight-up handsome like Tayshawn.

"We're both sure then," he said, kissing me.

I pulled away. "Why'd you ask me? If you never say it yourself."

"Keeps things uneven. Get the girl to say it, but never say it to her."

"That's nasty." It was but he didn't say it in a nasty way. "What happens if you fall in love?" I didn't think I was in love with Zach, but I was happier when I was with him than when I was with anyone else. But best of all was being alone. Do you want to be alone when you're in love?

"Then I'll say it. But not till then."

I wondered why it didn't hurt me that Zach was telling me he didn't love me.

"Okay, that's fair," I told him. "I'll do the same."

"So that's a no, then?" Zach asked, grinning so wide his face was about to split.

"A big fat no," I said, taking off up the hill at a pace I knew he couldn't match.

———

AFTER

"The cops asked me how he seemed. You know, last time I saw him," Tayshawn says. We're still in the cave, sitting, with the echo of Zach's funeral in our heads. I have no desire to be back there.

Sarah nods. "Me too. They came to my house. Dad was freaking out. He doesn't like cops. Doesn't trust them."

"Mine too," I say. "Dad says they're looking to bust a black man at the first opportunity. Specially when he's got an education."

"Your dad and mine should meet," Sarah says. "Seeing as how they say exactly the same things."

"Not mine," Tayshawn says, and I remember that Tayshawn's grandfather was a cop. I think an uncle is, too. He has firemen in the family as well. I don't remember ever seeing a black fireman. His mom, though, is an accountant and his dad's in business. Not a very successful business. They're as broke as my parents. But I guess they still count as a cop family.

"These cops were a lot meaner than any of your family, I bet," Sarah says. "The younger one—"

"Stein?" I ask.

Sarah nods. "He kept trying to make me and Zach going out sound nasty. He wanted to know if I was jealous of you, Micah. Didn't believe me when I said I didn't even know about you." Her voice changes tone, drops. "Not until after."

"Yeah," Tayshawn says. "They wanted to know if me and Zach ever fought. I mean, what if we had? Everyone fights. Doesn't mean you're going to go kill someone. Just 'cause you're mad at them. I don't think they have any idea what happened. Whatever it was, it was . . ." Tayshawn pauses, trying to find the right word.

Sarah and me both lean toward him.

"I heard it was done with a knife," Tayshawn says. "That his face was so cut up they didn't know who it was."

Sarah covers her mouth.

"If that's true, how did they find out it was Zach?" I ask.

"The DNA test we did in class," Tayshawn says. "It wasn't so useless after all."

I think of that class. When everyone was looking at a

piece of paper to tell them how black or white they were. I think of how Zach hadn't said a word. I shiver, imagining that somehow Zach knew his test results would be used to identify him one day. Mine were still sitting in my drawer.

"What else do you know?" Sarah asks.

Tayshawn shrugs. "They're working on it. He doesn't tell us a lot, my uncle, I mean. He's not homicide. But he hears stuff. He met Zach a few times. Knows he's my best boy. He tells me what he can."

"Such as?" Sarah says louder. "I'm sorry. It's because I don't know anything. His parents won't talk to me. His mom just cries and his dad says he doesn't know. I offer to help but they say there's nothing I can do. I know he's their son. I can't imagine . . . But, I mean, I *can*." She's crying now. Mascara-tinted tears run down her face. "I lost him, too. I thought we were going to be together forever." She sniffs, wipes at her face, smearing makeup. "I know. I'm seventeen. I know most people don't stay with their first boyfriend forever, especially if he's cheating on them. But, I really thought that. I still think that. I didn't know he was cheating on me. I didn't know there were all these other girls."

"Not girls," Tayshawn says. "Just Micah."

"How do you know?" she demands. "You didn't know about Micah! There could've been tons of other girls."

"Well, let's figure it out then," Tayshawn says. "How often did you see him, Sarah?"

Sarah gulps. "Pretty much every Saturday and Sunday night. Most Fridays, too. After school when he didn't have practice."

"And at school?" Tayshawn asks.

Sarah nods.

"What about you, Micah?"

"On the days we skipped. Sometimes after school, but not often."

"So how many times a week then, Micah?"

"Two or three times. Sometimes only once."

"And, me," Tayshawn says. "I saw him at practice and most Saturday or Friday nights if there was a party. How many days you think that leaves?"

He was staring at Sarah. She was still crying, but slower, not sobbing.

"I think we got him covered," Tayshawn says. "No way could he've had another girl."

I know he didn't have another girl. I would have smelled her on him, but I only ever smelled Sarah. I don't tell them that. I'm smelling them both strongly right now. The cave is getting warmer, more closed in.

"Makes sense, right?" Tayshawn asks Sarah. He touches her cheek briefly.

She nods. "It still doesn't feel good, though. I'm sorry, Micah, but, well, how *could* you?"

She's staring at me. Angry like she might hit me. I know I'm stronger than her but I wouldn't stop her. She'd be right to hit me.

"Why, Micah?"

I don't know how to answer. I can't tell her that I didn't really think about her. Because I did, but not like that. I shrug. Sarah's face gets tighter. "It just happened," I tell her. "I wasn't thinking. I don't think Zach was either. If it wasn't for the running it wouldn't have happened more than once. Honest, Sarah. He didn't think about me the way he thought about you. He thought I was a freak."

"Well," Tayshawn says, "you kind of are. You don't hardly talk at school and when you do it's a whole bunch of bullshit. I know your daddy isn't any kind of arms dealer."

"He isn't?" Sarah asks, letting go of her purse to wipe her face some more.

Tayshawn laughs. "Doesn't even sell switchblades. He's a magazine writer."

"How'd you know that?" I ask.

"I got my ways."

"You saw one of his articles?" Sarah asks.

"My mom subscribes to a million travel magazines," Tayshawn says. He grins.

"Don't you think being a travel writer would be the perfect cover for an arms dealer?" I ask.

Tayshawn laughs even harder.

"Why do you lie so much, Micah?" Sarah asks. She's still staring at me. I remember when she was afraid to. I'm not sure I like her lack of fear.

"I always have. I don't know. It's a habit." I'm not about to tell them about the family illness.

"A stupid habit," Tayshawn says.

It's gotten a little darker outside. I wonder what time it is. It doesn't feel that late. Might be dark clouds.

Sarah is still staring at me. Tayshawn, too. The air has gotten even warmer. The air smells like musk.

I hug my knees tighter. If Zach hadn't been killed we wouldn't be here. Sarah never would've talked to me so much. Tayshawn neither. Though we'd shot some hoops a few times. Almost four years I'd known them. Without knowing them at all.

"I miss him," I say. Even though I know Sarah might slap me for saying it. Who was I to miss her boyfriend?

Instead, she leans toward me. I think there's something on my face and she's going to wipe it off. She doesn't. She kisses me. The shock of her lips against mine travels from the nerve endings in my scalp to my feet. Her mouth is opening. I feel her tongue lightly press into mine. She tastes clean and faintly pepperminty. Her mouth is warm and her lips smooth. I feel hot and then cold. I'm kissing her in return.

Tayshawn stares.

Then, when Sarah pulls away, he leans forward and presses his lips against mine, which are still damp from Sarah's. His mouth is a little cooler. He presses harder, but his lips are as smooth. He puts his hand to my cheek, both hands, opens his mouth wider, kisses me harder.

I'm shaking. So's he. I have no idea what's happening but I wonder if Zach can feel it.

When Tayshawn lets go I fall back blinking and watch as Sarah and Tayshawn kiss. My heart is racing. I'm not sure what I think except that I want them to kiss me again.

I know that none of us killed Zach. We don't have it in us.

PART TWO
Telling the True Truth

I will not tell a lie. I will not tell will not tell a lie. I will not tell a lie. I will not tell a lie. I will not

CONFESSION

I am a werewolf.

There, I've said it.

The heart of all my lies.

Of the family's lies.

You guessed it already, didn't you? What with the fur I was born in, the wolf in my throat, my weird family. She's a werewolf, you said to yourself, from a werewolf family. That explains everything.

Now you're thinking, "Well, she killed him then, didn't she?" This proves it. And accounts for the how as well: a werewolf. Micah the werewolf.

Except that I didn't kill Zach. I have never killed a person. Not as a wolf and not as a human.

Or you're thinking, "She's crazy. She's not just a liar—she's insane."

Werewolves don't exist. Not anywhere outside of

dreams and stories, and yet she says she is a werewolf. Might as well claim that you're a doorknob or a space station. Micah the doorknob; Micah the space station.

You think my being a werewolf is the biggest lie of all 'cause it means I'm not the regular kind of liar who pretends she's a boy, a hermaphrodite, or that Daddy's an arms dealer.

No, it's worse than that: you think I believe it. That I am such a nut job I'm delusional.

You think I killed him, too. Trapped in my delusional state, believing I am a werewolf, I killed Zach. Believing I'm a werewolf is the only way I can live with what I did.

Except that I didn't.

That was a different werewolf.

Yes, there's more than one of us.

HISTORY OF ME

The change comes with my period.

It hurts. Every nerve, every cell, every bone, the shape of my eyes, nose, mouth, my arms, my legs. All of it. Shifts and grinds and groans. Bone stretches, elongates; the muscles, too. Fibers twitch and snap. It's as if every bone in my body has not only been fractured, but broken open, the marrow spilled. Muscles sheared from bone. Eyes pop. Ears explode.

I howl.

For the duration. For the twenty minutes of change I am nothing but a howl. It breaks and deepens and stretches and snaps. Starts human, ends wolf. It's just as bad when it starts wolf and ends human.

The cells in my brain. The gray matter. Squeezing and breaking my memories.

I, the girl, I, the human
is not
I, the wolf.

I could not do it every month. I would not survive.

Three or four times a year—in the summer—is the most I can manage.

That's why I am so good about taking my pill. That's why in the city I take one every morning without fail.

Because the shifting of my spine from human to wolf, that alone is enough pain for a lifetime.

I could not do it every month.

But I miss my wolf days and long for the summer, for the days between those two twenty-minute bursts of change—human to wolf, wolf to human. Days when I run free and kill and eat raw and never think once about where I fit or who loves me or what I'll be when I get out of school.

I just am. I know where I belong.

Until I'm human again.

BEFORE

My father told me about the wolf when I was ten. That's when he decided that I was old enough to understand the weight of the secret. He'd have waited longer, but he had to tell me before puberty, before my first blood brought my first change. The Greats judged that he was already leaving it too late. One of my cousins changed when she was nine.

Ten was a bad year for me. I was miserable. The hair I'd been born with returned and every day it seemed to be getting worse, not just on more parts of my body— my feet, the palms of my hands—but coarser and thicker. No doctor had any solution. No hair-removal technique worked for more than a few days. I hated school. The teasing was constant.

Dad decided to tell me the truth up on the farm. He said a week away from the city would be good for me. We could relax with the Greats and their assorted children and grandchildren.

I was grateful. I knew they wouldn't say anything about the hair. Some of my cousins were every bit as hairy: the family illness. It wasn't that they wouldn't tease me. They would: about being a city girl, about the color of my skin, about how I dressed, how I talked. Before I'd hated it. Now it seemed like nothing.

When we played they weren't as vicious or violent as they normally were. They didn't lead me out into the depths of the forest and leave me there. Didn't make me do their chores: cleaning out the stables, spreading compost, feeding the pigs.

They liked me better when I was covered in hair. They didn't laugh at me as much and I didn't rag on them for being the same age as me and not reading as well as my little brother.

When Dad called me into the house, we were playing soccer on a cleared patch of land where corn had grown, but was now left fallow.

I kept playing. My cousins stopped, looking at each other and glancing at me. As if they knew what Dad wanted. I kicked the ball at the two cans that marked the goal. Even with the goalie paying no attention I missed.

"Micah!" Dad called again. I headed toward him slowly, looking back at the cousins. They knew something I didn't. I wanted them to tell me. I wanted to keep playing. Instead I followed Dad through the trees and into the house.

Grandmother and Great-Aunt Dorothy were sitting in front of the fireplace. Their dog, Hilliard, curled up in a silvery gray ball at Great-Aunt's feet. His white snout with the brown stripe that started on the top of his head and ended at his shiny black nose rested on his paws. He raised his head and looked at me and then put it down again.

Dad sat on the chair next to the couch. I sat in the one on the other side, closest to the fire. Despite all the extra hair I was cold.

"You know we have an illness in our family," Dad said.

I nodded even though it wasn't a question. I didn't point at my hairy arms or say anything sarcastic.

Grandmother and Great-Aunt tutted. I couldn't tell if they were disapproving of Dad or of me.

"Well," Dad said, "it's not quite what we said it was."

Both the Greats harrumphed.

"She's only ten," Dad said. "She needs me to break it to her slowly."

"Break what to me slowly?" I asked, feeling a prickle of irritation at being called "only ten." Dad knew I wasn't dumb. It was true my grades weren't that good, but what else would you expect with all the moving from school to school? He just liked hiding things. How bad could it be anyway? I was already covered in hair. I could take whatever it was they were going to tell me. "I want to know."

"You're a wolf," Grandmother said, jerking her head toward their dog. "Same as your great-uncle there."

The farm dog was my great-uncle Hilliard? Great-Uncle Hilliard who'd died? Not just named after him? Grandmother wasn't smiling. Not that it would have made a difference. She never joked.

"Werewolf," Dad said, glaring at his mother.

I looked at Hilliard. I looked at Dad. Then at the Greats. None of them were smiling.

Great-Aunt Dorothy nodded. "Same as your grandmother, your great-uncle, your aunts Jill, Christine, Hen, and uncle Lloyd, and your cousins Sam, Jessie, Susan, Alice, and Lilly. The rest of us are carriers, passing it on, but not wolfish ourselves." She sounded a little sad. "That's why you're hairy. Once you start turning wolf the hair will go. When you're human, that is. You'll be hairy only as a wolf. A gray wolf to be exact, *Canis lupus*. Though most werewolves are *Canis dirus*, the dire wolf what's extinct except for werewolves. That's why we Wilkins are smaller than other werewolf families. Gray wolves only get up to 175 pounds or so. Mostly not even. Same as us. Long and skinny."

"Lean," Grandmother said, stretching out a stringy well-muscled arm. "Strong."

"We're a werewolf family?" I asked. The hair on my

arms and face was silvery and coarse. Like animal hair. Like Hilliard's coat. I felt the skin on my entire body tighten.

"I told you there's no point pussyfooting about," Grandmother admonished Dad. "Micah already understands. Should have told her years ago. It's not right growing up not knowing what you are."

Dad shot his mother a poisonous look. I didn't know why then but now I'm sure he was thinking of his unknown father, of battling through all his mother's lies to find him, and failing.

Even at ten I'd known my family was a mess, but I hadn't realized how messy. If they were all lying . . . I looked at their faces. They weren't lying.

"I'm a werewolf?" It made more sense than the doctors' explanations for my hairiness. Hormone imbalances and all that. Great-Aunt said the hair was going away. She had, hadn't she?

Grandmother leaned forward and patted my knee.

"It's not so bad as all that," she said. "You can live up here with us. Plenty of space for wolfishness here."

Hilliard was still looking at me. I thought of all the times I'd petted him and played with him. I hadn't even known he was a wolf. I thought he was a regular dog. Named after my dead great-uncle. Except that Great-Aunt Dorothy and Grandmother and the others always talked to him as if he was a person. But then I'd seen people in the city carrying dogs in their purses and talking to them as if they were babies. People with animals are weird. Except Dad and the Greats were saying Uncle Hilliard wasn't even a regular wolf.

He was a werewolf. Like me.

"Can he understand what we're saying?" I asked.

"Mostly," Grandmother said. "Though it's hard to tell. Hilliard doesn't change anymore. He's a wolf all the time."

Would that happen to me? Did I *have* to live up here? Did Mom know? Would it hurt?

"When will I become a wolf," I asked. "How long for?"

They told me. They told me everything they knew about the signs that would tell me the change was coming, about cycles, what the wolf me would know and what the human. How to control it. How to live with it.

They told me how long the Wilkins had been wolves. (Always.) What the family legends were. (Many and varied.) Why they'd come to America. (Space. Freedom.)

When they were finally done my butt was numb, my head was spinning, and I was so hungry my stomach growled. Yes, like a wolf.

FAMILY HISTORY

When The Change—menopause—comes most of us stop the other kind of change. One way or the other. Grandmother stayed human, greeting each new month with a tightening of the skin, with headaches and hot flashes, sometimes an itchy layer of fur that's shed within hours. Human still.

Hilliard went the other way. He's wolf all the time. Prowling, howling, stuck on a farm that isn't even a tenth of the size of a normal range.

He strays of course. How could he not?

He takes deer and raccoon and rabbit. Sheep sometimes. But not often.

Humans? you ask.

Never humans. Wolves don't eat people. Neither do werewolves. Not unless there's a reason. We never kill a person for food. Too dangerous. Too suspicious. Besides—rabbit, deer—they taste better.

Upstate, when those sheep disappear, everyone blames it on coyote. Coyote bigger than anyone's ever seen before. Coyote *are* bigger in the Northeast. But *that* big?

There aren't any wolves in upstate New York. So it can't be wolves taking them.

There're hardly any wolves in North America anymore. A few in the far north: Alaska, parts of Canada, tiny bits of Minnesota, Wisconsin, and Michigan. Those they reintroduced into Yellowstone Park—they're the only wolves that aren't in danger of being shot at or trapped.

North America used to be all wolves. All wolves and many werewolves, too. Now it's humans and highways and hubris. At least that's what the Greats say. But sitting on their porch in the middle of summer all I can see is honeysuckle and hummingbirds. And Hilliard.

He's lonely. The lone wolf—except for when my cousins change. Then they run like a pack, playing, hunting, howling. In summers I'm there, too. But my cousins and me change for only a few days each month. The rest of the time it's just Hilliard.

Wolves are social. They need their pack.

I wonder if Hilliard misses changing. Living life as both.

I know Grandmother does.

———

THE MOON

The moon has nothing to do with it. Not unless you cycle with the moon.

You must be wondering about the males. They don't

menstruate. They don't go through menopause. How do they turn into wolves? How do they stop?

There are always more female werewolves than male. Because it's the females who cause the change. A male werewolf who grows up alone, far from his own kind, never becomes a wolf.

He has to be around females. We start to change, they start to change. We hit menopause, they hit menopause.

This is why so many of us live in packs. Those of us who aren't extinct.

Those of us who aren't hiding in the cities dutifully taking our pills. Or, if they're boys, avoiding their own kind. A boy wolf can stay human forever—all he has to do is never go near a girl wolf.

THE ANIMALS

You're wondering about the other animals on the farm: the chickens, geese, pigs, goats, cows, and horses. How do they cope with wolves around? Not just Hilliard, but when the other Wilkins wolves change together?

First of all, geese aren't afraid of anything, not even human wolves. They're not like regular animals, so they don't shy from us when we're human. (There's a good side to most animals fearing us: there's never been a rat or a mouse in our apartment in the city—or on the farm—you'd think my parents would be grateful.)

But the animals freak when we change. The minute one of us feels it coming we get away from the house and stables and pens and into the woods. Of course, the freaking at the change is nothing compared to how the animals feel about having a wolf anywhere near them. When the pack is out in force, to be on the safe side, the Greats make sure none of the animals are loose.

Though we wolves know to leave them alone.

Rabbits and deer, yes. Anything domesticated, no. Too much trouble, whether they're our own or our neighbors' animals.

———

BEFORE

My pill?

Sometimes, not often, I forget.

My desk?

The one that clangs? That's made of metal?

It's a cage: three feet by six feet.

When I forget my pill that's where I am imprisoned.

It's where they put me the first time.

It was like this:

I was twelve. My skin started to itch. The way it used to when the extra hair was growing in. I was in middle school. The hair had disappeared. I'd been in the same middle school ever since.

My skin started to itch on the walk home from school. I had the cell phone my parents gave me to call them in an emergency—the emergency being any of the signs that I was about to change—but my school was only five blocks from home: one avenue, four streets. I was sure I'd make it. I quickened my pace. Bolted up the stairs, through the apartment door, hung my backpack from the coat rack by the door.

"Hi, Dad," I said. He was at the kitchen table, surrounded by a pile of glossy magazines and pamphlets, laptop open, typing furiously. He looked up, nodded, turned back to the screen.

I opened my mouth to tell him about my skin itching, but that was the do-not-disturb look. Instead I went into the bathroom. There was blood. Not a lot. Tiny spots of it on my pants.

Two of the signs the Greats had told me to watch for.

Hot flashes was another. Also aching teeth.

I washed my hands and felt my forehead. I didn't feel particularly warm. My teeth felt fine. How many signs before I tell Mom and Dad?

I went back into the kitchen, leaned against the fridge. "Dad?" I said tentatively. The whole thing seemed unreal. *Hey, Dad, I think maybe it's about to happen. It might be time to lock me in the cage.*

He didn't look up.

Maybe I should wait for another sign? But the Greats had said that even one sign was enough. Sometimes the first change comes on scary fast.

"Dad," I repeated.

"What, Micah? I'm kind of busy." Dad looked up.

I felt idiotic. What if it was nothing? The blood spots were really tiny.

"What, Micah?"

"Um," I said, "I think it might be about to, or, you know, going to happen."

"What's going to happen? This is due in"—he glanced at the screen—"two hours."

"The change. I think—"

Dad jumped up, narrowly missing whacking his head on the bicycle above. He put his hand to my cheek. "You feel hot?"

"Not yet. Just my skin." I held out my arms. Red bumps were starting appear. "And there was blood. Not much but—"

"Damn," Dad said. He almost never swears. "This is it then. You ready to go in?"

I wasn't, but I nodded. The Greats had said it could

happen quickly. I felt strange, like my heart was beating too fast, but I couldn't tell if that was the change starting to happen or me being afraid it was about to happen. Then I remembered: rapid heartbeat was another sign.

I crawled into the cage. Dad locked it behind me. I sat on the thin mattress we'd put in to make it more comfortable. At three feet high there was no standing up. There was a bucket in the corner for my toilet and a roll of toilet paper. In the opposite corner sat a jug of water and a plastic cup.

"You okay?" Dad said.

I nodded. I wasn't.

"I'll be back in a minute," he said.

"Okay," I said, wishing he would stay. I'd never minded being alone. I liked it. Not that time.

He closed the door behind him. I wished he hadn't. I instantly started worrying that he wouldn't come back, that the door wouldn't open again until I was a wolf. Or not even then.

The room was so dark. I wished I'd asked Dad to open the blind. Though it would be getting dark soon anyway. I tried stretching out. The cage was big enough that I could do sitting-down stretches. Problem was I didn't know that many.

I'd only been in the cage a few minutes but already I wanted to stand up. I wasn't sure how much more of this I could take.

The door opened. Thank God.

"Your mom will be home soon," Dad said. "I called her." He put his laptop on the bed and sat down next to it. Fridays Mom stays at work late to teach an advanced French class. Jordan is in chess club.

"I'm glad," I said. "About Mom I mean."

"Yes," Dad said. He put his hand on his laptop but didn't open it. "How do you feel now?"

We stared at each other. He looked away first.

"Okay," I said. "This is weird."

"Yeah, it would be a lot easier if you were up at the farm."

"Dad," I said, "you promised."

"I know. It's just—"

"Dad! I'd kill myself. This won't be so bad, right? It's not as if I can get out of this cage. We'll figure something out."

"I hope so," Dad said. He didn't sound convinced. I couldn't believe he was willing to sacrifice me to the Greats. Did he want me to be uneducated? To grow up without a computer?

I crossed my legs and leaned back against the bars. It wasn't comfortable. "Can I have a pillow?"

"Sure." Dad grabbed one from the bed. "You feel hot yet? How's your teeth?"

"Not hot. Teeth are fine."

Dad opened the cage, handed me the pillow, squeezed

my hand. "It's going to be alright, Micah," he said. He let go of my hand and locked the cage again. "I promise."

I fought the urge to cry. I believed every word Dad and the Greats had told me, but sitting there in that cage *waiting to turn into a wolf*, it seemed so stupid. What if it was bullshit? They were all so full of lies. What if this was their biggest?

When Mom got home they traded places. Dad went to finish his stupid article for whatever stupid magazine, but not before I made him promise that Jordan would not be allowed in. My idiot brother was not going to see me like this.

Mom came in with two cheese, ham, and tomato sandwiches, handing the plate through the horizontal gap in the bars and patting my hand.

I wolfed them down. Hungrier than I realized. Mom chatted about her day, acting as if watching her daughter sitting in a locked cage eating sandwiches was perfectly normal. "Jordan is staying at Karl's place for the weekend," she said, finally saying something that had to do with the bizarre situation we were in.

I was glad. Not because it's always wonderful when the brat's away but because they hadn't told him yet. I hoped he'd never find out.

I handed back the plate. "Thanks."

"You are most welcome, *chérie*." She reached her hand through to pat my knee. "How does it feel?"

"Fine. My arms are still itching but, look"—I held them out for her to see—"no hair yet. I don't feel hot either. My teeth don't hurt and my heart's not beating fast anymore."

"Did your grandmother say how long it would take?"

"She said it varies. Sometimes it's very fast after the first sign. Sometimes it can take a couple of days."

"Days!" Mom gasped. "We must keep you locked in for those days? I hope it happens soon."

"You and me both," I said.

BEFORE

It didn't.

Sunday morning I was still not a wolf. My arms had stopped itching and the bumps had cleared. When I used the bucket there was no further sign of blood.

"I think it was a false alarm," I told my dad. "Does that happen?"

"I don't know," he said. He held his hands out in front of him. He couldn't call the Greats—they had no phone. "I'll have to drive up. Ask them. I can't leave you in the cage if it's a false alarm."

He did two hours up (breaking speed limits) and two hours back (breaking them all over again) to learn that, yes, false alarms happen and that if the change hasn't happened in that first twenty-four hours and the signs go away, then the change is not coming.

I could have screamed.

If the Greats had been there I'd've killed them.

Dad came home as fast as he could and opened the cage and let me out before he explained a thing.

I staggered. I had never gone so long without running, let alone standing. I was not sure I could do it again. Go back into that cage?

Mom and Dad held me tight despite the way I smelled. Despite the smell from the bucket.

I kept my back to the cage. When they let me go I went and showered.

It was only then that I wept.

I would not go back in that cage. I would not live with the Greats.

There had to be another way.

TOOTH & CLAW

"You may feed the wolf as much as you like; it will always glance toward the forest."

Grandmother says it's an old Polish saying. (Great-Aunt Dorothy says Russian.) What it means is that wolves are wild. Their other oft-quoted saying is Latin: *lupus non mordet lupum.* "A wolf does not bite a wolf." Which leaves the rest of the animal kingdom free for the biting.

We can't be tamed. We shouldn't live in cities.

Grandmother quotes those to me a lot. Said them even more back then, when she was trying to persuade me and Dad that it would be best for me to live on the farm. To stay there for the rest of my life.

I cannot explain to her why I love the city so. I have tried. But how can I describe it to someone who has never been there? To someone who fears it?

She hates the city because she says it destroys nature. She thinks there's no nature here.

She's wrong.

Nature is everywhere. I don't even have to go into the parks to find it. There are weeds and grass poking up between cracks in the sidewalk, out of the sides of buildings and walls. In the city there are no streets without plants. There are gardens in abandoned lots, on balconies, even on the roofs of buildings.

Plants mean insects, microbes in the soil.

Nature's the same in the city as in the country. It's just tougher. There are not many varieties of woodpeckers in the city, no deer, precious few raccoons. But rats, pigeons, mosquitoes, flies? They all do fine.

Nature's everywhere. Under my feet, rats and insects. Over my head, pigeons, sparrows, even the occasional red-tailed hawk. There's nowhere in the city—in the world—that a spider isn't within reach. There are bigger animals, too, not just the people, the cats, the dogs, but the occasional pig or llama, the horses, and the squirrels, the foxes and woodchucks and snakes and lizards.

The Greats cannot see how strong nature is. How it survives even in the least hospitable circumstances. Just like them.

FAMILY HISTORY

The Greats are divided on werewolf origins.

Grandmother says it goes back to the beginnings of humans. We evolved from wolves; they evolved from monkeys.

So why don't humans turn into monkeys once a month?

Grandmother has no answer to that.

Great-Aunt Dorothy tells about a deal made between a man and a wolf way back in the early days. They were escaping a predator bigger than either of them. They both ran for a narrow cave opening. There wasn't enough room for both of them so they fought. The predator came closer. The wolf proposed they share the space. He cut his belly open and told the man to crawl inside. Then the wolf wedged his way into the cave.

But when it came time to separate they couldn't. They were bound to each other. A mannish wolf, a wolfish man.

Dad said his grandfather told him that there was no cutting involved and that it was a woman, not a man. The wolf and the woman had squeezed so tight together trying to get into the cave that they melded into each other so that you couldn't see where the wolf began and the woman ended.

Great-Aunt laughed at that one. She said that's not how she heard her daddy tell it. The woman and the wolf fell in love, lay together, and werewolves were their babies.

The other story Grandmother told was that the Wilkins had made a deal with a pack of wolves way, way, way back before countries had names, when people lived in tribes, eking out an existence, moving from spot to spot. The pact was to keep from moving, to stay in the one spot, safe and sound even in the winter. The Wilkins would share food with the wolves; the wolves would fight their enemies.

The Wilkins were able to shift from hunting and gathering to planting and harvesting, raising goats and pigs and grains and vegetables. They fed the wolves; the wolves defended them.

They lived so close together that it wasn't many seasons before the human tribe and the wolf pack were indistinguishable. Not too many years before they were all part wolf and part human.

They're interesting tales though I doubt they're true.

Here's what I think:

Horizontal gene transfer.

You have brown eyes and the ability to curl your tongue, and your kids have brown eyes and can curl their tongues. That's because you passed on those genes, which is the regular way genes get passed on: vertical gene transfer.

But genes can also be transferred horizontally from one organism to another. It's called HGT. I know there's no documented case of HGT happening between big organisms. Humans and wolves are big. Each with at least twenty-three thousand different genes, way bigger than bacteria and viruses, who can have as few as eight. But if it can happen between bacteria why can't it happen between bigger organisms? If a tomato can have fruit fly genes in it or, more relevant (since humans put the fruit fly in the fruit), if cows can acquire a gene from a plant to help their digestion, then why can't wolves and humans do the same?

Though I'm not talking the one gene, I'm talking many. There'd be the gene (or genes) that makes the change possible. A gene no one's ever heard of, let alone mapped. Then there's all the wolf genes that express when I'm wolf and human genes for when I'm human.

Not to mention *why*. Could it be a means to preserve genes—wolf genes—that were approaching extinction? That would explain the *Canis dirus* werewolves. Increasingly the *Canis lupus* ones, too. Though when the first werewolves emerged gray wolves were everywhere. There are other animals of roughly human size that have gone extinct. Are there were-saber-toothed tigers?

I would love to map my own DNA. What would it show? Humans have 85 percent the same DNA as wolves. What do I have? Ninety-five percent? Ninety-nine? Or do I have the same 85 percent as everyone else? Along with hidden werewolf DNA.

When I'm a scientist—a biologist who specializes in wolves—I'll find out. I'll map my own DNA. Secretly. I'll prove that it is HGT. That we were made by a horizontal transfer of genes a few million years ago.

Unless it was a virus. Something that attacked an ancestor's DNA and caused massive mutations resulting in unstable genes that express both as wolf and as human.

There's so much I don't know and that I can't ask Yayeko without making her eyebrows go sky-high.

Why am I *Canis lupus* while most werewolves are *Canis dirus*? Is that even true? How do I find other people like me? Does that mean there are two kinds of werewolves?

Or are there more? Are there African werewolves who are *Canis simensis?* The sole African wolf? Or *Canis rufus* were-wolves? Or are they both too small? There are many rec-ognized wolf subspecies. Are there werewolves for every one? Or only the ones that are roughly human-sized?

I don't know where I come from. Or what I am. I don't know *how* I am. I don't know anything.

———

BEFORE

The real change came on me four weeks after the false alarm. The warning signs were the same but this time I ignored them. I did not want to sit in that cage waiting, getting filthier and more wound up and miserable by the hour.

The first sign was a tightening of my skin as I walked to school. It felt itchy in the exact same way it had with the false alarm. I kept walking. It didn't feel so bad. At recess there was a tiny bit of blood. Spotting, same as last time. I figured that even if the change was real I still had plenty of time to get through the school day and then walk home.

Like before, I didn't feel hot. My teeth didn't hurt.

It was in math class. Second-to-last class of the day. We were learning number puzzles. We had to draw three shapes but make sure they were all touching, then four, then five. Five was impossible. I was trying to make it work when the first wave of heat hit me. Then more itching. Then sharp pains in my belly, dots in front of my eyes. My head began to throb. My teeth hurt.

Inside me things were moving. I knew what it was. I had to get home.

I stood up.

"Micah, sit down," the teacher said, without looking at me.

I fell down.

I didn't mean to but the muscles turned to liquid in my legs. At least it felt that way. But when I looked down they looked like human legs.

"Are you alright, Micah?" The teacher was staring at me.

"No," I said, amazed that my tongue and mouth were cooperating. I tried to stand up, clutching the desk for support. My bones were turning into knives. "It's my illness."

I had a file. The note about my illness was in the file. All the teachers knew about it.

"I have to call my dad."

I think that's what I said but the next thing I knew my body was buckling. It felt as if the spine was coming out of my back. "I have to go. Call my dad. He knows."

I have no idea if the words came out or not.

I reached for my bag while crawling to the door, groped inside for the cell phone. The pain was spreading all over my body.

I was sure I would die.

Somehow I got out of the classroom. Somehow I got the phone into my hands. Pressed for Dad. Screamed for him to come get me. Told him I would be getting home as fast as I could. The school was only five blocks from home: one avenue, four streets. Running was fastest. Ordinarily I would be home in minutes.

But liquid muscles, moving bones, pain in every fiber, every cell.

I kept moving: toward the exit, down the few steps, out onto the street.

I didn't know if I was going to make it, if I was going to turn into a wolf on First Avenue in the daylight of a busy Thursday afternoon.

The teacher was still hovering, I think. Had she followed me? Maybe it was someone else. More than one. My eyes weren't processing right. There were less colors. I saw red. I saw yellow. But mostly red. But I knew which way to go. Down. South. West.

I kept moving.

They were calling my name. I concentrated on breathing, willing the change to slow, for the one foot after the other to turn into a run. I think I progressed to a shuffle. I don't know how many blocks I got before Dad grabbed me, pulling me along.

I heard shouting and questions. I squeezed my eyes shut.

By the time Dad pushed me into the elevator there was fur all over my arms and I was bent double. I could smell the fear and sweat of my father. Or was that me?

I'd never been in so much pain. I was going back into the cage. I wasn't sure which was worse.

As Dad dragged me into the apartment, into my room, into the cage, the bones were trying to push their way out of my face. I could no longer see. Or hear. My eyeballs and eardrums had exploded.

Then I was a wolf.

In a three-by-six cage and hungrier than I have ever been in my life.

Dad told me afterward that I howled for twenty minutes straight. He'd lied to the neighbors to keep them from calling the police. I don't know what lies he told, but after that they all looked at me funny.

FAMILY HISTORY

My biology obsession ignited after my first change. I'd always been interested but now it was a passion, no, it was a *necessity*. I had to know what I was, how I was. I had to learn more.

How was it possible? How did mass reshape itself like that? I was a 105-pound twelve-year-old. I became a 105-pound wolf. It made sense when I thought of the conservation of matter. Equal weight. Both mammals. Both warm-blooded. It would be much weirder if I were to turn into a snake, go from warm-blooded to cold. From human to python. Or what if I changed into a slug? No blood, no bones. No slug has ever weighed even close to 100 pounds.

Human to wolf: matter is conserved. But *how* do I change?

How does the hair come and go, bones shift and grow and shrink? How can I be a wolf *and* a human?

When I change back, am I the same human I was? Is it the same skin, the same cells? Or am I re-created each time? A new wolf, a new human. If so, why do my memories not change? Or do they and I just don't know it?

Who am I? What am I?

To understand, I was sure—I am sure—I had to learn how humans function. How we absorb and expend energy. What happens when we breathe. What we are made of. Genes, DNA. I had to learn the same about wolves.

I have to understand *how* I am in order to understand *what* I am.

I know so little. I don't know if I'll ever know enough.

I can say "werewolf." But I don't know what that means. Not below the surface of my skin, of my hide.

I've asked Grandmother, Great-Aunt Dorothy. They have a few answers, but not enough. Most of the time they don't even understand my questions.

I asked Grandmother why she'd tried to breed the werewolf out of her children.

She denied it.

"But your story?" I asked. "About finding someone who wasn't a werewolf to have a baby with . . . about marrying out so you could weaken the family illness?"

Grandmother clucked. "That was a story for your father. I'm proud of the wolf in me. In you. I would never try to kill it. Why do you think I work so hard to keep this place the way it is? To make it bigger? Why do you think I want you here?"

"Then why?" I began. "Who, I mean. Who was my grandfather?"

"You won't tell your father?"

I thought of all the lies he'd told me, everything he'd kept hidden. "No. I promise I won't tell him." I thought of the lies Grandmother had told me. I could break my promise.

"Your father's not a wolf. He doesn't understand." For a second her eyes seemed yellow. "Your grandfather was a local boy. Never saw him more than once or twice. He wrote me letters. I never answered. That was that."

"Is he still alive? My grandfather?"

Grandmother didn't answer at first, looking at her bony hands, her scarred knuckles. "He's long gone."

———

HISTORY OF ME

Grandmother said that taking the pill to stop the change was an abomination. That we were killing an essential part of me. That if we kept the wolf in me down it would eat away at the human. It was too dangerous. I could explode. I *would* explode. Her arguments were not rational.

Grandmother says it gets easier. That putting it off only makes the next change worse.

I didn't care. I would not live on the farm. Not for more than the summer. I could not be a wolf in a cage. Even if it was possible, which it wasn't. The neighbors might not have called the police that first time, but it was unlikely they'd refrain twice. What would happen when the cops found a wolf in a cage? It's not legal to keep a wolf as a pet in New York City. What if they came and it was human me in the cage waiting to change? What if they saw me change?

Never again, Dad decided. Never again would he deal with me changing in the city.

They decided to send me to the farm.

Forever.

Living without electricity, without hot water, without my parents, without anything I cared about. With my grandmother, my great-aunt Dorothy, my aunts and uncles and cousins who could barely read and write, let alone do calculus or trigonometry. Who know as little about fast-twitch muscles or mitochondrial DNA as they know about how to catch a cab or how to order a pizza.

No college. No future. No life. I would never unlock werewolf DNA. I would never understand what I am.

I would rather die.

I cried for two days straight. While Mom and Dad told me in turns why my living in the city was impossible.

I would not listen. There had to be another way.

Dad found it.

He learned that the pill can be used to suppress menstruation. He figured it would stop me turning into a wolf, too.

It did. It does.

But the first time we tried it was on the farm where it wouldn't matter if it went wrong. I refused to go up unless they promised I'd get to go home. No matter what happened.

They promised, but I'm not sure what would have happened if it hadn't worked. It wasn't as if Dad had never broken a promise to me before. My hopes were pinned on Mom. If she let me down, then I was going to run all the way back to the city. I would not stay on the farm.

Didn't come to that because it worked. I didn't bleed, I didn't turn into a wolf. I can keep the wolf inside. One pill a day.

My life wasn't over. Though Grandmother kept telling me that it should be, about the terrible mistake I was making, Dad was making. That this would rebound on me a hundredfold.

She calmed down a bit when we agreed to my returning each summer. Not taking the pill, being a wolf, running wild. It makes her and Hilliard happy. I can give away three months of my life each year. For their sake.

HISTORY OF ME

Grandmother is right. When I am a wolf I cannot be in the city. When I changed that first time the pain of the change was worse than anything I'd ever experienced. The Greats had talked about the pain but they hadn't explained that changing back would be as bad.

Wolf to human. Curled wolf nails retracting into flesh. Everything in reverse, but every bit as searing, bone-breaking, cell-crushing. There is nothing of a human that is the same size as that of a wolf. Not our lungs, our toes, our livers, our teeth, not even the shafts of our hair. Nothing is the same. All of it has to change.

Going from one to the other and back is the worst pain I have ever experienced and yet being trapped in that tiny cage . . . I thought I would lose my mind.

I could not run.

I could not even pace.

There was no hunt, no play, no running. The smells were metallic and dusty and human but what I heard was worse: machine hums and rattles and beeps, electricity in everything, loud thuds and thrums, squeaks and squeals from the street below. The noise was unendurable. The wolf-me wanted to run. Had to run. Couldn't run. Couldn't close my ears either.

I was unjointed, jangled, discombobulated. Many more times in that cage and the wolf would go insane.

I was more than glancing at the forest. I longed for it with every cell.

I could not be a wolf in the city. But I could not be a human on the farm.

HISTORY OF ME

That's not entirely true. (You're shocked, I can tell.)

I don't spend summers upstate solely to make my grandmother happy. I *hate* being on the farm when I'm human, but I *love* it when I'm a wolf.

There is nothing better. Happiness is flat-out full-bore wolf speed. The taste of raw deer that I killed myself. The ease of sleeping, of waking, of being. Hanging out with Great-Uncle Hilliard.

The first summer I was there after the change was the first time I was a wolf without a cage. My second time as a wolf.

I loved it.

No, that's too weak a word. I adored it. Worshipped it.

After I changed, after the blood and hair and teeth of me shifted, after the pain, my universe expanded.

My hearing surged. Wolfish me can hear everything: the faintest movement of rabbit, fox, deer, even rays of sun hitting the ground. Good sounds. Because there's no electricity on the farm there are no buzzes and clicks to make my fur stand on end.

I ran.

When I run as a human I'm fast, but it's the faintest echo of how it is when I'm a wolf.

Hilliard knocked me over. Nipped me. Butted me

with his head. Showed me how to run like a wolf. Taught me how to hunt.

Wolf life is cleaner, safer, happier.

When I want to play, I play. Sleep, I sleep.

There's no angst or hesitation or doubt or anxiety or madness.

Turning human, the world closes in. My perceptions dull. For a human my senses are sharp, but I don't smell or hear anywhere close to how I do in my wolfishness. When I'm human my head is hammered with dark thoughts and feelings and confusion.

When I'm the wolf I don't remember much of the human, but sometimes when I'm human all I can remember is the wolf.

I want it.

I want to throw the pills in the trash, flush them down the toilet. Never take one of those tiny pills again.

I want to run wild. I want falcons above, rocks, dirt, plants, and mulch beneath my paws. Trees all around. Drink from a stream, eat what I kill.

Wolf kin makes sense. Human? Not so much.

FAMILY HISTORY

There's one other thing that can (rarely) bring on the change: going into heat, rutting.

That's why I'm not allowed to have a boyfriend. Why my parents grounded me when they found out about Zach.

They don't want me to run any risk of changing in the city. Even so unlikely a risk has to be avoided, even if the precedent is rare and disputed.

Great-Aunt Dorothy remembers it happening; Grandmother says it's horseshit.

Great-Aunt also says that the same werewolf who changed when he went into heat also changed at the smell of blood—not menstrual blood, *any* blood—as well as at the scent of prey. In fact, the reek of fear—even anxiety—set him off, whether it came from prey or not. So many things triggered change in him that by the time he was twenty-five he had become a wolf permanently.

I am not like that.

My dad listened to all their tales but the only thing he took away was that I must not ever have sex.

My parents did not notice that blood does not set me off, prey neither, and the scent of fear? Of anxiety? The rooms and halls of my school exude it. So does every street of the city.

I am not like that long-ago, hair-trigger wolf.

My parents do not listen. When they found me with Zach they went ballistic.

HISTORY OF ME

I have thought about not taking the pill in the city, not climbing into the cage. I'd like to see what would happen. How would a wolf hide in the city? Where would they hide? Central Park? Too small. Too overcrowded. Inwood? Maybe. In some ways it would be safer than upstate. Not so many shotguns and coyote-hating farmers in the city.

I would love to know if it's possible. I would love to try.

I imagine myself living off the ducks and turtles and rabbits in Central Park.

What about when I changed back? How would I—filthy, naked, most likely covered in dried blood—make it all the way back home? Even at four in the morning there are people on the streets. Would I be arrested? Probably not. I'd be confused, they'd think I'd been attacked. They'd take me to a hospital. Would my blood be tested? Would I be discovered? Locked up? Turned into an exhibit? I can see the headlines:

First Werewolf Discovered!
Stranger than Fiction: Miss Wolf!

I can never do it. The risk is too great.

But I would like to. I think of the challenge. I think of
the fun.

Besides, I am *so* much faster than any police officer.

If it weren't for my parents, I would do it in a heartbeat.

———

BEFORE

Hilliard was ahead of the deer, me and Jessie flanked it.
The fear it gave off was so pungent I would've gagged if
it hadn't smelled so delicious, like swimming in choco-
late.

We'd waited out of range of the herd's eyes, ears, and
noses for so long that I'd forgotten what moving was like.
Hilliard is strict about waiting for the perfect moment,
for the wind to be in the right place for us to start moving without setting the deer off, for us to be able to cut
off their exits. Healthy deer can outrun us. These were
very healthy deer: glossy hides, sharp eyes, and musky
inviting odors.

I waited, salivating.

Hunting is six-tenths waiting. That's the worst part. Then there's the three-tenths of running, and only one-tenth of bringing the animal down. That's the best part.

When the herd bolted, we'd already surrounded the slowest: an older doe. Hilliard went for the neck. I buried my teeth and claws in her belly. Jessie bit in deep on the deer's hindquarters. The deer went down.

I clawed the belly wide open, tore at the guts, the innards spilled out so hot they steamed, filling the air with the smell of blood, gas, and acid.

We hunkered down and ate everything: eyeballs, entrails, ears. When we were done the deer was nothing but hooves, bones, fur, and stringy bits of sinew. No carrion left for the birds, barely enough for ants and flies to nibble on.

———

HISTORY OF ME

I've made wolf life sound more romantic than it is.

When I'm a wolf I have ticks. Parasites suck the blood in my belly and mites breed in my ears. Tapeworms come from the deer I eat, fluke from the fish.

It's true that I hunt, that I run and play. Most enjoyable, all three. Except when they're not. When the prey gets away, which is most of the time. A part-time wolf is not as competent as a full-time wolf. A wolf as part-time as me? Three or four times in the summer. I am the least competent wolf of all.

Mostly I sleep. When I'm awake all I want to do is scratch and eat and play and go back to sleep.

When I'm a wolf I itch, I ache, I'm hungry all the time, and if I stray too far off the farm I get shot at. The farm is smaller to the wolf-me than our apartment is to the human-me.

But both are better than time spent in a cage.

PART THREE
The Actual Real Truth

I will not tell a lie. I will not

HISTORY OF ME

Being a liar is not an easy business. For starters, you have to keep track of your lies. Remember exactly what you've said and who you said it to. Because that first lie always leads to a second.

There's never ever just one lie.

That's why it's best to keep it simple—gives you a better chance of tracking all the threads, keeping them spinning, and hopefully not propagating too many more.

It's hard work keeping all those lies in the air. Imagine juggling a thousand torches that are all tied together with fine thread. Or running the world's most complicated machine with cogs on wheels on cogs on wheels on cogs.

Even the best liars, even the ones with the longest memories, the best eye for detail and the big picture, even they get caught eventually. Maybe not in all their lies, but in one or two or more. That's the way it is.

I hate when that happens. When people figure out that what you were saying wasn't true and your elaborate construction crumbles.

The lies stop spinning, there's no lubrication, gears grind on gears. That's the moment when Sarah stared at me after I laughed, and said, "You're a girl."

That moment could have lasted a week. A month. A year.

I was ashamed and angry and hating being caught and already spinning more lies to explain it all away.

But it was also a relief. It's *always* a relief.

Because the air is clear, now—*at last*—I can tell the truth. From this moment on everything will be true. A life lived true with no rotten foundations. Trust. Understanding. Everything shiny and new.

Except I can't, not ever. Because my truth is so unbelievable—

What did you do over the summer?
Turned into a wolf, tore deer and rabbit apart . . .

—lies will always be easier.

Spin, spin, spin.

I have been through the moment of being found out a hundred times, a thousand times, maybe even a million.

I'm only seventeen, but I've already seen that look of shock—she lied *to me*—so many times I have lost count.

It never gets any better.

Yet that's not the worst danger of being a liar. Oh no. Much worse than discovery, than their sense of betrayal, is when you start to believe your own lies.

When it all blurs together.

You lose track of what's real and what's not. You start to feel as if you make the world with your words. Your lies get stranger and weirder and denser, get bigger than words, turn into worlds, become real.

You feel powerful, invincible.

"Oh sure," you say, completely believing it. "My family's an old family. Going way way way back. We work curse magic. Me, I can make your hand wither on your arm. I could turn you into a cat."

Once you start believing, you stop being compulsive and morph into pathological.

It happens a lot after something terrible has happened. The brain cracks, can't accept the truth, and makes its own. Invents a bigger and better world that explains the bad thing, makes it possible to keep living. When the world you're seeing doesn't line up with the world that is—you can wind up doing things—*terrible* things—without knowing it.

Not good.

Because that's when they lock you up and there's no

coming back because you're *already* locked up: inside your own head. Where you're tall and strong and fast and magic and the ruler of all you survey.

I have never gone that far.

But there are moments. Tiny ones when I'm not entirely clear whether it happened or I made it up. Those moments scare me much more than getting caught. I've been caught. I know what that's like. I've never gone crazy. I don't want to know what that's like.

Weaving lies is one thing; having them weave you is another.

That's why I'm writing this. To keep me from going over the edge. I don't want to be a liar anymore. I want to tell my stories true.

But I haven't so far. Not entirely. I've tried. I've really, really tried. I've tried harder than I ever have. But, well, there's so much and it's so hard.

I slipped a little. Just a little.

I'll make it up to you, though.

From now on it's nothing but the truth.

Truly.

———

LIE NUMBER ONE

Yayeko Shoji, my biology teacher, did not describe the decomposition of Zach's body.

I made that up.

Yayeko did not tell us about the pooling of Zach's blood, his calcium ions' leak, his rigor mortis, the breakdown of his cells. She did not tell us about bacteria, flies, eggs, or maggots.

I told you what I wished she'd told us. Because I wanted to know. Because I wanted to understand. How Zach could go from living, breathing . . . from how he was to . . . bacteria, flies, eggs, maggots.

Everyone lied.

They talked about him being gone but not what that meant. I heard Principal Paul say that Zach had "passed on." He didn't "pass on." Zach died. Like we all will. Only he went sooner and more violent, with blood pooling inside and outside his body.

So I read about death and decomposition and I try to understand.

But I don't.

The first thing that happens after death is that blood and oxygen stop flowing through the body.

The body falls apart. Slowly.

In the end all that's left is the beating of my heart, the in and out of my breath. Sarah's. Tayshawn's. The rest of us who are left behind.

We still tick. We still tock.

It hurts.

———

AFTER

On the day of Zach's funeral I leave Tayshawn and Sarah, I walk south to the park, Central Park, to the place where Zach and I first kissed.

I'm not sure what I think this will achieve. It's more like a compulsion. I want to pay tribute to him. The park seems a better place for that than a church crowded with people who mostly didn't know him. Not the way I did.

A better place than in Sarah and Tayshawn's arms.

I haven't been there since. I've run along the path but I haven't stopped. Haven't stood there under the bridge and thought about that day. That first kiss.

There are no icicles hanging from the bridge now.

It doesn't look the same. There's still green. Leaves, not snow, underfoot. The air isn't sharp to breathe.

Nothing's the same.

I can't think about that.

I slip my mom's shoes off and, holding them in my right hand, I run home, the wide skirt of Mom's dress ballooning and twisting around me. I'm too tired, too jangled, too encumbered by the dress to play the dodging game. My head is full of thoughts of Zach. And of Sarah and Tayshawn, of the feel of their mouths against mine. It makes my longing for Zach burn in my chest. Breathing starts to hurt. My eyes burn.

Running past Twelfth Street on Third Avenue I smell something rank, then I hear feet pounding lightly behind me. I tense but don't turn. Then the white boy who's like me is running beside me. He smiles. His teeth are more yellowy green than white. He doesn't look very old, yet his skin is lined. Not as old as me even. He must spend a lot of time outside.

I run faster but I'm fighting the dress.

He keeps pace.

This is the fourth time I've seen him. Once on Broadway when I played the dodging game. Once in the park when I ran with Zach. Once on the last day I ever saw Zach.

I can hear his breathing. It's as even as my own.

The white boy dodges the crowd as well as I can. With me in this dress, he's better.

He's fast but his technique is terrible: arms flapping like wings, shoulders too high, no lift in his knees, he thumps down hard on his heels. I wonder if my technique was that bad before Zach taught me. I hope not.

This close he smells worse. He's so filthy I wonder if

he's ever washed. I breathe shallow and wrinkle my nose. There's something familiar in his stink. I know it.

"You're a wolf," I say as we run past St. Mark's.

He reeks of it.

But how can that be?

The Greats say our kind mostly avoid cities. Except for boy wolves who don't want to change. Is that what he is? Then why follow me?

He stops in his tracks. I stop, too. But too slow. When I've turned around he's already off again, half a block away. I sprint hard to catch him. Watching his ungainly form weaving along the sidewalk, avoiding other people, elbows sticking out. I should be able to catch him but the half-block lead is opening up to a full block. I am tempted to tear Mom's dress, but she'd kill me. I press harder, dashing across Eleventh, narrowly avoiding being hit by a taxi, who hits his horn and screams abuse.

The boy is even farther ahead, dodging the traffic on Fourteenth.

I pull up short of Union Square. Tonight I don't have the reserves to catch him. They were drained away by the funeral, by Sarah and Tayshawn, by Zach. I'm spent.

I am unnerved. I head home. It's a necessity. As I regain my breath, I find myself wishing the Greats didn't live so far away. I have a hundred questions. If the white boy is what I think he is, if he did what I think he did, then I need their knowledge, I need them to tell me what to do.

Right now I'm wondering what it would be like to tear open his abdomen, watch the innards fall out.

I wonder what I should tell my parents.

As I pull out my keys and unlock the door to our apartment building I turn. Across the street in front of the supermarket the boy watches me.

LIE NUMBER TWO

I kissed Sarah first.

In the cave, after the funeral, when me and Sarah and Tayshawn were entwined, it was me who started it, not them.

I don't know why I lied. Does it matter who kissed who first? All three of us kissed. No one pulled away. There was no hesitation.

I guess I wanted it to be that way. For them to start it, not me. As we sat there talking, I could feel my lips getting warmer, along with my skin—the cave, too—the air between us. I knew it wasn't only me. Their mouths were glistening, redder than usual. Their eyes clear. They were as much in heat as I was.

Sarah *wanted* to kiss me. I'm sure of that. Tayshawn, too. Otherwise why would they have responded? They needed me to set their heat free.

But it does matter. Me making the first move? They'll always be thinking I'm easy.

By kissing them first I confirmed the thousand *slut* calls as I walk by.

When I leaned toward Sarah, she was already leaning toward me.

I should have waited.

AFTER

Dad is waiting, sitting at the kitchen table with his laptop.

"Hi, Micah," he says, looking up, smiling at me. He's showing his concern, that he knows what day it is, and he cares. There's no reason for me to be annoyed. I am annoyed anyway.

"Hi, Dad," I say, hoping that I can get this over with and be in my room quickly.

"How'd it go?"

I shrug. How does he think the funeral went? Well, probably not how it actually went. I am not going to tell him about walking out, about Sarah and Tayshawn. Nor about the white boy following me home. I'm not going to tell him anything that matters.

"It was weird," I say, because he needs to hear something. "I mean, the funeral was weird. All these people I never saw before and the preacher said stuff that was all wrong. Not like Zach at all. It was like no one had even *met* him, let alone knew him well. They were all talking about imaginary Zach."

"Funerals are always that way," Dad says, closing his laptop to show that I have his full attention. "Everyone talks about an idealized version of the dearly departed. All their warts are removed and they become someone they're not . . ."

I lean against the fridge, knocking off a magnet and causing one of Jordan's vomits on paper to fall to the floor. I ignore it. "The party after was worse. I only knew his friends from school and none of them like me. And they were all drinking—"

"You didn't—" Dad begins.

"No, Dad. Of course not." I'm not allowed to drink because they're afraid I'll turn wolfish even though the Greats say that's horseshit. Well, mostly horseshit. Great-Aunt Dorothy remembered that it had happened once with her grandfather, but only once, and she doesn't remember it happening to any other wolf. "I've still never had a sip of alcohol. Even if I wanted to try it, I wouldn't surrounded by those creeps. They think I'm a freak. Which is true, just not the way they think I am. I can't wait till school's done," I finish, hoping I've said enough for Dad to feel as if we've had a talk and he's done his fatherly duty. I'm pretty sure that's how it would have been if I had gone to Will's place.

"I'm sorry," Dad says. "You okay?"

I nod. Even though I'm not. I wonder what he'd say if I told him about the white boy. About what I suspect.

"Your mom wants to talk to you."

"She in bed?" I ask, even though it's obvious. It's not as if there's anywhere else she could be.

"Uh-huh," Dad says, reaching out to pat my shoulder. I don't brush his hand off though I want to. "You sure you're okay?"

"Yeah," I say. "Tired." Confused, guilty, sad, angry, worried, mourning. I am many things. I want to know who that boy is, why he's following me, what he wants. I want to know if he killed Zach. I want to know why.

I want Zach to be alive.

I knock on the door to Mom and Dad's room. "Mom?" I call, not bothering to be quiet for Jordan asleep a thin wall away.

"Come in," Mom says.

I open the door. Mom's in bed, wearing her frilly pajamas that make us both giggle. She pats the bed. I sit. She pulls me into a hug and kisses the top of my head.

My throat hurts so much it closes over. For a moment I can't breathe, tears stream out of my eyes. I can't seem to stop. I cry and cry and cry.

"There, there, *chérie*," she says, stroking my hair. "There, there, my love."

BEFORE

Me and Zach, we raced each other a lot after that first time in Central Park. The result was never in question. He was fast, I was faster. I knew that. He knew that.

But it was Zach who taught me how to run right.

Running beside him, matching stride for stride, hearing his breath, smelling it. Duplicating it. Teaching myself to run as he did. No one ever taught me, you see. I had no technique. Learning from Zach made me even faster, copying all the things Zach learned from his coach: landing light on my heels, knees higher, longer stride. Fists pumping, elbows in tight by my side.

I even tried to get my heart to beat at the same pace as his.

I could hear his beating when I slept, taste his breath. It was as if he had crawled into my skin. Under it, always there.

Even after he died.

Maybe *more* after he died.

I've never been as comfortable, as happy with another person as I was with Zach.

I wish I hadn't had to lie to him. I wish he knew what I really am.

If he had lived longer I think I would have told him.

Maybe.

I told the police that I would never hurt him. I don't think they believed me.

Biology was Zach's favorite class. Mine, too.

Maybe if he'd known about me he would have wanted to help me figure out how my wolfishness works.

Right now I'm thinking about how Zach was made, was unmade.

Once in class we had to put together a model of the human body. We looked at how the organs sat together: spleen and pancreas behind stomach. Gallbladder behind liver. Kidneys in the middle of the back. Large intestine nestling the small. All shiny and plastic.

Yayeko warned us that real bodies were only vaguely like the model. That spleens, pancreas, stomachs, gallbladders, livers, kidneys, large and small intestines are as varied as the nose and eyes and mouths on our faces.

Does that mean the model is a lie?

Zach's organs are even less like that model than they were. They no longer fit together. Even before they started to rot, they were pulled apart, shredded, blood breaking through the veins and capillary walls that were supposed to keep them housed safe, sound, and circulating.

Zach's blood got free, drowned all his organs.

But I don't know how. I don't know who did that to him. At least, I'm not sure. My suspicions are without any proof.

All I know is that he's gone forever.

I wonder if I would have loved his lungs, his voice box, his pancreas if I'd seen them nestled safe within him. If you love someone, do you love all of them? Even the mucus in their throat, the cankers in their mouth, the cavities in their teeth?

I want it to be winter always. Because I met Zach in winter. Really met him. Talked to him. Kissed him. Ran with him. All the things we did together. Those were winter things.

In winter he was alive. Organs well-knit.

In summer I was away, aching for him, being a wolf.

But here in the fall, he's gone. All the layers gone, too. Right down to his skin.

I'm not sure what to do without him.

The last time I saw him we were running. All the way from Central Park to his apartment building in Inwood. But I kept running, turned, ran backward slowly, waved, and then ran all the way down to the Lower East Side. To my apartment building, my tiny little room, where he had never been.

I never saw him again.

Not alive. Not with organs intact.

———

LIE NUMBER THREE

There were never any doctors.

My parents were too afraid of blood samples being taken. Too afraid of what the doctors would find. Of what lives in my blood.

I have never been to a doctor. Not one. I've never had any tests done. Never been vaccinated. Never had my ears or eyes tested. When I run a fever my parents give me aspirin, put cold cloths on my forehead, and hope that it will come down.

No doctor ever told me to keep taking the pill. Mom wasn't horrified by the suggestion. She's the one who gets the prescription from her doctor. I added that detail to make it seem more real.

There were hair-removal specialists though. By the time I was ten I swear we'd been to every single one in the city: electrolysis, waxing, laser, creams, and unguents. Mom found an old French woman who made me drink a foul-smelling herbal drink that tasted like dirt and made me throw up. Chinese and Spanish herbs and ointments. There was acupuncture, even a spirit worker.

None of it worked.

The hair came, stayed for more than a year, then the hair went, to return only when I am a wolf.

SCHOOL HISTORY

My school was founded by Quakers. They believed in equality and justice and wanted to make a school in that image. One of them was very wealthy, that's why there's so much scholarship money—that's how they've kept the school fees low. Well, not low by my standards, but low compared to most private schools in the city. Low enough that with scrimping and saving my parents can pay the half of my tuition that isn't covered by my scholarship.

But that rich Quaker—isn't that a contradiction? I thought Quakers were supposed to be poor—anyway, that Quaker left his Quaker wife and his many Quaker children and ran away with a much younger woman who was a dancer, not a Quaker. He moved to New York City to watch her dance every night. Until she up and left him, leaving him with a broken heart and—according to Chantal—a bad case of the clap.

That's when he founded the school and poured all his money into it.

He founded it in this building that used to be a prison. A women's prison. They kept the bars on the windows.

None of the students at the school are Quakers and only one of the teachers: Principal Paul.

I wonder if the Quaker sense of equality and justice extends to werewolves. Does it extend to me?

I realize I don't know much about Quakers.

But I know a lot about cages, about prisons. I've been kept hostage by lies all my life. Imprisoned by them.

This is how it is:

I'm alone.

Bars surround me. Prison guards bind my arms, bring me pills several times a day. They ask me—beg me—to tell them the truth.

I am.

Every single word.

Truth.

They don't believe in my wolves.

AFTER

The day after the funeral, I almost stay home from school. I'm not sure I can face Sarah and Tayshawn. The thought of seeing them makes my cheeks hot. I don't want to have a conversation about how it was a mistake, how we should forget about it, move on. I don't want to talk about it.

I keep my head down and go back into invisibility mode, which is much harder than it used to be. Zach is buried, but they still talk about him, still look sideways at me. Except now it feels as if there's more reason for them to be staring. I'm sure everyone knows what we did after the funeral.

No, not after. *During.* That makes it so much worse. Who noticed us leave together? Does everyone already know what happened? My cheeks get hotter.

I take my lunch—burned meatballs—into Yayeko Shoji's classroom, pretty sure I'll be safe from them there. I sit down under the poster of the carnivores' evolutionary tree, noting the branch where the gray wolf and the domestic dog split apart. It's very recent. There's 0.2 percent of mtDNA sequence difference between a wolf and a Pekingese . . . dogs and wolves can still interbreed.

The door opens while I'm contemplating how much DNA I share with black bears. Dogs and humans have 85 percent shared genetic material; wolves and bears share—

It's Sarah. I look away.

"Okay if I join you?" she asks.

I nod.

I wish it hadn't happened.

No, that's a lie. (See? I told you I was done with lying.)

What happened, it was . . . I didn't . . . I did . . .

I liked it. It felt good. I wish we would do it again.

But I don't know how it happened. Sarah can't really have meant to return my kiss. Neither did Tayshawn. It was something else overwhelming us.

Grief.

We were trying to find traces of Zach in the layers of our skin.

"How you doing, Micah?" Sarah says, sliding into the seat beside me.

"Fine," I say.

She puts her hands on the table and accidentally touches the side of my little finger. We both pull away quick.

"Sorry," Sarah says. "I didn't mean . . ." She pauses. "Kind of creepy eating lunch here, don't you think?" She's looking at the plastic model of the human body. The guts are jumbled, the pancreas resting on the heart, the gallbladder on the place where the genitals would be if the model had them. The large and small intestines and the voice box are on the floor.

"It's quiet," I say, wishing I didn't have to speak. Zach didn't like talking all the time either.

"We should talk," Sarah says.

She never used to talk to me when I was invisible. But I'm not anymore.

After my first two lies were exposed—they knew I was a girl, they knew I hadn't been born a hermaphrodite—after that, I started to disappear. I didn't talk in or out of class. If your mouth's shut, lies can't come streaming out. There were still whispers. But after a year they dulled down.

I liked being invisible.

I watched. I thought.

Zach never saw me. I know that. I noticed him, sitting with Sarah, nuzzling at her neck, kissing her. Playing ball with the guys.

I imagined what it would be like to be him. But I didn't envy it. I wasn't happy, but I wasn't *not* happy either. Invisibility suits me.

"I like you, Micah," Sarah says. "Aside from Zach and all that . . ." She blinks, takes a deep breath. "Aside from that and from you being a crazy liar, too." She smiles at me and my cheeks feel hot again. I don't know where to look except at her. "Yesterday was the best I've felt since . . . Zach. The talking, I mean. The three of us being friends. I don't want to lose that, too. We can stay friends, right?"

I nod, though I really doubt it.

"Good," she says. The top she's wearing clings to her arms. They're slim and not at all strong-looking. How exactly do they think a girl like Sarah could have killed Zach? He was stronger and taller and bulkier than her.

And Tayshawn? Why on earth would he kill his best friend? His boy that he'd known since the third grade.

Sarah's waiting for me to say something, but I have nothing.

"Could you help me with bio?" she asks.

"Help you?" I repeat, not understanding.

She gestures at the plastic model pieces. "I'm not doing as well as I should. Biology's not really my thing."

"Sure," I say.

"I can help you with your other classes."

"Okay." I'm not bad at any of them, but biology is what I'm best at.

Sarah's looking at me, expecting more words, but I have no idea what to say. She hasn't said anything, not really, about what happened. It's as if it didn't.

It did. When I'm not thinking about Zach, I'm thinking about what happened between me and Sarah and Tayshawn after the funeral. Would Zach be mad at me if he knew? I know he's dead. But I can't help thinking that he knows, that he cares. I'd undo what we did, I'd undo *anything*, if it would make him alive again. I'd stop lying. Tell everyone about the wolf within.

I miss him.

The ache of where he isn't is so large that sometimes I can barely manage to stay upright. Even with his coffin lowered into the ground, with soil on top of him, I cannot believe he's dead.

"Micah?" Sarah asks. She puts her hand on mine. Hers is warm, a little dry. Her touch makes me tingle. I wonder if it makes her tingle, too. I'm about to say something stupid when Tayshawn joins us.

Sarah pulls her hand away. "I was asking Micah if she'd help me with bio."

"Uh-huh," Tayshawn says. He pulls up a chair, sits. His eyes are red and he's a little sweaty, as if he's been running. I brace myself for what he's going to say. Is he mad about finding us alone together with Sarah's hand on mine? Does he think we're leaving him out? Is he going to be weird?

"Erin Moncaster isn't dead," he announces, looking at both of us.

———

AFTER

Erin Moncaster was found in a hotel in Fort Lauderdale, Florida, with her skeezy eighteen-year-old boyfriend. Now she is back in the city and back in school.

In class they're not talking about me. Erin the slut replaces Micah the liar and possible killer.

I see her later that day between fifth and sixth periods. She's dressed the part, walking down the hall with too much paint on pale white skin, making her look as garish as a clown. Her short skirt and low-cut top are supposed to be clingy, but she's so skinny they hang off her, like the white boy, but she looks fragile, not fearsome. She keeps her head high like she doesn't care, but her eyes are red, and her lips tremble.

Everyone is staring at her. The whole whispering, giggling thing that I am so used to. It belongs to Erin now.

"Hey, Micah," Tayshawn calls, coming down the stairs.

I wave. To my right I see Brandon "accidentally" knock into Erin.

"While your boy's in jail," he breathes at her, "you can get some from me." He's licking his lips the same way he did at me that day under the bleachers when he was making me the same offer.

I don't remember moving.

My hands are around his neck. I'm pressing Brandon into the wall. The Amnesty International poster behind him tears, leaving barbed wire floating at his left shoulder. My face is inches from his. He's gone red. He's coughing, struggling to breathe, clawing at my fingers.

I step away, dropping him.

"Bitch!" he screams, sliding to the floor, rubbing his throat where my fingers have left red marks. "Fucking bitch! Is that what you did to your boyfriend?"

My urge to hurt him floods back. I step forward.

Brandon cowers. "Bitch," he whispers.

"Don't," Tayshawn says, grabbing hold of my upper arm, pulling me away. "Leave the wuss on the floor. Beaten up by a girl again, Brandon? How many times is that this week?"

Several people laugh.

"Fuck off. She's no girl," Brandon says, but he's mumbling, looking down. "Girls don't fight like that." The bruises are starting to show on his neck. "Bitch."

I'm realizing what I've done. Shown how fast and strong I am. In front of everyone. Any doubts they might have had about my ability to kill Zach are gone now. I've done what Dad's always told me not to do. I'm lucky no teachers saw. Now it's down to whether Brandon tells or not. But at least he will respect me.

"Stop looking at me," Brandon says quietly. I doubt anyone but me can hear.

"Why would I look at you?" I say. "There's nothing to see."

"Come on," Tayshawn says, pulling me farther away. The hall has thinned out. Classes must be starting.

We pass Erin. She's staring at me. I wonder if she's grateful that I pulled Brandon off her. Though that isn't why I did it. I don't feel sorry for Erin; I just hate Brandon. After all, Erin isn't dead, is she? Her boyfriend isn't dead either. She's not a wolf. Her life is fine.

"That was amazing," Tayshawn says. His hand is still

around my upper arm. "Where'd you learn skills like that?"

"Dad used to be a boxer," I lie.

LIE NUMBER FOUR

What I told the police isn't what really happened the last time I saw Zach.

School was out for the day. We were in the library. Both of us on giving-back-to-the-school duty. Brandon and Chantal weren't there. They'd forgotten.

"How did you find those foxes?" Zach whispered. We were in front of the fiction shelves. Zach was shelving and I was pulling out the books that did not belong.

We weren't the only ones there. The librarian, Jennifer Silverman, and a handful of freshmen, working on a project that seemed to involve a lot of loud talking and giggling.

"Wasn't a big deal," I said.

Zach wasn't listening. "I saw how you followed them. I've never seen anything like that. The path was lit up for you: *this way there's foxes*. I never saw a fox in the park till you showed me. You're like magic or something."

I looked down to hide my grin.

"What?" he asked. He was paying attention now.

"I kind of cheated."

"That's a shock. She lies. She cheats."

He touched my forearm. I tried to ignore it. Just pheromones. Chemical receptors. Biology. Controllable. Ignorable.

"It looked real to me," Zach said. "How'd you cheat?"

"I'd seen the burrow before," I confessed. "So I knew where the fox was going."

"Ah. Okay. You already knew? Damn."

"You should see your face."

He looked mad, annoyed, and kind of impressed all at the same time.

"You're a piece of work, you know."

I did know.

"You suck. You can't track shit. And here was me thinking you were some kind of wild girl of the woods! Damn."

"I am. I could have tracked those foxes, I just didn't have to is all."

"Why would I believe you?" Zach asked, and I could tell he was really angry. "You lie about everything."

"Not about this. I know a lot about tracking animals, hunting. Every summer I'm upstate with my grandparents. We hunt together all the time."

"So you say."

"Scout's honor," I said.

"You're not a scout and even if you were I wouldn't believe you. You're a liar, Micah."

"I could track you," I said. "You go hide yourself in the park and you'll see how damn easy it is for me to find you!"

"Shhh!" the librarian said, walking over to us. "I know school's out but there's no need for you to be yelling."

"Sorry, Jennifer," Zach said.

"Sorry," I mumbled.

She walked back to her desk.

"How do I know you won't cheat?" Zach said.

"I can't cheat on this one. I won't know where you're going."

Zach considered, shelved the book in his hand, turned back to the cart for another. "Alright," he said. "How you want to work it then?"

Jennifer the librarian walked over again and handed Zach some more fiction to shelve.

I ducked down and straightened the lowest shelf. She smiled at both of us and returned to her desk. Two of the books were mis-shelved: one about censorship in the USSR and the other an inorganic chemistry textbook. Neither of them belonged with novels written by people whose names began with Q or R.

"We'll both come in on the Columbus Circle side," I said to the shelf. "Me a half hour after you."

"What's to stop you following me?"

"I won't."

Zach didn't bother to answer. He was still angry. I wondered if it was weird of me to really want to kiss him. He returned to shelving.

"Okay then. I'm leaving now. You come and find me in the park when Jennifer lets you go."

He kissed my mouth quickly and I almost blushed, looking around to make sure no one had seen. He walked over to Jennifer's desk and started sweet-talking her into letting him go early. It was three thirty. We were sup-posed to be shelving until four.

She let him go. Zach almost always got what he wanted.

HISTORY OF ME

Details. They're the key to lying.

The more detailed you are, the more people believe. Not piled on one after another after another—don't tell too much. Ever. Too many details, that's too many things that can be checked.

Let them tease the information out of you. Lightly sprinkle it. One detail here, the smell of peanuts roast-ing; one there, the crunch of gray snow underfoot.

Verisimilitude, one of my English teachers called it.

The details that give something the appearance of being real. It's at the heart of a good lie, a story that has wings.

That, and your desire, your overwhelming desire, not to be lied to. You believe me because you want what I tell you to be the truth. No matter how crazy.

And because I promised no more lies.

Which I've stuck to: nothing but the truth.

BEFORE

It wasn't summer but it felt like it. Spring had sprung for a day and then turned hot and sweltering. Central Park was entirely green. Not like winter, with the city leaning in on the leafless skeleton trees, making sure it is never out of view. The reprieve from the city buoyed me, but it was scary, too: city is city and forest, forest. I don't like them getting muddled.

It feels as if I'm seeing myself reflected in the leaves, and in the glassphalt sidewalk. That hurts my head.

I caught Zach's scent coming out of the subway. I followed it, jumped over the fence, into the park, trying to name the parts of his scent: the meatiness, the sweat, and the something else underlying it, something sweet. No one else smelled like that. Just Zach.

The smell of him warmed me, drew me toward him. As if the finest thread stretched out between us. He was reeling me in. Tracking him would be easier than finding the foxes.

I slid into a jog, following the molecules. If they had been visible they would have glowed brighter than neon.

Before I got to the lake the strange white boy crossed my path. He didn't turn to look at me. Just ran past me in his wild and uneven way. Erratic but fast. He was out of sight down the path almost instantly, leaving a lingering pungent smell.

I shivered and continued chasing Zach.

AFTER

"Come on," Tayshawn says, leading me down the front steps, past reception, out onto the street. We're seniors so we're allowed to go off campus for lunch but it's not lunch, it's fifth period.

"Where are we going?"

"Away," Tayshawn says. "I gotta tell you stuff."

"Like what?" Is he going to talk about what happened? Between him and me and Sarah?

Tayshawn stops on the sidewalk, leans in to whisper in my ear. "It was dogs," he says. "Zach was killed by dogs."

My knees stop working, as though the cartilage has melted. I stumble. I would fall but Tayshawn's holding me. I'm not thinking about dogs; I'm thinking about wolves. That's why Brandon kept calling me "bitch." He meant it literally. Will the cops be coming after me?

I'm screwed. How will I tell my parents?

How does Brandon know about me? No one outside my family knows.

"Micah," Tayshawn says. His eyes are bruised. "I know." He puts his arms around me, holds me tight.

What will they do to me?

"I know," he says again. His voice sounds thick like he's trying not to cry. "How could dogs have killed him?"

Dogs. Tayshawn's not talking about me. I breathe. He makes a kind of crooked grimace with his mouth. He's looking at me, but not accusingly. The thought of me being a wolf hasn't occurred to him. Or to anyone else. Why would it?

I'm being crazy.

"Dogs," I say, though dogs didn't. That strange white boy did.

Tayshawn wipes at his eyes, drags me into a dark café that's all coffee: huge coffee-making machines, giant sacks of beans. The smell so overwhelming that when we're sitting in back and drinking it hot and burned it becomes the murk we're floating in.

Tayshawn switches off the lamps on either side of us. Darker is better.

Dogs. This is what the cops haven't been telling us. This is why the coffin was closed. Zach's body was torn apart. Like prey.

I take another sip. I've never drunk coffee before. It's something else I'm forbidden. I think I like it.

Dogs. But then why were we ever under suspicion? I ask Tayshawn.

"The autopsy report was a big surprise to the police. They thought the dogs"—Tayshawn pauses, swallows— "that they got at his body *after*. They never thought the dogs were what killed him."

"But now they're sure it was dogs?" I sip more coffee, feeling it make my eyes widen, my spine straighten. I want to run. "Your uncle told you?"

"Yeah. He called me last night. Dogs. Not a murder. It'll be all over school pretty soon."

I reach across and put my hands on Tayshawn's. His are shaking. "Where?" I ask. "Where did they find the body?"

"Central Park."

That's what I was afraid of. Zach found dead, torn to pieces in the place we spent the most time together.

"Well," I say, "at least the cops won't be bothering us again."

Tayshawn manages half a laugh. "No more killer Tayshawn rumors."

"No one really believed that shit," I say, though it's not true.

"Right. You just believe that. Not that it matters. Because those rumors are gone now. No killer Tayshawn, no killer Sarah, no killer Micah. Just a pack of dogs." His voice breaks on *dogs*.

I wish I could tell him it wasn't dogs. That it was wolves. A lone wolf. But surely the police can tell the difference? Aren't the bites of dogs and wolves different? I want to ask Yayeko. Or do the police know? Is "dogs" a cover story?

Tayshawn is crying again. I squeeze his hands. "It's a lot," I say. The coffee is making my head spin. I'm not allowed anything with caffeine in it. It's like avoiding alcohol. We don't know what could happen to me, what could trigger a change. No sex, no drugs, no alcohol. No nothing. That's my parents' policy.

I take a much bigger sip—to spite them. The more I drink, the more I like it. Bitter, but not as bad as it smells. I think it's making my blood move faster.

I have to find the white boy.

Then what?

Kill him?

I've never killed a person.

Or a wolf.

I need to talk to the Greats. I need to get upstate.

"Sorry," Tayshawn says. His eyes are red. "I keep imagining what it would have been like. Dogs . . ."

"Yeah."

"I guess it's better, right?" he says. "At least Zach wasn't murdered. I was afraid . . ."

He was afraid that it was me or Sarah or someone else he knew? He doesn't say it though. I never suspected them. I think I always knew it was the white boy.

"God," Tayshawn says. He touches his bottom lip, pulling at it. I want to kiss him. I wonder if it's wrong that I'm thinking about that. I'm pretty sure he isn't thinking about kissing me.

"Have you told Sarah?"

He shakes his head. "I was going to, you know, at lunch. But then I didn't find you until just before the bell."

"So you told us about Erin Moncaster?"

"Funny, huh? I saw you both there and I couldn't do it, couldn't figure out how to tell you. I still can't believe it's true. Dogs?"

"Yeah," I say. "I know."

"My uncle, he says there's a pack on a vacant lot in Hell's Kitchen. There've been a ton of complaints. That pack's attacked other dogs. They're vicious. Their owner's a crazy old guy who owns the lot. Says he has the dogs under control, but he doesn't."

"Hell's Kitchen?" I ask. I know that pack. They might be vicious but they back up when I run by. Snouts to the ground, cowering. They smell what I am. The lot is a long way from Central Park. Too far for a pack of wild dogs to roam. There's at least ten of them. How would they get all the way up and into Central Park without someone seeing and freaking? It's not exactly an empty part of the city.

We look at each other. My eyes are on his mouth. Tayshawn looks away.

"What a way to die," he says, shuddering. "I can't even imagine."

I can. I know exactly what it would be like. I've torn creatures apart. I've watched them die. It's mostly quick.

"My uncle told me if they can prove it was the old man's dogs, they'll put them down and press charges against him."

"What charges?" I ask. "Murder?"

Tayshawn shakes his head. "I don't know. I don't think so. My uncle didn't say."

"Didn't they use to do that in the old days?" I say. "Set dogs on people? Could the old man have done that?"

"But Zach's white," Tayshawn says.

"Hispanic," I says.

"White Hispanic. He didn't even speak Spanish. Plus it's now."

Not to mention that dogs had nothing to do with Zach's death. I sip at the no-longer-hot coffee. Lukewarm it's not so good.

There have been so many rumors. I'm not sure how I feel now that we have the official truth and dealing with Zach's murderer has become my responsibility.

AFTER

The week after the funeral seems unending.

Erin Moncaster brings a tiny bit of distraction from thinking about Zach and the white boy, about Tayshawn and Sarah. Erin's certainly occupying everyone else's thoughts. I think it's because the idea of Zach being killed by dogs is too weird, too horrible for them to dwell on. So instead we hear about how Erin wept when her boyfriend was arrested, how she insisted that they were married and that they couldn't take him away from her.

They could, though. She's only fourteen and her parents didn't give permission, so the marriage isn't real.

Next I hear she's pregnant. Then that she's diseased. Or both.

Everyone is talking about her. No one's talking about me and Sarah and Tayshawn. No one knows that happened.

When Zach's name is mentioned, it's followed by silence and then a change of subject. No one's wondering who killed him because now we know. Except we don't.

I'm the only one who *really* knows. I'm the one who has to do something about it.

I haven't seen the white boy since after the funeral. I'm nervous, but not as nervous as if I'd seen him. Either way is bad. Friday after school I'm going upstate. I'm hoping the Greats will have answers for me. Instructions.

I need someone to tell me what to do.

Sarah, Tayshawn, and me don't talk about what happened between us. I still want to kiss them, they show no signs of feeling the same way. I wonder if maybe they're getting together when I'm not there. I work hard to keep that thought out of my head.

My body is hollow.

The end of rumors about Zach and his death brings another kind of relief. I was sick of people, like Chantal, who'd hardly known Zach, acting as if they'd been best friends. As if his death was her own personal tragedy. Now she's forgotten all about Zach and is all gossip about Erin all the time. She's newly best friends with Kayla so she can stay up on juicy Erin gossip. She shakes her head and tsks as she passes along each new scrap.

Chantal's a hypocrite and every bit as big a liar as I am.

It makes me want to tear out her throat. How can anyone forget about Zach so easily?

But at least he's more mine now. Mine and Sarah's and Tayshawn's.

Though it's me who has to avenge him.

LIE NUMBER FIVE

I don't have a brother. I made Jordan up.

What did you think? That after having me, the wolf girl, my parents would risk a second child? A second freak? Two cages in the already overcrowded apartment? Even if the kid wasn't wolfish how would you keep it from blabbing about its monster for a sister?

Not likely, is it?

Good-bye, Jordan. Imaginary or not, he sucked. Vile, sticky-fingered, foulmouthed, nasty, smelly brother.

But you want to know why, don't you?

Why did I lie about having a brother?

I wanted to see if I could do it: invent a person. Make them believable. Real. Whole. I wanted to see if you would buy it. And you did.

You buy everything, don't you?

You make it too easy.

BEFORE

I found Zach high up a tree in the North Woods in Central Park, not near any of the paths. The tree had wide, thick branches and plenty of leaf cover. He did a good job of keeping still. I couldn't hear or see him, but his scent gave him away. It was everywhere.

The branches started a few feet above my head. Zach was using his height against me. He is—he *was*—over six foot four. I'm not. He could jump and touch the lowest branches. Not me.

I prowled around the tree, quiet. I couldn't feel the telltale prickles of someone looking at me. Zach was high up. Maybe he'd fallen asleep. It happened. He trained so hard, worked such long hours keeping up with home-work that he was often coasting on two or three hours of sleep a day. I'd seen him fall asleep in classes, at lunch. Sometimes when we ran together he'd be close to falling asleep on his feet. If he'd gone for a ball scholarship he could've gotten the sleep he needed, but he wanted a full ride courtesy of his brains.

Zach wasn't crazy.

He'd seen what a sports scholarship can do to you. He'd seen what happened to his brother. Shredded knees and back leaving him too crippled to even walk right. No pro career for him, but his grades were only so-so, and he'd never figured out anything else he wanted to do.

Zach wanted options.

The trunk wasn't that wide. I spread my arms around it and slipped my shoes off, gripping with the soles of my feet. I was going to climb it like a coconut tree.

It was harder than it looked, but I was strong and didn't care about cutting up my hands and feet.

"Hey, there," Zach said, leaning down from halfway up the tree. I'd reached the first branch. "Want a hand?"

"Nope." I grabbed the branch over my head and hauled myself up to straddle it with my legs. Wolves might not be wild about climbing, but I like it fine.

"Well done, shorty."

"Thanks." I wiped my hands on my pants. "Told you I'd find you."

"You did. You are a superhero." He climbed down to my level. "Strong and brave with magical tracking skills. I'll never doubt you again." He was grinning to undermine his words, but he meant them. "How'd you do that?"

"Do what?" I asked, playing dumb. "Climb the tree?"

He snorted. "Find me, stupid. The park's I-don't-know-how-big. Must be thousands of trees. You can't have seen me from down there. It's not possible . . ." He stopped, leaning in, looking at me closely.

I could see the pores of his skin, tiny hairs, a few blackheads nestled against his nose.

"You're not like anyone else. What are you?"

That could have been the moment. I could have told him. I almost had a few weeks before, but, well . . . we were distracted before I could get the words out.

"There's something, isn't there?" Zach said.

What would have happened if I'd told him? Would he have laughed?

I ran my fingers over his cheek, over the light stubble.

"Tell me, Micah."

Instead I leaned forward, kissed the tip of his nose, and then his mouth. We made out, tentative and cautious, because we were up a tree, and gravity isn't kind.

When we climbed down it was getting dark.

"Run home with me?" he said. I did. More than a hundred blocks side by side, backpacks bouncing. We'd done it before. I figured we'd do it again.

We didn't.

Outside his building we stopped. Zach wiped sweat from his forehead, his upper lip. We kissed again.

"Tomorrow," he said.

I nodded.

"Will you tell me then?"

"Maybe."

He laughed.

It was the last time I ever saw him.

AFTER

Brandon hasn't told on me; he avoids me. But he doesn't avoid Erin. He harasses her whenever he can. Erin, who he never looked at twice and didn't give a damn about before she ran away. Or after she ran away, for that matter, when we all thought she was dead like Zach.

It's only now that she's back in school and her boy-friend is in jail in Florida that he's giving her lots of quality Brandon attention. Because now she's prey. She twitches, looks around, checks all possible exits. She's always ready to run, to cower, to hide. She exudes the prey scent: fear.

Brandon thinks because she's prey, she's easy. She's someone he can take. He's probably right.

Lucky Erin.

I want to prove him wrong. I don't like to think of Brandon and me having anything in common. I'm the predator, not him. I can teach him that. I *will* teach him that.

I wish dogs would take Brandon. I think about how I can arrange it. I can make him prey.

Instead I make it a habit to be in Erin's vicinity as much as I can. Brandon doesn't say a word if I'm there. He can't even look me in the eye.

He's scared of me.

He should be.

AFTER

The week after the funeral I eat lunch with Sarah and Tayshawn most every day. We don't talk about what I want us to talk about. We don't talk about Zach or what happened to him either. I don't tell them anything about the white boy or what I have to do.

On Thursday after school we meet at Sarah's place. Supposedly to study. I am hoping not.

Her dad is working late and her mom's away at some lawyer conference. Turns out Sarah lives a few blocks from my place, but her building is shiny and new. There's a doorman. He sits behind marble and writes down my name and checks my school ID. I've never been in a doorman building before.

He hands back the ID and tells me that Miss Washington is expecting me.

"Okay," I say.

"Eighteenth floor," he tells me, pointing to the bank of elevators.

"What apartment number?" I ask.

"Eighteenth floor," he repeats. "That's the number."

The elevator opens up to Tayshawn. We're standing in a room that's bigger than my kitchen. It's lined with racks for shoes.

"You have to take your shoes off," Tayshawn tells me. He points to where his are already resting on a rack. "Pretty weird, huh?"

"Yeah." I slip off my sneakers and put them beside his, looking up at him, smiling. I've always liked Tayshawn; he's the only one at the school who's always been nice to me.

Tayshawn holds his hand out to help me up. I take it and feel a jolt of intense longing.

I kiss him lightly, my lips on his. I lean into it, easing onto my toes so our lips stay aligned. My mouth opens a little, so does his. We're kissing for real.

The feel of it is strong. I grab hold of him, grip his biceps to keep from falling.

He pulls away but I don't want to stop. He pushes me off. The heat is still on me, so intense my legs shake. I have to steel every muscle to keep from throwing myself at him again.

"Sorry," I mumble.

We're here at Sarah's to study together. I'm not sure I can. I thought Tayshawn felt that way, too. He's not shaking.

"Wow, girl," he says, showing me his palms. "Slow down."

I look away. There's sweat on my upper lip. I don't know what to say. Zach would have responded. Zach would have exploded with me.

"This way," Tayshawn says, opening the door, careful not to touch me.

It's the biggest apartment I've ever seen. We're standing in a living room that's as big as an entire floor of my building. Everything is clean and shiny. The couches are made out of real leather. A television takes up a whole wall.

I walk toward the glass walls that look down on Astor Place. Beyond I can see both the Chrysler and Empire

State buildings. To my right, I can see all the way to Brooklyn.

Tayshawn mock punches me, and even that light touch of knuckles on my bare shoulder is enough . . . I cough. He looks down at his hand, as if he didn't know what he was doing.

"You're staring," he says at last. "You never seen a rich person's place before?"

"Nope," I say. "I thought Zach's place was big."

Tayshawn laughs.

He thinks I'm joking.

"Where's Sarah?"

"Here," she says, from behind us. "Welcome."

She sounds like a hostess at a party. Or at least how I imagine one would sound. She looks like one, too, even barefoot. Her pretty black curls spill down her back.

I knew Sarah was better off than me. I didn't realize just how much.

I am looking at her mouth. I am thinking about kissing her.

"You bring your books?" she asks. I tap my backpack. We're there to study bio. It's the only class Sarah isn't acing.

She leads the way into her bedroom. The room is huge and has a view of the Woolworth Building. With binoculars you could probably see the Statue of Liberty. There's a teddy bear and a floppy giraffe on the bed.

Compared to the acres of stuffed toys I was expecting it's not too bad. The room's painted blue and white, not pink.

The door to the closet is open. It's not a closet so much as another room. Outside of a department store it contains more clothes than I've ever seen before.

She leads us into a room on the other side of the closet. Her study, I guess. There's a desk, a couch, chairs, a stereo, and lots and lots and lots of books. I didn't realize one person could own so many.

Sarah's bedroom is made up of three different rooms. My entire apartment is made up of four.

"I know," Sarah says. "It's a bit much, isn't it?"

She sits on the couch and crosses her legs. Her skirt rides up a little so that I can see her knees. They're smooth, not ashy like mine. She probably bathes in milk or something. She makes me feel gangly, awkward, ugly. But I still want to kiss her. I wonder why either of them wanted to kiss me. If they do anymore.

I'm pretty sure it's because of Zach.

"How rich are your parents?" I ask, knowing I shouldn't.

"Not that rich," she says. She shrugs. "I mean, they're above average."

Neither me nor Tayshawn says anything.

"Okay, a lot above average but I wouldn't say rich, you know?"

"Damn," I say. "What did you think when you saw my place?"

The walls of our apartment haven't been repainted since before I was born, the paint flakes and chips off. We don't have a living or dining room, the pipes clang so loudly in winter sometimes it's hard to sleep, the hot water shuts off randomly, and water from the upstairs apartment's bathroom seeps through the ceiling even though the super's fixed it a hundred times.

Sarah blushes. "I didn't think anything. I mean, not that I thought *nothing*. I . . . your place is lovely. It's—"

"Shit," I finish for her. "You don't even have to compare it to this place to see that."

"It's not my fault we're rich," Sarah says.

"It's not our fault we aren't," Tayshawn replies, mocking both of us. Though mostly Sarah, I think.

"I'm sorry," I say. Though I'm not. "I didn't realize."

"I'm still me," Sarah says. "With or without money."

I doubt that, but I don't tell her so. Her being rich makes understanding her easier. The way she acts, the way she talks, how she's always dressed right—the dress she wore to the funeral was definitely *not* borrowed from her mother. She might be scared of some things, and girly and all, but there's a certainty about her. She knows she's going to college. She doesn't need a scholarship or student loans. She doesn't worry about any of that.

She's not a wolf either. She's not going to wind up

living the rest of her life on a crappy farm without electricity or hope. Suddenly I want to hurt her.

"Can I use the bathroom?" I ask.

She points to a door I hadn't noticed. I close it behind me.

Her bathroom is four times the size of my bedroom.

HISTORY OF ME

You're wondering why I lie, aren't you?

The shrinks and counselors I've seen over the years have had a million theories, but they boil down to just two:

1) Resentment.

   Of my brother. (Who I made up.)

   Of people with more money than me. (Which is almost everyone. Not just Sarah.)

   Of people with less hair than me. (When I was a hairy little girl. Before the change came.)

   Of people who are smarter than me. (Which doesn't leave many to resent, does it?)

2) Anger.

   At all of the above.

Plus at my parents for loving my imaginary brother more than me. At my father for passing on the family illness. (And various other reasons only shrinks and counselors would come up with.)

Also at all my teachers and all the students.

Really, according to the shrinks, I am angry at everyone ever. Especially them.

I am all anger and resentment all the time.

Not one of them has ever suggested that maybe I lie because the world is better the way I tell it.

AFTER

hen I come out of the bathroom Sarah is still sitting the couch and Tayshawn is in a chair opposite her. As r away as he can manage.

"Nice bathroom," I say. I don't know where to sit. The empty chair is too close to Tayshawn and I can't sit on the couch next to Sarah. I don't want them to think that I want us to do what we did after—during—the funeral. Even though that's exactly what I want. I sit down on the floor. The carpet is soft as fur.

"You don't have to sit there," Sarah says. She pats the couch next to her.

"That's okay," I say. Neither of them is flushed or sweating. They don't have the same fever I do. Is it because I'm a wolf and they're human? Humans don't rut whenever and wherever they want to. But we did before, in the cave in Inwood. What's different now?

Tayshawn coughs. "We all miss Zach," he says.

I turn to stare at him. For once I hadn't been thinking about Zach.

"Yes," Sarah says.

I realize that the only time I haven't missed Zach is when the three of us are together. I look at Tayshawn, legs wide, elbows resting on his knees. On the wall behind him is a framed photo of Sarah as a child. Sarah is cross-legged on the couch, bouncing her fingers on the armrest.

"There's no bringing him back," Sarah says. It's one of those sentences that's been said a hundred times before. I don't know what it means.

"If we did he'd be a weird-ass zombie freak," Tayshawn says. He's smiling but it's not very convincing.

"Ha," Sarah says. Her laugh is less convincing than his smile.

I want to tell them about the white boy and what I have to do. I want to kiss them.

I cross my legs the opposite way to Sarah. I should remind them that we're supposed to be studying. I don't want to be studying.

Sarah and Tayshawn exchange a look and I wonder again if they are seeing each other without me. Tayshawn pushed me away when I kissed him. Maybe because they are together and he was too embarrassed to tell me. On Sunday I left first. Did they keep kissing?

Them together is natural. They look good. It makes sense, too: Zach's girl winding up with Zach's best friend.

"Nothing's ever going to be . . ." Sarah trails off. "I miss him."

"We all do," Tayshawn says.

"Micah?" Sarah asks. "You okay?"

"Yeah," Tayshawn says. "You're kind of bouncing there."

"Huh?" I ask, before I realize that I'm crouched down on my heels rocking back and forth. "Sorry." I can't say *I just want us to make out again*, can I? "It's weird being here. With you two. If Zach weren't dead I wouldn't be. Here, I mean."

"It's true," Tayshawn says. "I've never been here before."

"You came to my birthday party last year," Sarah says.

"Not like this. Not the three of us alone," he says, taking a deep breath. "Are we going to do it again? 'Cause I liked it."

Sarah flushes. I laugh.

"I want to," I say. A shiver of warmth covers my whole body.

"Sarah?" Tayshawn says.

She nods.

We don't move. We've all said yes, but no one's ready to be first.

I stand up, spring up, really. I nod toward the bedroom. "I'm game if you two are."

Then we're on her king-sized bed, teddy and giraffe pushed aside.

It's more awkward and ashamed than it was before. I'm certain this is the last time it will happen, but I don't care, I'm getting what I want. Some of the fire and need that has built up so large in me drains away.

I can face the white boy. Stronger and better now. I can go upstate to the Greats, find out what to do, and then do it.

Sarah and Tayshawn give that to me. It would be greedy to want more.

LIE NUMBER SIX

That didn't happen.

I mean, yes, I went to Sarah's home and, yes, her

apartment is crazy big. Yes, she has a whole room for her clothes. But nothing happened. We studied. We talked about Zach. Cried. Studied some more.

The room was full of everything we didn't do.

We didn't kiss. We didn't touch.

I wanted us to. I think Sarah and Tayshawn, I think they wanted it, too. The air between us burned. I'm not lying about that. We were all in heat.

But Sarah and Tayshawn . . .

I don't know how they did it. Somehow they managed to turn it off. They made it not happen.

No kisses, no touching, no skin. No nothing.

The air did not ignite.

Except here, in my dreams.

———

BEFORE

Besides the last time I saw him, up in the cypress tree, there was one other time I thought of telling Zach about the wolf inside me.

We spent so much time together. Sure, we ran way more than we ever talked, but when we did talk the lies bent my words out of shape, created a wall between us.

I wanted to tell him the truth: I am a wolf.

Zach would have believed me. He knew how fast I run, how strong. He'd seen the residues of the wolf in the human. "What are you?" he'd asked me more than once.

I thought of showing him. Though I never figured out how. Not without scaring him or killing him. I hated the idea of him watching me change.

If Zach had lived, I would have told him.

Eventually.

Zach was good at keeping secrets.

I'd like to be able to tell Tayshawn and Sarah, but there's no way. First, I don't know how they feel about me. Second, however they feel, I don't think we're going to be friends for long. Third, if I tell them the truth and they believe me they will think I killed Zach. Our friendship will be over.

I am afraid of losing them.

The first time I started to tell Zach, we were making out in Tompkins Square Park. I had to be home but we were elongating the good-bye, wrapped around each other on a park bench as far from the dog run as I could get. Sometimes dogs go crazy if I get too near.

Making out in Tompkins Square was stupid of us. It's way too close to home and there's not exactly much cover. But it was after dark and we couldn't keep our hands off each other.

Zach's hands were on my waist under my shirt, his fingers on my bare skin. Mine held his face. We were kissing deep and long, heating up. I felt a stirring inside me. Like, but not like, when I change.

"Zach," I said, pulling away. "I have to—"

"Go," he finished for me. "I know, I know. Just a little bit longer . . ."

"No, not that. I have to tell you something."

"Now?" he asked, kissing me again, pulling me onto his lap.

"Yes, now," I said. He ran his fingers lightly along my flank. I felt it down deep inside me, where the wolf lives. "Oh," I said.

"Mmmm," he murmured, kissing the side of my neck. Warmth spread from flank to neck. My lips buzzed, my toes.

"I'm . . . ," I started, determined to tell him. "I am . . ." I paused, thinking how to phrase it, trying not to be distracted by how warm and good and buzzing I felt. Should I say, *I am a wolf?* Or *I am a werewolf?* Which would sound less crazy? What should I say next to prove I wasn't nuts?

"Micah?" said a voice that sounded just like my mother's. "Is that you?"

I twisted on Zach's lap. Mom and Dad. Right there in Tompkins Square Park.

"What the hell?" my father said.

Zach and me, we jumped up, but we were tangled, his

chin hit my cheekbone, my elbow got him in the chest.
I fell. He fell. We stumbled up and away from each
other. He looked down. I looked at my parents standing
there, glowering.

"I don't know who you are, young man," my father
said, "but you need to leave."

"It's a public park," I said, not sure why I was fighting
them. I was busted.

"Go," my mother said to Zach.

Zach nodded, his head still down. "I'm sorry, ma'am.
I didn't—we didn't . . . I respect—"

"Go *now*," Dad said.

Zach went, looking back at me for half a second, hand
half raised. I smiled back at him.

"Wipe that smile off your face!" Dad yelled.

I tried not to laugh. He'd never said stuff like that
before: "Young man," "Wipe that smile off." It was like
he was quoting from a ye olden days handbook of angry
parenting.

"Are you insane?" Dad asked in a lower tone, aware
now that some of the hipsters and homeless were looking at us, wryly amused. "Why would you take such a
crazy risk?"

He grabbed my arm. I didn't shake him off despite
really wanting to. Mom gave me her most powerful I-am-
disappointed-and-ashamed-of-you look.

"We're going home. We'll talk about this there." Dad

turned on his heel, pulling me along behind him. I kept my eyes down, dragging my feet all the way along Seventh Street.

Home was more haranguing. Lots of words repeated over and over: *trust, dangerous, responsible, disappointed.* They yelled; I listened.

Except for when they demanded to know if we'd had sex and I insisted we hadn't.

That was that. I was grounded.

Zach died the next weekend.

———

LIE NUMBER SEVEN

Me and Zach slept together. Made love. Had sex. Fucked. Explored every inch of each other's bodies.

Not once, many times, lots of times, all the time.

I liked it. He liked it.

Other than running it was what we did most.

We couldn't keep our hands off each other. It was like the pull of magnets, magnets that sparked when contact was made. Not sparked, exploded.

It was worst in school. We had to avoid each other. Sit nowhere near at lunch. Opposite sides of the classroom. The only way I could not look at him was to keep my eyes down. Otherwise it was impossible.

I burned. He burned.

Sometimes in class—even in bio—my concentration was shot. Even when I couldn't see him, I could smell him, which was worse.

There were days I didn't think I'd make it. I'd close my eyes. Imagine pulling him into the janitor's closet. Or worse, leaping across desks, jumping on him, demonstrating the reproductive systems, then and there, in front of Yayeko and the whole class.

Sometimes it would make me sweat, make me damp between my legs. I'd have to run to the bathroom. Stick my head under the cold water faucet. Slap my face. Do anything but think about Zach. Plug my nose with cotton balls so I couldn't smell him.

Every day at school I managed not to touch him, not to look his way was a triumph. It was also a lie. Other than keeping my wolfishness hidden, my biggest lie.

I don't understand how we got away with it for so long. How did no one notice? Except Brandon, and that was only because he saw us.

People are blind.

Same as you, if you believed what I said earlier, that we never made it past first base. How dumb can you be?

About as dumb as everyone at school. When they found out they didn't believe it.

It was a relief to be busted. Except that Zach was dead, so there was nothing to hide.

Now I'm not lying. I lied to my parents, but not to you.

They can't know because I swore to them that I hadn't, that I wouldn't. They were so freaked when they caught me and Zach kissing, so afraid of me fooling around. Afraid that it would unleash the wolf, afraid that I'd get pregnant and make more beasts. Afraid of me.

So I lied. When they caught us I told them that was the only thing we'd done together: kissing, nothing more. And the only time. I told them I was curious. That I wouldn't do it again.

But that's not why I lied to you. Not entirely. I mean, I was in the habit of keeping it hidden: from my parents, from everyone at school, most especially from Sarah.

I wanted you to think that I'm a good girl. Good girls don't kill.

Sex is beastly, animal, out of control. The feeling I get from fucking is not so far from how I feel when I hunt, when I bring down prey. The two are too close. Too intimate. Too likely to get confused. Not by me, by *you*.

I did not kill Zach.

AFTER

"You need to bring him here," Grandmother says. We're out on the porch in rocking chairs. Grandmother has a rug over her legs. Great-Aunt Dorothy is knitting some-thing orange. I'm staring at the trees and trying not to scratch my arm where the new hair has come in. I've timed my visit badly. The place is overrun with wolves. The pull of so many changes is fierce: the hair starts to sprout within three hours of getting there. I can feel my heart beating faster.

Great-Aunt nods. "Get him out of the city. Bring him here. We'll take care of him." The click of her needles takes on an ominous sound.

The packet of birth control pills is in the breast pocket of my shirt. I keep them there when I'm with the Greats and don't want to change. That way Grandmother won't find them when she looks through my stuff. I put my hand over the pocket. Maybe the hormones will soak through the foil and cardboard and cloth into my finger-tips, keep the change at bay.

"Take care of him?" I ask, though I think I under-stand what they're saying.

Grandmother tut-tuts and presses her index finger to her bottom lip. I'm not sure if she's shushing me or tell-ing me not to worry.

"It means he won't be killing any more people," Great-Aunt Dorothy says.

"Not ever," Grandmother says.

"Because you'll kill him?"

Grandmother nods and Great-Aunt clicks her nee-dles louder.

"Good. He deserves to die. How will I get him up here?" I don't even know how to find him.

Grandmother laughs. It's a weird sound. More of a bark really. I'm not sure I've heard her laugh before. "Ask him. He'll follow."

I'm not sure I want him to. I'm relieved they haven't told me to kill him but I'm also angry. Which emotion is stronger? I don't know. What would it be like to kill another human being? I don't want to know. Yet I do. Part of me wants to fuck Zach's killer up.

Can I just leave it to them? The Greats didn't even know Zach and if they had, they don't give a damn about anyone who isn't family, who isn't wolfish.

"We told you," Grandmother says, "that it's dangerous having wolves in the city. We don't belong. None of us belong there."

I don't roll my eyes because this time they're right: if the white boy wasn't in the city he wouldn't have killed Zach. He doesn't belong there. But I'm different: I can control the change.

"Is he *Canis lupus* or *dirus*?" Great-Aunt wants to know.

"*Lupus*, I think. He's scrawny. Not as tall as me."

"That doesn't mean anything," Grandmother objects. "How old is he?"

"I don't know. I think he's my age. Maybe younger."

"Hasn't hit his growth spurt then, has he?" Grandmother tuts at my stupidity. "Besides, *Canis dirus* isn't much bigger than us."

"Teeth are," Great-Aunt says. Her needles click to emphasize her point.

"A bit," Grandmother says, waving Great-Aunt Dorothy's words aside with her hands. "They're slower than us anyhow. Shorter legs. Doesn't matter what size their teeth are. That's why *they're* extinct."

"Except as werewolves," I say.

Grandmother tuts at me for saying the obvious.

"What difference does it make then?" I ask. "Whether he's *dirus* or *lupus*?"

Grandmother and Great-Aunt exchange looks. I'm supposed to already know, or this is information I'm not ready for, or they're tired of talking. It's hard to know which.

Out in the forest one of my kin howls. The too-dense hair on my arms stands on end.

Grandmother tuts again. "That's where you should be," she says. "Not sitting on a rocking chair."

—

AFTER

I don't change, but it's close.

On Sunday, my one non-wolf uncle takes me to the

train station in the horse and buggy. I wear long sleeves and pull my hat down low over my eyes to hide the eyebrows that now meet in the middle, threatening to take over my face. My back is aching and my eyes hurt.

I'm hoping that getting away from the farm, from all the wolves, will reverse the change.

The horses shy away from me when I climb onto the seat. They take coaxing to head into town. I try not to scratch at the coarse hair all over my body. I tell myself it's receding. My heart beats too fast. I ache.

"Coming back in the summer?" my uncle asks.

He's not a talker so the question startles me. "Yes," I say at last. "Always."

Neither of us mentions that if the change doesn't slow soon we'll have to turn the cart around and go back to the farm. He grunts and there's no further conversation.

It takes an hour to get to the station. Not until we're at the fringes of the town can I be sure that the change is unwinding: my heart slows, the aches dull.

My uncle glances at my now normal hands and lets me off at the station. He rides away without waiting to see if the train's late. It is. It always is: on time leaving the city; late, late, late going back.

I'm hungry but I don't have enough money for even a candy bar out of the vending machine. What little I had went on the return ticket up here. Metro-North doesn't come this far upstate, and Amtrak's expensive.

On the train, everyone around me is eating: Mc-Donald's, bags of chips, sushi. The old man next to me has two huge meat sandwiches wrapped in wax paper, oozing mustard and pickles. The smell is sharp in my nostrils. I press my face to the window and watch the Hudson, trying not to think about food, or the white boy, or Zach, or anything else that makes the muscles of my stomach contract. It's not easy. I wish once again that Zach had not died, that my life was where it had been.

By the time I'm back in the city the hair's gone completely, my heart is normal, and the spotting has stopped. Now all I have to do is find the white boy and lure him upstate.

I don't think it will be as easy as the Greats say.

AFTER

I walk home from Penn Station. I wish I could afford to refill my MetroCard or had the energy to run. I'm starving. The train was two hours late and then it was another three back to the city. I'm finding it hard to think about anything other than food, but I force myself to look for traces of the white boy as I head home.

The sooner I find him the sooner he'll be taken care of.

Taken care of. I feel like I'm Mafia. *Cosa Nostra. Lupo Nostro.* Or something.

I can't smell the boy. Will I be able to find him if he doesn't want me to?

The city reeks in ways the farm never does. There are so many scents it's hard to track older odors. Not that the boy's smell is subtle. But I'm looking in places that thousands—hundreds of thousands—of other people have been. Not to mention dogs, squirrels, rats and then closer to the park—horses, and all the smells that go with all those people and animals: urine, shit, vomit, garbage, sewage smells worming their way up from underground. There's also bicycles, cars and taxis and trucks with their gasoline fumes, construction sites that smell of brick, mud, soldered metal, rusting metal, plastic, plaster, sand, cement.

The food smells are the worst: meat grilling, hot dogs exploding under the weight of pickles and mustard and ketchup, fruit rotting, pretzels burning, cotton candy, gum chewed and spit out. My stomach growls so loud it hurts.

I put my hand over my nose, try to breathe out of my mouth. But then stop because I'm *trying* to smell him.

When I unlock the door to our building I haven't caught the faintest whiff of the boy and I'm too hungry to think straight.

What happens if I can't find him?

I can't bear the thought of the white boy not paying for what he did. I think of Grandmother's saying: *Lupus non mordet lupum.* "A wolf does not bite a wolf."

They don't bite, they kill.

BEFORE

There was another time I encountered the white boy. A time I forgot.

I was with Zach. We were making out on a blanket in his secret cave in Inwood.

Yes, I'd been there before the funeral. Yes, I made out there before that time with Sarah and Tayshawn. It had been our special place, mine and Zach's. I didn't like the idea that he'd brought other people—other girls—there. That it wasn't just his and mine.

So I lied.

How many lies is that now? I'm losing track.

But surely it's not so big a lie, really? I don't think I'll include it in the official tally. It was just to Sarah and Tayshawn. And you.

Now I'm telling the truth: me and Zach, we went there, more than once.

I thought it was our place. Uncomfortable, cold and stinky, but ours.

And one time—with Zach's mouth against mine, my track pants pushed halfway down, my T-shirt riding up, my skin tingling from his hands, from the cold, from the heat—one time, my skin contracted, not from cold or desire, but because the white boy was near.

I pulled away, ignoring Zach's complaints, shielded my eyes to look out of the cave. I couldn't see anything, but I knew he was there. The tiny human hairs were now standing up all over my body. I scrambled out of the cave, pulling my pants up, my top down, I could smell something that hadn't been there before.

Zach called to me to come back.

I turned and hissed at him, "Shhh!"

Something was there, someone.

I peered out into the trees and bushes bright with sunshine. Somewhere in the distance a dog barked. The wind made the trees move, leaves and branches rubbing against each other. I could feel someone looking at me, but I could not see them. I recognized the odor, but I could not name it. Not till later—after Zach was dead—did I finally put that smell and the white boy together.

But I think I knew even then that the smell, that the boy, was dangerous.

FAMILY HISTORY

We used to take vacations. Back before I changed for the first time, my parents would try to take a vacation once a year. Nothing fancy. We've never had much money. One year we went to the Jersey Shore and stayed in a friend of Mom's family cottage. It was a bit rundown—her friend apologized for it—but it was about a hundred times bigger than our apartment. I loved it. Loved inhaling the tangy salt of ocean and sand only a few blocks away. When I climbed onto the roof I could see it: vast and blue and flecked with white peaks. None of the gray oiliness of the Hudson and East rivers.

We went swimming every day for a week. Our skin—even Mom's—became warmer and darker and happier. I wish we could have stayed there forever.

Another time, Dad had to review a new top-of-the-line Winnebago. We drove it all the way down to Florida, stopping at every campsite on the way. We couldn't afford Disney World but we drove past signs for it. I was having so much fun out of the city, seeing new places every day, I didn't even mind.

Dad bought me my first cotton candy as a Disney World apology. It was tall and blue and dissolved into sweet chemical acid on my tongue. I ate it slowly, savoring it, wishing I could have cotton candy every day.

We went into the ocean in North Carolina, South Carolina, Georgia, and Florida. It was the same ocean in every state. The same ocean as the Jersey Shore. When I was little, that didn't make any sense to me. It seemed magical.

After I changed there were no more vacations. Not for me. It was the city or the farm or nothing.

I suggested it once. Asked my mom if we could go to France, to where she came from. She gave me such a look, an are-you-crazy-you're-not-going-anywhere-ever look. "We have not the money," is what she said. But what she was thinking is, *How can a wolf travel? What if you forget your pill and start to change on a plane? In a hotel room? Out on the streets of a foreign city?*

No travel for you, Micah. Not ever.

The change has closed down every part of my life.

———

AFTER

It's late when I get home but my parents are awake, both sitting at the kitchen table, looking at me, wanting to talk. I try not to groan.

"How'd it go?" Dad asks, before I have time to dump my backpack or go to the bathroom, or ask—beg—for something to eat.

"Fine," I say.

"Everyone is well?" Mom asks, even though she doesn't care. She doesn't like any of the Wilkins. Nor do they like her. But none of them bothered with the fake politeness of asking after her health.

Their questions make me nervous. This is not about my trip, there's something else. My stomach growls so loudly they must have heard. No food is offered.

"Funny thing," Dad says, "I ran into your biology teacher, Ms. Shoji. She wanted to know how you were doing. I told her and she said something about dogs killing Zachary Rubin. How dreadful it was but what a relief it was to finally know what happened. She thought I already knew."

"Dogs," Mom says. "We are wondering why you didn't mention this fact to us."

I sink down against the fridge, leaning on the backpack between me and it, and close my eyes. My stomach growls even louder. I have a hunger headache. They were bound to find out. I'm lucky they didn't see it in the newspapers. "It wasn't me," I say at last. "It really wasn't."

"Four days, Micah. Four days you were missing."

"You came home barefoot in someone else's clothes," Dad says. "You were torn up."

I know that. Why are they telling me what I already know? "I didn't kill him."

"How do you know?" Dad asks. His eyes are wet. My father rarely cries.

"Because I would remember. I remember all my kills." Dad flinches at the word. Mom looks away, but I push on. "Every single one. I've never killed anything bigger than a deer."

"Deer can be large," Mom observes. Her lips are pressed tight. Her eyes are clear. "Zach was skinny."

"He was six foot four. He weighed a lot more than a deer," I say. I'm not sure that's true. Some of the bucks I've killed could easily have been 170 pounds. "Besides, I've never killed a deer alone. Hilliard always hunts with me. My cousins, too."

"The police say it was dogs. How likely do you think that is, Micah?"

"They'd know if it was a wolf. They'd say!"

My parents are quiet now. The tiny kitchen is full of their disbelief, their sadness, their disappointment. The air reeks of it. I'm not sure I can stand it. If I were my wolf self my fur would be standing on end.

"There's another one," I say at last. "Another wolf. That's why I went up to see the Greats—to tell them about him. To ask them what to do. They told me to bring him up to the farm. I *know* he killed Zach. He's been following me, too. He saw me with Zach. I think . . ." I'm not sure what I think. "I think he killed Zach to get at me. He must have smelled me on Zach or something," I say, before I realize what I've said.

"Smell you on Zachary?" Mom asks. Her tone is even,

but she's angry. Her back held straight. Her lips go thinner still. "Why would Zachary have your smell on him? Unless you have lied to us. Again. That you still see this boy? Kiss this boy? Make love with this boy? After you've told us you do not. That it's only happening once, you say, and that now you're only friends. You lied to us?"

"Zach's dead—"

"Micah," Dad says. "Don't. You need to tell us what happened. Did you change that weekend because you . . ." He pauses, made squeamish by the thought of me having sex.

"I told you. I told you what happened. I forgot," I say. "I forgot my pill. I didn't realize. By the time I was changing it was too late to get home."

"So you hid in Inwood Park?"

I nod.

"You didn't go anywhere near Central Park?" Dad asks. He doesn't believe me.

I shake my head. I'm telling the truth. Why don't they believe me when it matters? Okay, I know why. But can't they think rationally? How would a wolf get from Inwood to Central Park without being noticed? That's almost a *hundred* blocks. It's not possible. I was lucky to get up to Inwood before the change was complete.

"You must stop, Micah," Mom says. "No more lies. If you kill this boy we'll still love you. Nothing changes that. I think always I know this." She's so upset her

English is crumbling. "What you do. I know it, but I can't let myself believe."

"I didn't, Mom! I *didn't*. I could never kill Zach. Not as a human, not as a wolf. I loved him."

"So much that you slept with him, changed, and killed him?" Dad says quietly. I'd almost prefer if he yelled.

"I didn't!"

"Didn't what, Micah?" Dad rubs at his eyes, making the tears that didn't quite fall disappear. "Didn't kill him or didn't sleep with him?"

"Didn't kill him."

I look down at my hands. There's no sign of the wolf in them. They're almost hairless. The fingernails are short and square. My stomach growls so loudly they must hear it in the apartment next door.

"So you slept with him," Dad says. It's not a question.

"Yes," I say softly, addressing my words to the backs of my hands.

"You lied to us," Dad says. "About your relationship with that boy. You knew it was dangerous. You promised us you would be careful. Smart. You were neither, and now he's dead. You killed him."

"I did not! The white boy did!"

"The white boy? Oh, Micah," Dad says. "Don't. We've had enough of your bullshit." My father never swears. "This is what happens . . ." He stops, too full of despair to give me a lecture. This is bigger than that.

"You're going up to the farm. You can't stay here. You're not killing anyone else."

"Dad! I didn't kill him. I didn't. The white boy did. He's a wolf, too. He did it. Not me. You have to believe me."

Dad shakes his head. He's not even looking me in the eye.

"You can't send me upstate. I have to finish school. I've worked my ass off to get this far. I've sent off my college applications. I've—"

"Let's say it is true," my mom says. "That there is this other wolf. It is quite a coincidence, no? That he is changed the same weekend as you?"

"Well," I begin. It *is* a coincidence, I realize.

"The white boy, you say. He is a boy wolf?"

I nod.

"A boy wolf needs a girl wolf near so that he may change? That is how it works, no?"

"Yes," I say.

"This boy wolf? He changes the exact same weekend as you?"

"Oh," I say, realizing. "He changed because I changed."

Mom is right. Without a female around, male wolves don't change. The white boy changed the same time I did. Even though I'm sitting on the floor, I'm dizzy. This means I killed Zach. No. Let there be other wolves. A secret den in the city. Please don't let me have made the white boy change. All because I forgot my pill.

"Whether this white boy wolf exists or no, you must go upstate. You are a wolf," Mom says. "You cannot ever forget this thing that you are. Not ever."

I don't. How is that even possible? It governs everything I do and say. Something they will never understand. "I never forget," I say. "I'll find that boy. I will take him up to the Greats like they said. I'll fix this," I say, even though there is no fixing it. Zach stays dead no matter what I do.

"Even if he exists, that boy is not the one who must go to the farm. You are. Your *grandmère* was right. There is no place for you here. You are too wild for the city. Too much for the city, too much for us." Mom stands up, ducking to avoid the bikes, steps over me, careful to make no contact, and goes into their bedroom, closing the door firmly behind her. My mother has never not kissed me good night before. Not even when . . . not even the last time they were this angry.

Dad is leaning forward, his head in his hands. He's quiet but I'm afraid he's crying.

I get up, open the fridge, and pull out the remains of their dinner: half a chicken. I slip back down to the floor and finish it off, not bothering with knife and fork or napkin or ketchup, eating with my fingers, shoveling the food in so fast I don't even taste it.

Dad looks at me. I can see the disgust. *My daughter eats like an animal*, he's thinking.

I'm not an animal.

I am.

If it weren't for me Zach would be alive.

I can't think about that. I open the fridge, looking for more food. I think I will eat till I puke.

———

LIE NUMBER EIGHT

So, yeah, I was a wolf the weekend Zach was killed.

Yes, that was a lie—yet another one—but not a total lie. I did track Zach in Central Park, did talk to him in the cypress tree, like I said. Just not that day.

There's truth in most of my lies. You can see that, can't you?

You can see, too, why I couldn't tell you? Think about it for more than half a second: back then I wasn't admitting the wolf within me. Once I did admit it, if I'd told you the truth about that weekend—what would you think?

That I killed Zach.

I didn't.

You want to know how I know, don't you?

I can remember what I do when I'm a wolf. Not every

detail, not crystal clear. But hunts, I remember. Food, I remember.

Those four days, hiding in Inwood—*not* Central Park—I remember everything I hunted, everything I ate.

I ate fox, a feral cat, squirrel. Fox tastes god-awful. I remember every foul bite.

I did not eat Zach.

I did not *see* Zach.

Not while I was a wolf.

How could I have killed him?

In Central Park there aren't many places for a wolf to hide. Over the course of four days I'd've been found, locked in a cage at the zoo or something. And then—surprise!—I'd've changed back and they'd have a naked seventeen-year-old girl in a cage.

I couldn't allow that to happen.

But Inwood, Inwood is more wooded. There are caves to hide in, marshland, less people. That's why I headed there when the change started to hit and I knew I wasn't going to make it home.

Yes, I know Zach lived in Inwood but *that's* not why I went there. I'd figured out a long time ago that it was the safest place. Hell, it's probably the *only* place on the island a wolf could hide for four days. The only place that's how it was before white people, before cars, and pollution, and skyscrapers. The biggest and wildest the island has to offer.

I did not see Zach. I did not kill him.

I wouldn't. I *couldn't*.

———

AFTER

Before Dad goes to bed he tells me they're taking me up to the Greats first thing in the morning.

"What about the white boy?" I ask. "He's real. I didn't make him up."

"I don't need this now," Dad says.

"I promised the Greats I'd bring him."

"Stop it, Micah." I know he thinks I'm lying, that the white boy doesn't exist. He thinks I killed Zach. Not indirectly by causing the white boy's change, but directly with my teeth and claws. I think my mom believes the same.

"I didn't—," I begin.

"Shut up, Micah," Dad says. "I don't care, okay? First thing in the morning we take you up to my mother's and you stay there. If this boy actually exists then he's no danger with you gone, is he? Now, go to bed."

"But I—"

"Micah, we are not having a discussion. This is final."

His face is cold, narrowed. He's never looked at me that way before.

I go to my room and shut the door behind me. It's never seemed so small before. The cage is most of it. Christ, I hate that cage. There's no cage up on the farm. There's no life there either.

I could have defied Dad. I am stronger than him. He cannot physically make me obey. But I love him and Mom and I want them to love me. I don't think they do anymore. I think it's a long time since they loved me. I have broken our family. Once they leave me at the farm, will they visit? Or will it be the end?

I slide down to the floor, my back against the door.

How can I make this better? How can I get their love back? How can I keep them from sending me away?

I have to find the white boy, bring him to them, prove that he exists, that he killed Zach, not me. Then they can take him up to the Greats and I can stay. I'll promise never to forget the pill again. In the five years I've been changing, I've only forgotten twice. I can do better than that. Then I can finish high school, go to college, have a life.

I should be exhausted. I'm not. I climb out the window, quiet as I can, raising it the barest fraction, squeezing myself through.

I will find the white boy.

AFTER

I walk around the neighborhood, concentrating on smell—the white boy's smell. I'm torn on whether I want to find him. Taking him to the farm is what he deserves. The Greats'll take care of him.

But what if it's not enough for Mom and Dad? What if even finding him, proving what he did, bringing him to them is not enough, and they still condemn me to the Greats?

I could not stand it.

Can I stay in the city, finish school, get into college without them?

I don't think so.

I could get a job, but it wouldn't be enough to pay for a place, for food, for the pill I must take every single day. Is there some refuge that would take me in? Could I ask Yayeko Shoji to help me?

I hate the white boy. I hate him more than I've ever hated anyone. If I find him now I will kill him. Even though it would make everything worse.

I think about when and where I've seen him before. What did all my sightings of the boy have in common?

I've seen him in Central Park most often. But also down here, not far from my apartment building. That's the where.

When is all times of day, but never at night. It's dark right now. 2:00 a.m.

What else?

I was running. Every time I've seen him I've been running. Except that once at Inwood. But I didn't see him that time, just smelled him.

I take off. Shoot up First Avenue, fast as I can.

At Forty-first and Broadway—weaving my way through the drunken, wobbly crowd, touching no one, not even getting close—the white boy joins me. Comes out of nowhere to run by my side.

I smell him before I see him. Gasp from the reek of it. I doubt he's ever bathed. He's ripe.

My first impulse is wolfish: tear open his belly, watch his innards drop out. But my human nails and teeth aren't strong enough. Also, we are running up Broadway, approaching the park, surrounded by people.

He doesn't smell like prey. He smells like enemy.

My brain almost breaks in the tumble of thoughts. Ideas of what I should say. Why did you? Who are you? It's too much. I don't know where to start. Easier to keep running.

In the park, after hours, breaking the rules again, I run even faster. He keeps pace easily. Wolf. Wolf. Wolf. Wolf. Wolf. Stays with me even when I accelerate on Heartbreak Hill.

The boy doesn't say a word. I start to wonder whether he speaks English.

Yet I don't speak to him.

The boy who killed Zach. How can I run with him?

He's so dirty he probably still has Zach's blood on him. How can his parents let him run around like that? Don't they care?

I look at him out of the corner of my eye; I don't want him to know I am looking. There are scabs on the side of his neck. Though maybe that's just dirt. Food he hasn't washed away.

Bits of Zach?

The anger is building in me again. It never went away. Every stride it builds and builds and builds. If I open my mouth I will yell at him.

I have to speak to him.

"You did something to me," he says as we scream down Heartbreak Hill.

———

HISTORY OF ME

I remember when I was very little, before the hair started covering me, before I knew about the wolf within, I remember wanting to be a cop when I grew up, or a basketball player, or, possibly, a fireman.

I remember having a future.

I remember having friends in preschool and then in

grade school. I remember jump-rope contests. I remember hide 'n' seek. Learning how to juggle. Spelling bees and red rover and dodgeball. I remember not hiding how fast I could run. I remember having tiny secrets that didn't matter—like knowing that Janey liked Cal, that Keisha still had a blankie, and how babies are made.

Before the family illness started showing itself, before Dad and the Greats told me what it was, before I became a wolf.

I remember not being a freak.

Mom and me and Jordan—no, not Jordan, I made him up—being a family without scary family secrets. Without the wolf being at the center of everything we thought and did.

I liked those days. I wish they could come back. I wish—often I wish—that I was not what I am, not who I am. That my father's family were just a bunch of weirdo rednecks. Anything but what they really are.

I liked having a future.

I want it back.

BEFORE

The last time I saw Zach? Like I said, it wasn't up the cypress tree.

It was the Tuesday before he died. I'd felt pissed all day. Pissed with him, with school, with my parents, with the world.

Turns out that's another symptom. One the Greats never mentioned: the feeling that nerves are grinding on nerves, that everything is at right angles and can never work again. I spent the whole day wanting to scream. Definitely a symptom that the change was on its way, but also the way I feel on most days of my existence. It didn't warn me.

"Wanna hang with me late Saturday night?" Zach asked.

I wanted to snarl a reply at him. Instead I said, "Dunno."

He was already telling me the details, where and when. I was full of venom and bile thinking, *He's not listening. I said, "Dunno," not "Yes." He thinks I am so easy that I will do whatever he wants.* Before I could open my mouth to tell him, he'd moved away, making sure no one'd seen us talking.

That's the last time I saw Zach alive.

Not very romantic, was it? I didn't linger for a last look or snatch a final kiss.

I stomped my way into the library. I had a study period. I opened up my bio textbook—straight onto a picture of a wolf—and slammed it shut.

"Micah!" Jennifer the librarian said.

"Sorry," I muttered, shoving my book back into my backpack and hauling out of there. Out of school, too. Couldn't stand it another second. My skin didn't fit. My head hurt. My eyes. Everyone was driving me crazy.

I was deep into my run in Central Park when my spine began to elongate. I staggered, bent double, saw my hairy wrists sticking out of my sleeves, and realized I'd forgotten my pill. It was too late to make it home. I was way up north in the park, practically in Harlem. I sprinted farther north, ran every step of the way to Inwood. By the time I burst into the park I was on all fours and had a tail.

Fuck.

I came out of it—naked and bloody—with no clue where my backpack was, I washed myself as best I could with river water, then went on the prowl for clothes. I was lucky it was the early hours and dark and the streets were empty. I was lucky, too, I was in Inwood, one of the few parts of the island that still has a few houses and backyards and clotheslines.

I stole clothes from one, dressed, and then went to Zach's apartment building and up his fire escape, through his kitchen window—left open specially for me—and into his room.

Only Zach wasn't there.

I lay on his bed, waiting. I fell asleep. Woke up. 3:00 a.m. and he still wasn't there. Slept again.

4:00 a.m. Shit. Weren't his parents coming home that morning? I called his cell from his landline. No answer. Thought about leaving a message. Thought about Sarah finding it.

Then I was out on the streets again. Running all the way to Central Park barefoot.

Yes, when it was closed. I'd done it before. 1:00 a.m. to 6:00 a.m. Those are the best hours to run. I'd even done it with Zach. You have to stick to the less trafficked paths, away from the night patrols. I thought he might be running, and even if he wasn't I needed to stretch out, get rid of all the pent-up waiting energy. Also, I wasn't ready to go home and face my parents. I'd never gone missing before. They'd know what happened. They'd be . . . well, I didn't want to think about how they'd be.

Which is where I found him. It.

Now I know it was him, but I didn't think so then. I didn't even realize it was a body.

Not a human one.

Certainly not Zach's.

I smelled it first. Blood smells salty, thick and metallic, but I didn't only smell blood—it was like a toilet had exploded. Awful, filling my nostrils, making my stomach churn.

I slowed my pace, then I slipped—didn't fall, just skidded a little—stopped running.

There was a lot of blood. It was dark, but light enough to see that and the mangled bits of . . . flesh? Nothing recognizably human. Nothing recognizably anything. There was no face. How can you recognize someone when their face is gone?

I thought I was going to be sick. I slipped again as I turned and ran away. Blood on my bare feet. I wiped them in the grass as I ran.

You want to know why I didn't tell anyone, don't you?

What did I have to tell? I didn't know it was a person. I didn't know what it was. Dumped meat from a restaurant? No, the blood was too fresh. The remains of some freaks' sacrifice of a pig or goat?

Someone else would find it and report it during the hours the park was actually open.

That's what I told myself. Besides, I'm a liar, remember?

I am often in trouble. Mostly for things I have not done.

I can't expect to be believed. I am the girl who cried wolf.

My parents wouldn't believe me. Or if they did, they would think I'd done it.

The cops would believe me.

They'd want to know what was I doing there. I found

the body around 4:30 a.m. The blood smelled fresh. They'd want to know that. It meant he hadn't been dead long. I could have helped their investigation.

They'd want to know what I was doing in the park after hours. How I came to find the body. Me, who knew him. Me, who was his after-hours girlfriend. Such a coincidence! They would think I had something to do with it.

Nothing I could say would convince them otherwise.

But you mean *after*, don't you? Why didn't I report it when I found out Zach was dead and realized what I'd seen?

But I didn't realize. I didn't know it was him until Tayshawn told me about the dogs. When it was too late. When the police already had the autopsy report.

It never once occurred to me to think that mess had once been a person.

That it had once been Zach.

—

HISTORY OF ME

You want to know why I didn't smell him? Why I didn't realize it was Zach? I told you I smelled the blood well enough to know it was fresh. So why didn't I know it was Zach's body?

You're right. I'm a wolf. My sense of smell is excellent. Even when I'm human.

But not when I've just changed back. The wiring's all wrong. This way and that. Sometimes I hear with my fingers. Smell with my ears. That kind of weirdness. Takes hours, sometimes a day, to be normal again.

I'd only just changed back. I got the basics: blood, innards. But not a lot more.

And the memory of the smell didn't stay with me. (Thank God.)

That's why I didn't know.

AFTER

"I did something to you? What do you mean?" I scream at the white boy as we near the bottom of the hill. We keep running. I don't know why I'm not confronting him, wrestling him to the ground, pinning his arms, dragging him to my parents. *See? Here's your killer, not me.*

"You're the same as me," the boy says. He has a strange accent. Not New York. Or maybe it's a speech impediment. He doesn't talk right, whatever it is. "You're just me."

I have an urge to tell him, no, *I* don't reek. But it's true.

We're both wolves. He's not breathing heavy the way Zach would be by now. His stride is too short and his arms are flopping all over the place, but he keeps pace easily.

"It happened after I saw you. Running like me. You did magic on me. Made me into an animal."

He doesn't know what he is?

"It hurt. Your magic hurt so bad. Why'd you do that? You could've warned me."

What do I say? I concentrate on the swing of my arms, on keeping my shoulders down and my knees high.

My head hurts. What about his family? Why haven't they told him what he is?

"Why'd you do it?" he asks.

"I didn't," I say. "The wolf's already in you. Your parents should've told you."

"Got no parents," he says. "Wolf? Is that the animal you magicked me into? Huh. Thought I was a bear."

"I didn't do it to you. There's no magic." No parents? How could he have no parents? "What about your other family?" I ask. "Brothers? Sisters? Grandparents? Aunts?"

"No family. You made me a wolf? I like wolfs."

"Wolves," I say.

In the distance there's a patrol car. I jump the fence and head deeper into the park where cars can't go, enjoying grass under my shoes. Springy, more give. The boy follows, not missing a beat. He's not sweating any more than I am. Just as well. I can't imagine how much worse he'd smell.

"I didn't make you into anything," I repeat, though it's not entirely true. "You were born that way. Comes from your family. Mine are all wolves. That's why I'm one, too."

"That mean you're my family then?"

"Maybe," I say, hoping not.

"You're black. Can't be family."

I groan. I'm starting to think he's simple. How can I explain anything to him? "How old are you?"

"Dunno. Thirteen? Maybe fourteen."

"How can you not know how old you are?" This is impossible. "When you turned into a wolf you killed someone. Did you know that?"

The boy grunts. I'm not sure if it's a yes or a no.

"You killed someone."

"Yeah. Your boy."

I turn my head to watch him. He looks as bad as he smells. Not just dirty. His skin is uneven, blotchy, pocked, sprinkled with zits and blackheads, large-pored. There are scars on his forehead and under his right eye. Maybe his left, too, but I can only see his profile. His teeth are so crowded and crooked they threaten to overwhelm his mouth. They're green.

"My belly hurt," he continues. "It was all angry and hungry. Smelled him first. Knew him 'cause he was with you all the time. I've been following you. I ate him," he says. Some snot dribbles out of his left nostril. "Didn't know I could till I did it."

I lurch to halt and punch the boy in the face with all my might. My hand explodes. "Ow. Fuck."

The boy goes down onto the grass. I kick him hard in the ribs and then again and again. He makes no sound. Like he's been beaten before and knows to keep quiet. I stop. "Fuck."

The look he gives me is wounded but unsurprised. His left eye reddens. It will be black before long. I don't know what he was expecting from me but this wasn't it. I pace in front of him, my hands curled into fists. "You killed my boyfriend. What did you think I was going to do? Kiss you?"

The boy doesn't say anything. He sinks lower, preparing himself for more violence. It makes me wince.

"You live on the streets, don't you?"

He's homeless. A street kid. He's poor. Poorer than poor. He doesn't have *anything*. He's as much poorer than me as I am poorer than Sarah. He has no family. I don't think he's been to school. Or if he has, it was a long time ago. He had no idea he was a wolf until I forgot to take my pill.

This is my fault.

"I hate you," I tell him. "You killed Zach and I will never forgive you for it. Why couldn't you eat a fucking squirrel? A cat or a dog? Hell, even a tourist would have been better. Why'd you have to kill Zach?"

"He smelled good."

No more violence, I tell myself. The Greats will take care of him. I just have to get him upstate. But the white boy didn't know. He didn't know anything. He still doesn't know anything. How can I take him to his death?

Fuck.

He killed Zach. He knew Zach was human and he killed him. This boy has no moral sense. He'll kill again. Taking him to the Greats is a mercy killing.

What's his life worth now? No home, no family, no friends, no nothing.

"Didn't mean it," the boy says. "If I knew how mad you'd get I wouldn't've done it."

I think I'm going to scream. I pace faster.

"Can you turn me back?" he asks. "I'd like to be a wolf again."

I squeeze my fists tighter. I won't hit him again. "What part did you like best?" I can't help asking him. "Killing my boyfriend? Or eating him?"

He ducks his head. Doesn't answer.

If I take him to Mom and Dad they'll know what to do. They'll see that I didn't kill Zach. They'll let me stay. They'll stop looking at me like I'm more beast than human.

The white boy's so beaten, so desperate, he'll do whatever I tell him.

"I'm going to take you somewhere," I tell him.

"No," the boy says firmly. "You're mad at me."

"It's somewhere safe," I tell him.

"Where?" He looks at me warily.

"Upstate. Where you'll turn into a wolf once a month."

"Promise?"

I nod. "There are other wolves there. My relatives. You'll like it."

"Wolfs like you?" he asks.

"Yeah."

"Alright," he says, standing up. "I liked being a wolf. It's better."

Death is better than what he's got.

———

AFTER

It's dawn when I push the white boy into our apartment and slam the door behind us. I shove him past the shoes and coats and into the kitchen. He falls bonelessly to the floor, glaring up at me.

"This isn't—," the boy begins.

"Micah?" Dad calls out from the bedroom, before joining us in the kitchen. Mom behind him. "Where have you been? Who's he?"

"This is him," I say. "Zach's killer."

"Didn't mean to," the boy says.

"*Mon dieu*," Mom says, covering her nose.

There's no getting past the boy in such a tiny kitchen. He's sprawled and sullen, reeking even worse inside than he does outside, with no breeze to mitigate the smell. The three us are crowded into the hallway not wanting to get too close. I wonder if I reek from being so near him the last few hours. My hand hurts and I need a shower.

"Why'd you bring him here?" Dad puts his hand over his nose.

"Because you didn't believe me. Well, here he is: the boy who killed Zach."

All three of us stare at the boy, who pulls his knees to himself. "Was me," he agrees.

"He is a wolf?" Mom asks.

"Only once," the boy says. "I liked it. She says I can be a wolf again. Once a month."

Mom and Dad exchange looks. There's no doubt they believe me now. Maybe they'll let me stay.

"He's disgusting," Dad says. "I'm running a bath."

Our bathtub is barely a half tub. The whole bathroom is tiny. Skinny as the boy is it'll be a tight squeeze.

"Not washing. Don't like water."

"No kidding," I say.

"Come on," Dad says. "I'm cleaning you up. Putting you in fresh clothes."

"Don't like water." He doesn't move.

"I can see that," Dad says. "But wash, you will."

"If you don't go with Dad, we won't take you up to the farm."

"The wolf farm?"

"Yes, the wolf farm. But you have to be clean. Wolves are clean animals."

"Alright," he says, standing, slowly. Mom and I move toward the front door to avoid touching him, trying not to get tangled up in the coats hanging there.

"This way," Dad says, as if there were another way. The boy follows him.

"Should I help?" Mom asks.

Dad shakes his head, leads the boy into the bathroom, closes the door behind him. There's a few seconds of silence, then the boy starts screaming, but it's too loud and angry for me to pick words out. It sounds like water is going everywhere.

"Will Isaiah be alright?" Mom asks. "He won't hurt him, will he?"

I press my ear to the door. Dad's talking soft, trying to soothe the boy, coax him. "Dad's okay." The boy's unhappy but not murderous. "It'll be okay."

"He killed your Zach?" Mom asks. "You are sure?"

I nod.

"He's not slow? He understands?"

"He's slow but he understands. He's like me. You should see him run. No style at all. Totally spastic, but he runs as fast as I do."

"Oh," Mom says.

"Yeah. There's no doubt." I walk the length of the hallway, twisting to get past Mom. It's not very long. I walk from the front door past the coats, the kitchen, the bathroom, my parents' room, mine. Fifteen not-very-big paces. Then back again. Water is trickling out from under the bathroom door. But the yelling's died down. Mom grabs a tea towel and shoves it under the door.

"Where did you find him?"

"He found me. I didn't know, Mom. I didn't know he was like this. A street kid! He had no idea what happened to him. Didn't know he was a wolf."

Mom looks distressed. She puts her hand on my shoulder. It's the first time she's touched me since last night. I am so relieved I almost cry.

"He doesn't have any family to tell him what he is, Mom. He's homeless. I don't think he's had much education. Or food for that matter. Did you see how skinny he is?"

"Yes. He is a wretch. It will be good for him upstate," Mom says. "The Wilkins will help him." She goes into the kitchen. Opens the windows. Then gets out the mop and cleans the floor.

I pace. Now's not the time to tell her what the Greats plan to do with him. Each time I pass the bathroom door, it smells a little less bad. Dad is probably washing away evidence. Zach's blood and DNA from under the boy's fingernails. Not that it matters, because we won't be turning him over to the police. But still. It bothers me.

I am imagining how Zach's blood and DNA got there. A surge of hate sweeps through me.

I can't wait till he's up on the farm meeting the Greats. I can't wait till they tear him apart limb by limb. I hope they let me join in. Werewolves punishing their own. I wonder if there's a special ritual for it. I doubt it. It's not like the Greats have much of a ritual for anything. Stuff just happens the way it's always happened.

I want to make a fuss. I want to celebrate killing the white boy. Let off fireworks. Not that they allow fireworks on the farm. Makes the horses skittish and freaks out my kin. We wolves don't hold much with fire or loud noises. Too often it's gunshots and a bullet in our side.

But he *knew* it was Zach. *Your boy*, he said.

Dad opens the door, nods grimly at me, then closes it behind him before I can peek. "His name is Pete," Dad says, before disappearing into his bedroom.

Pete? It hasn't occurred to me to ask the boy's name. Hasn't occurred to me that he'd *have* one. Dad comes back out with some clothes and a towel, then returns to the bathroom.

If I didn't know better, I'd say Dad was enjoying himself.

I'm not. Nor is Mom, in the kitchen, cleaning.

I wonder what the white boy—what Pete—thinks of all of this.

———

AFTER

Clean, the white boy still looks bad. He's got scabs and scars all over him, and the black eye I gave him is already a lurid mess of greens, blues, and purples. He smiles at me, which only renders him more hideous and makes my heart contract with guilt. How could I have punched someone so beaten down? So pathetic?

Dad inventories Pete's injuries, old and new. His ribs are bandaged as well as Dad could manage. "I think at least one of them is broken," Dad says, and I try not to cringe. "Pete's had a rough time."

No kidding. When we take him upstate it's going to get rougher. But half of me wants him to die. I want my life back. I'm willing for Pete to give his in exchange. He killed Zach; he deserves what the Greats give him.

Dad is on the phone, trying to borrow a car. Mom hands the boy a cold pack. I slouch against the fridge, watching.

"Cold," he says, dropping the pack.

She picks it up. "It's for your eye," she tells him.

"My eye?" he asks. He's sitting at the table under the bikes, where he's eaten practically all the food we have, including four bowls of cereal. He tore into the food worse than I ever have, pulled each plateful close, and hunched over in case we change our minds and snatch it from him. I can't help thinking that this may be his last meal.

He looks at me for confirmation.

"Yes," I tell him. "It's to stop the swelling."

He lets Mom put the pack on his eye.

"'S there more food?" the boy asks.

Mom pours him another bowl of cereal with the last dribble of milk. He plows into it. One hand holding the pack to his eye, the other spooning cereal into his mouth.

The boy's skinnier than I thought. Dad's clothes hang off him like he's made of string and air. He's younger, too. Looks more twelve than fourteen. That might account for how stupid he is. Or it could be all the beatings he's had. Or the lack of food. Brain damage or malnutrition or both. Mom asks him how long since he last ate. He shrugs.

She shakes her head and tuts, sounding for a second like Grandmother. I don't tell her so.

"You are sure you killed Zachary?" she asks, sitting opposite him at the table and giving him her warmest smile.

The boy pauses briefly in his eating, nods. "Was me,"

he says almost cheerfully. A little bit of cereal flies out of his mouth.

Mom discreetly wipes the fleck of cereal from her cheek. I can see she's struggling to comprehend. "Where were you born, Pete?"

"Dunno."

"Where are your parents from?"

"Dunno."

"What happened to them?"

He shrugs.

Mom sighs. "Why are you not in an orphanage? With a foster family?"

"Dunno."

"You live on the streets?"

"Parks, too. Benches. Stoops. Slept in sewers. I can sleep anywhere." He sounds proud of his sleeping skills.

"*Mon dieu.* Does anyone know how you live?"

He looks up. The cereal's all gone. "How'd you mean?"

"Do you have any friends? Anyone who looks after you?"

"Nope. Just me." He's not sad or upset. It's how things are, that's all.

"I cannot believe you live like this!" Mom says, her voice rising. She's plenty upset on the boy's behalf. "With no help or support? Pete, it is so wrong."

The boy shrugs.

Mom takes his plate, ducks her head to avoid the bikes, and washes it in the sink. Her eyes are red.

"When do we go to the farm?" Pete asks.

"As soon as we get a car," she tells him, putting the plate to drain in the rack above the sink.

He nods. At least he doesn't smell so bad now. There's still a funk to him, though. You'd have to take all the layers of his skin off to get rid of it. He may never smell okay, let alone good.

Not that it will matter for much longer.

"Got a car," Dad announces. "I'll be back in half an hour. Be downstairs and ready. I'll call when I'm close."

"Good," Mom says. "Hurry."

Light is streaming in through the windows. I go into my bedroom and take my pill.

———

BEFORE

Sometimes I don't think Zach felt the same way about me that I felt about him. Okay, not sometimes, often. Often I felt like that. We didn't have that long together. That one winter, a little bit of spring. Then I was away for the summer. Then early in the fall he was dead.

He didn't try to contact me once during the summer. Admittedly that was hard. No internet, no phone. I gave him an address for letters—the gas station. But who writes letters anymore?

I wrote him exactly one:

> *Dear Zach,*
>
> *I run every day. I'm not sure how many miles. It's not like we have a real track or anything. I do the dynamic stretching. Knees to my face and that. It's not too hard. I think I'm faster.*
>
> *See you in the fall.*
>
> *Micah*

I didn't send him kisses or love or tell him I missed him. But I did.

That was the longest summer of my life. I wish I could have been a wolf the whole three months. Wolf time was golden. Human time stretched out long and aching and not a word from Zach.

I wish we'd had longer.

I can measure our time together in minutes. Sometimes a week—two even—would go by without seeing him. Glimpses at school, his scent. Nothing real.

He didn't miss me the way I missed him.

He didn't love me the way I loved him.

There was nothing constant about his heart. Not like mine.

———

LIE NUMBER NINE

I do have a brother.

I *did* have a brother.

If only I'd made Jordan up.

He died.

I was twelve. He was ten. It was an accident.

We don't talk about it.

I *can't* think about it.

———

AFTER

It takes Dad considerably longer than half an hour to show up. He's borrowed a car from one of his journalist friends. It's battered and has a top speed of about forty miles. Dad drives. Mom sits beside him. I'm in back with the white boy. I'm along because my parents want me to keep an eye on him. I said no, but Mom and Dad insisted, and as soon as they did the white boy declared that he wouldn't leave without me.

Here I am in a car so small I can hear my parents breathing in the front seat. The windows are down despite the chill because the boy's still a bit too rank. No one's talking. The boy's peering out the window. He's been stuck that way since we left the city and there started to be real countryside.

He's definitely not playing with a full deck.

The farther we are from the city the more fall announces itself. Trees on the side of the highway have turned to flame—gold, red, purple as far as I can see. In the city, trees are still mostly green and lush. Fall's come late. I'm glad. I haven't been looking forward to my first winter without Zach.

"Cows!" the boy announces. "And another one! And another! And another! Five cows!"

At least he can count.

"Seven cows!"

This is going to be the most fun drive ever. Slow and cold with the cow-counting savant to entertain us. Kill me now.

"Eleven cows! Two horses!"

Please don't let him count and name every animal we pass.

"You've never seen a cow before?" Dad says.

"No," the boy replies.

Mom turns from the front seat to look at him. "You have been outside the city before?"

The boy doesn't move from staring out the window. "Don't think so," he says. "Never been in a car before."

That can't be true. "What about a bus?" I ask.

"Nope."

"What about the subway?"

"Yeah," he says. "Used to sleep there. Don't see cows or horses out subway windows."

"No," I say.

"I like cows," he says.

"There are cows on the farm. Four of them."

He turns to look at me, making sure I'm telling the truth. "Really?"

"Yes, really. Cows, horses, pigs, geese, chickens."

He's impressed. "Horses? Can I play with them?" I revise my estimate of his age further downward.

"I don't know about *playing* with them but you can help feed them," I say. Maybe there'll be time before they kill him.

"Cool," he says, turning back to the window. He's reminding me of a puppy. A puppy we are taking to be put down.

———

AFTER

We arrive at the road to the farm well before sunset, which is a first. But then, we don't usually leave before noon or come up on a weekday. We're against traffic the whole way. It's the densest leaf coverage since we left the city. The trees are close to the side of the dirt road, they lean in over it, obscuring the sun. Golds, reds, browns, and purples surround us. The light shining through the leaves sets them ablaze. It is beautiful.

The boy is openmouthed.

If I'm going to tell my parents about what the Greats have planned for the white boy—for Pete—now's the time. We're only about ten minutes from the house, even driving as slow as Dad is. What do I say to them? What do I say to Pete?

What would Zach want me to do? Get vengeance on his killer? Or forgive him?

"Is that a house?" the boy asks. "It's covered in trees." You can see part of the porch and two of the windows. The rest is lost in the foliage.

Dad stops the car. "It is," he says. "My mother's house. I grew up here. I'm sure you'll like it." Because Dad sure didn't.

We all get out as Grandmother and Great-Aunt Dorothy walk down the front steps to meet us. Too late for me to say anything. I am a coward as well as a liar. But the boy's a killer. Zach's dead because of him.

"This is him, then?" my grandmother says, looking at the boy.

My cousins come crowding around. Pete cowers, ready to be struck. The wolfish ones stand back a bit, still scratched up. Yesterday they were wolves. But I can tell they're curious. More even than their human brothers and sisters and cousins.

"How old are you, boy?" Grandmother asks.

"Dunno."

"He told me thirteen or fourteen," I say, "but I think he's younger."

"Could be. He *is* scrawny," Grandmother says. "Come into the house," she says to my parents. "Micah, show the boy around."

"Okay," I say. I'm relieved the Greats will explain what's going to happen to the boy. Better them than me. My mother will try to save him. I'm not sure whether I want her to succeed or not.

"Get back to your chores and lessons," Great-Aunt tells the cousins. They melt away from the boy. He peers back at them, eyes wide. One of the youngest girls waves. He smiles at her.

This is not going to be easy.

"What's her name?" he asks.

"Um," I say, "not sure. I can never keep them all straight."

"I thought you said they were your family?"

"They are. They're my cousins, second cousins, like

that. The old ladies are my grandmother and great-aunt."

"Then why don't you know who's who?"

"I don't spend much time here and there's a lot of them." Also, I don't want to know. I've always kept myself as separate as I can. I belong in the city. I am only ever here temporarily. "And she's not a wolf."

I never wanted to belong on the farm. That's why I hardly talk to my cousins. I don't want to know them.

But I can't avoid knowing the wolves. When we change, we're a pack.

I do not want to be part of a pack with Pete.

"They're really your family?" he asks.

"Yes, they're really my family."

"But they're all white."

I roll my eyes. "You may have noticed that my grandmother's white and my dad's black. It's not that tricky to figure out."

"But none of your cousins are black?"

"No."

"So wolfs aren't all black?"

"Wolves. No. How could they be? You're a wolf. You're white."

"I thought they'd be black like you."

"I'm the only black werewolf I know."

"Huh," the boy says. "How soon will I be a wolf again?"

"In about a month. Give or take."

"Why does it take so long?"

"Only happens once a month. They've all just changed back so you missed it."

"Oh," he says. I can't tell if he's disappointed. His voice is too flat.

"You have to wait," I tell him.

"Can I see the horses?"

I lead him to the stables, wondering what to do. He's so young and stupid. So deprived. This is the biggest adventure of his life. He was excited about seeing a cow, and now about seeing horses. He's never been outside the city before. He's never seen or done anything.

My youngest cousin, Lilly, is mucking out one of the stalls with a spade that's almost bigger than she is. She's a wolf, but young. Her first change is a few years off yet. "This is Pete," I tell her. "Want to introduce him to the horses?"

"Sure," she says. "You're a wolf, too? I never met a wolf that wasn't a Wilkins before."

I leave them to it, running back to the house as fast as I can. I'm going to talk the Greats out of killing him.

———

FAMILY HISTORY

I'd like to tell you I have good memories of Jordan. But it would be a lie. There's not a single one. Everything I told you about him, everything I described? All true.

He was a shit. A selfish, whiny brat. I will never understand why my parents loved him so much.

His death didn't change their love, didn't make them start to love me more.

No, they still celebrated every birthday with an elaborate cake shaped like a dinosaur, because he loved dinosaurs.

Except he didn't. By the time he was six he'd forgotten all about dinosaurs and moved on to pirates. By the time he died it was all about superheroes, especially Batman. If my parents love him so much, why can't they remember that?

One year they had a cake made in the shape of a soccer ball because he'd played soccer. But they'd forgotten that he only played it for half a year and he'd played it badly. Very badly.

There was always cake, whether we could afford it or not. I had to wish my dead brother happy birthday, eat his stupid cake, and pretend to like it.

The anniversary of his death is worse.

They don't wear black. Mom says it would make Jordan too sad. Like Jordan ever noticed what anyone wore.

Instead they dress in bright, happy clothing. They make me do the same. Push me into one of Mom's summer dresses, which are too short and too loose on me. We eat his favorite food: hot dogs, which, at least, are cheap. Then we share our memories of beloved Jordan. Talk about how much we miss him. What we miss most.

I don't miss a single thing, so every year I make up something new. They watch me closely to make sure I mean it. But trust me, I don't lie as outrageously as they do. He did not sing like a bird, he could not play piano or speak French. There was nothing precocious or talented about him.

They love him more dead than they've ever loved me, even if I am the living child.

I know they wish it was the other way around.

———

AFTER

I go in through the back of the house. "Grandmother," I say as I barge into the living room, "you can't kill him."

"Can't kill who?" Grandmother says, dragging her gaze from the fireplace to me.

"Where are my parents?" I ask. They're not there. It's

just Grandmother, Great-Aunt, and Hilliard curled up in front of the fire.

"Can't kill who?" Grandmother repeats her question.

"The boy. His life is miserable," I say, standing between them and the fire. I pace as I talk. "He didn't know what he was doing when he killed Zach. He didn't even know he was a wolf. If it wasn't for me he wouldn't have changed. I did it to him when I forgot my pill. He's got no family. So no one's ever told him anything. He's a stupid, ignorant kid. You can keep him on the farm, can't you? Teach how to be a wolf? He won't kill anyone up here."

"*Lupus non mordet lupum,*" Great-Aunt Dorothy says. She's smiling. She looks like a Hallmark grandmother. White hair in a bun, rosy cheeks. She doesn't have the evil witchy look of Grandmother, but she's just the same.

"I know," I say. "You won't bite him—you'll put him down. But he's not a danger up here. Truly. He loves it here. I mean, he was excited about seeing horses. If you can believe that."

"We don't kill other wolves," Great-Aunt says. "We've never killed other wolves. Not unless they're rabid, or too sick, or the like."

"Only when there's no other way," Grandmother says.

"There's another way for the boy," I say. "Just being up here will change him. He's never had any—"

"Stupid girl," Grandmother interrupts. "We never

said we were going to kill him. Because we're not going to kill him. We need him."

"Wait," I say, stopping mid-stride. "What?"

"He's breeding stock," Great-Aunt says. "A new bloodline. A new *wolf* bloodline. He's gold, Micah. We won't be touching a hair on his head."

"But you said that you'd kill him. You told me you would."

"Didn't say that," Grandmother says.

"Yes, you did!" I can't believe she's lying so brazenly about it. "I asked if you'd kill him and you said *yes*."

"No, I didn't," Grandmother says. "I'm craftier than that. I just moved my head a little. Coulda been yes, coulda been no. Never said word one 'bout killing the boy. Said we'd take care of him and that we will."

"You *lied* to me." I don't know why I'm surprised. Not like I haven't seen them lie before. But it was a *nod*. I saw it clearly. Just because she didn't open her mouth doesn't make it less of a lie. How could they lie to me? If I'd known all along I wouldn't have gone through hell trying to decide what to do. How could they mess with me like that?

But: they're not going to kill him. The white boy gets to live, gets to be a wolf. I'm so relieved I sink to the floor next to Hilliard. I pat his head. His fur is hot from the fire. He shifts, resting his snout on my knee. I scratch behind his ears.

"Supper soon," Great-Aunt says. She gets up, heading for the kitchen.

"We said we'd make sure he never killed a human again," Grandmother tells me. "He won't. Not livestock neither. We'll teach the boy well. Like we taught you and your cousins."

"Do my parents know?" I ask, before remembering that they'd never known the Greats were going to kill him. I never repeated the Greats' lie. "Where are they?"

"Gone."

"Gone where?"

"Back to the city."

I freeze, my hand on Hilliard's head. My parents left without me? They couldn't have. "Why?"

"You'll be living here now," Grandmother says. "You'll be—"

I dash out the front of the house, down the steps to where the car was parked, but now there's only tire tracks in mud. I run down the road as fast as I can. The car's gone. I run until the house is out of sight behind me, and throw myself down on the ground, landing on mud and the mulch of fallen leaves.

My parents have left me here. They know I didn't kill Zach. I found the white boy. I proved it was him, not me. They still left me here.

This isn't about Zach. This is about Jordan.

My parents have destroyed my entire life. Without saying good-bye.

I howl. I weep and wail and scream. Throw mud and golden leaves in the air.

How could they?

———

HISTORY OF ME

I think maybe lying to you about Jordan was one lie too many. (Ten lies too many? A thousand?)

But there was a reason for it.

I wanted all that pain to go away. If I made you believe that he'd never existed, then maybe I could believe it, too. Forget about him. Forget how he died.

It would be easy. We never talk about him, you see. Except for his birthday and the anniversary of his death. But other than those two days it's like Jordan never existed.

I wish he never had. I wish I had invented him. I'd rather Pete was my brother than Jordan. Inventing Pete would be easier than inventing Jordan. He makes more sense.

Not that I invented Pete.

You know what I mean.

Making myself believe that Jordan was imaginary didn't work. I don't think I ever stood a chance. Even dead, he's there all the time. In the way my parents look at me. In the way they don't look at me. In the way they don't trust me.

Or love me.

It was an accident.

Why don't they believe that?

Why don't you?

———

AFTER

I must have fallen asleep. Up all night, and grief wearing me into exhaustion. I wake to the white boy patting my cheek. "Don't cry," he's telling me. "Why are you crying?"

"Because they fucking left me." I wipe my cheeks. I have cried in my sleep. I'm crying still. "Because Zach's dead," I whisper.

"But it's good here."

The boy's cross-legged in the mud beside me. It's dark but I can't tell if that's the dense tree coverage or because the sun has set. Either way it's late in the day and there's no electricity. Not that I care. My life is over. No city, no college, no future. I'll never see Sarah or Tay-shawn again. I might as well be in prison.

If I go home will Mom and Dad take me in?

I don't think so. If I go back to the city I'll have no money, no shelter, no nothing. I'll be a street kid like Pete.

My parents have taken everything away.

"We can be happy here," the boy says. He's patting the top of my head as if I was a dog.

"We?" I ask the boy, wishing my eyes would quit leaking.

"You and me. This is why I found you and you res-cued me. This is the happy part. We belong here."

He's not just stupid, he's insane. I belong here the way a homeless kid like him belongs at the Ritz-Carlton. Not at all.

"I like it here. I like the horses and the other ani-mals. And your cousins. Even though they poke. But when they knock me down they help me back up. They don't hit as hard as you do. There's lots of food. I picked an apple off a tree. Not just one apple. Lots. Ate them, too."

"You're brain damaged."

"When I'm a wolf they're going to teach me how to hunt. I want to be a wolf."

"Don't talk about that. I've seen the results of your hunting."

I sit up. It's cold. The chill runs through my whole body. I am never cold.

"They're going to teach me to ride a horse. How to make fences and fix them. No one's taught me how to do anything before. Not anything good. I like it here."

"You said." I bring my knees up, hug them to my chest. Every part of me is frozen but I don't care.

He leans his head against my shoulder. I almost stroke his hair. I pull my hand away just in time. He killed Zach.

"I'm glad you wolfed me," he says, still leaning on me.

"I told you, I didn't. It's the way you are. Like having brown hair, or big feet, or being tall. It's in your genes."

"I never thought I was people," the boy says. "I didn't belong in the city."

"Not you, too," I say, but he's not listening, he's telling.

"The city's mean. It's people pushing you around. Telling you where you can't go. Fall asleep on a stoop and people yell at you to get off. They yell at you for taking the food they threw away in the trash. Yell at you for being on the same subway car as them. People are all yelling and pushing and worse. Lots worse. It's not like that here because it's not real people—it's wolf people."

"They're not all wolves. Not even half."

"I like it here."

"Yay for you."

"Why don't you like it here? You're a wolf person."
He angles his head to look up at me. Even in the murky
light I can see that the black eye has gotten more lurid.

"Yeah, but I don't want to be. I belong in the city. It's
my home. I want to finish high school," I say, though I
know he'll never understand. "I want to go to college.
I've studied so hard. I sent off my college applications.
I want to study biology. Figure out what I am, how it
works. Map my DNA. These genes we have, you and me.
What are they? What are we? How are we? I want to be
the one to find out. I'm not going to find out anything
stuck here, am I? With a bunch of morons who haven't
made it past the seventh grade. None of my cousins have
been to preschool, let alone college. Half of them can't
even read!" I'm crying again.

"I can't read," says the boy. "Why does a wolf need to
read?"

I don't know what to say to that. I'm still crying. If I
stay on the farm I will lose my mind. I will lose who I am.
"I can't imagine what your life was like."

"Doesn't matter," the boy says. "It's good *now*. I'm
not going to think about how it was."

"Just like that?" I say. "You're going to forget the rest
of your life?"

He nods. "I never remember the bad stuff. But
now it's going to be all good stuff. I can remember

everything from now on. Everything from when I first saw you."

I try not to be angry with him. I substitute despair. He killed Zach after he first saw me. That's one of his treasured memories. I don't ask him about it. I don't want to punch him again.

"Why do you want to go back there?" he asks. "At your school if they knew you was a wolf would they still like you? I bet they don't like you. Not how you are. If you stay here you don't have to be a person. Everyone here knows what you are—a wolf. Like them. They like you because you're a wolf. Here's better."

How could this moron street kid know that? I stare at him. He blinks but doesn't look away. I'm grateful it's getting too dark to see the full glory of the black eye I gave him.

What if he's right? I am a wolf. Back in the city I have to fight what I am every single day. Take pills to keep it at bay. I have to tamp down all my impulses. Not leap at enemies' throats, not jump on the people I desire, not run when I want, not eat when and how I want.

Here I don't have to lie to anyone. I can be the wolf that I am.

I stand up. The boy does, too. He puts his hand in mine. His is smaller and all bones, but his squeeze is firm.

"Promise me you'll stay," the boy says.

I laugh. "They'll look out for you better than I will."
I'm tempted to tell him that he's breeding stock. "I hate
you, remember?"

"Stay."

"Fine," I say, feeling something break inside me. "I'll
stay." I don't have anywhere else to go.

"You promise?"

"Sure," I say. "Why not?"

We head back to the house. It really is dark now. But
our night vision is good—we're wolves, after all. Most
everyone is in bed already. Here on the farm they go to
bed early and rise earlier. Not much else to do once the
light's gone.

Grandmother and Great-Aunt Dorothy are still
awake. Great-Aunt leads the boy away.

Grandmother stands up and stares at me for what
feels like minutes and then, for the first time in my life,
she pulls me into her arms, mud and all, hugging me
hard before pushing me away and kissing my cheeks.
"We love you, child," she says.

She's never said that either. Maybe I do belong here.

It occurs to me that it was not the white boy who was
the puppy being abandoned in the woods, it was me.

AFTER

I wash the mud off in a metal tub in the kitchen. Grandmother heats the water over the wood-and-coal-fueled stove. She doesn't say anything. Hands me soap and a washcloth. Then a towel to dry me and a coarse nightgown that's probably a hundred years old. She dumps my muddy clothes into the tub and starts washing them.

She pats my cheek with her wrinkled, scarred fingers. "We're glad to have you here at last," she says.

"Thank you."

I climb the stairs to the bed I share in the summer. I slide under the covers, pushing the nearest cousin farther in so there's room. She stirs but doesn't wake. I curl inward, holding my knees and resisting the impulse to suck my thumb. Instead I cry as quietly as I can.

I wake up aching and swollen-eyed. I've never cried that much before. I vow never to do it again.

When I crawled into the bed there were two girl cousins in it. Now there's light streaming in through the window and just me. They're all up and working already, but this city girl has slept past dawn. I wonder how long they'll let me get away with that.

My chest feels tight and sore. Like my heart is broken.

My heart *is* broken.

I dress in the clothes I arrived in even though they're still damp. There's a suitcase full of my things but I haven't touched it. It's proof that my parents knew from the outset they were dumping me with the Greats.

They packed that suitcase.

It's their biggest one. They probably crammed everything I own into it. I'm not opening it. I don't want to see what they thought I would want. I'm not wearing any of those clothes. I don't want to see more evidence of how much they do not love or understand me. I'll wear the clothes I came in till they disintegrate.

I don't care that the suitcase is my last link to the city, that Zach's sweater might be in it, his jersey.

My resolution holds until I realize I have to take a pill.

I open the case, relieved to find several months' worth stashed at the bottom. I take one and put the rest of the pill packets in my pockets. I don't trust Grandmother not to find them and get rid of them. It's a miracle she hasn't already. I have no idea how I'm going to get hold of more. In a few months I'll change with the rest of them.

All control of my own body gone.

———

HISTORY OF ME

I'm not sure where I start and where I end. Is the human the real me? Or the wolf?

Every time I change from one to the other I lose bits of myself.

Or all of myself.

I don't know if the cells I start with are the same ones I end up with when I return to being human. Does the wolf-me destroy the human-me? And then does the new human-me destroy the wolf-me? How many Micahs have there been?

How can I know if I'm the same me I was back when I first started changing?

There are very few organs of the same size and dimension in both wolf and human. As I go from one to the other and back again my liver, kidney, eyes, ears change. *Everything* changes. What happens to the human cells when I'm a wolf? Are they hidden or are they gone?

If they're gone, then every time I change I lose more.

I become less me.

I am afraid of changing.

I am afraid of changing back.

———

AFTER

The breakfast is made up of farm produce: eggs, butter, milk, bacon, bread. This is a working farm. Even my littlest cousins lend a hand at churning butter, pulling weevils out of flour. There's wool to be spun, animals to be fed, canning and pickling, meats to be salted. Cleaning, washing, baking. Repairs to be made. I learn over breakfast that two of the barns need their roofs fixed before the first snows hit.

I try to be interested. This is my life now.

The eggs taste like slimy dirt. The bread is heavy and scratchy. It's the worst breakfast I've ever had.

Not that it's breakfast for them. They broke their fast around dawn with bread and cheese and pickles. This is the day's second meal. The one after they've already been hard at work for several hours. About half the family's there: Grandmother, Great-Aunt, an uncle, two aunts, and most of the kids. They eat steady and fast. The rest will come in and grab what's left on their own time.

Pete sits next to me, eating even faster, demolishing three helpings, then reaching across to grab more bacon.

"No," Grandmother says, pulling the plate of rashers away from him. "You're not the only one who needs to eat."

Pete shrinks into the bench.

"There'll be more food," I say. "Two more meals today."

"Really?"

"They eat four times a day."

"Every day?" Pete asks. He doesn't quite believe me, but he wants to. Across the table Lilly and one of her brothers giggle. Pete flushes. He'll have to get used to everyone's ears being as good as his own.

"Every day," I tell him. "Four meals. You'll have to work for them, though."

"I picked apples."

"Ate most of them, too," Grandmother says. "That'll stop."

Lilly waves at Pete and giggles again. Pete can't decide where to look.

I push my plate at him. I've eaten an egg and half a slice of the murky bread, my hunger muted by heartache. Pete inhales what I've left. "It's good," he tells me.

"Micah, clear the plates," Grandmother says, which means the meal is over. Most of my cousins are gone before Grandmother says plates. Not Pete though.

Lilly waves at him again. "More apple picking?" she asks.

Pete mumbles no and starts grabbing some of the plates and cutlery ahead of me. I busy myself stacking the cups. Some of wood, some of clay. All made on the farm.

I look across to Grandmother, who nods. "Slops go in the bucket in the kitchen."

Pete sticks to my side. I guess he wants to make sure I stay like I promised. Today the Greats let him. It's his first day. They'll get tougher on him soon.

After we scrape the plates into the bucket I wash, Pete dries (slowly), and Grandmother puts away. Great-Aunt sits at the kitchen table peeling and coring apples. Pete nudges me and whispers, "See? I didn't eat *all* the apples."

"You ate enough," Grandmother says, taking the now-dry plate from his hands.

Pete jumps and I laugh.

"Wolves," I say, "have really good ears. You might want to remember that."

Pete nods. "Good ears, fast legs, sharp teeth. Like me."

"Because you're a wolf," Grandmother says. "You're strong, too. But you be careful about eating so much. Keep going like you're going and you'll puke it all up."

"Won't."

"Can't fit that much food in such a skinny human. When you're a wolf, eat as much as you can. But you're human for the next few weeks. Got to act like one."

"Why are we wolfs?" Pete asks.

"We come from wolves is all. Most people come from monkeys."

I try not to groan. Then Great-Aunt launches into the tale of the man and the wolf and the deal they made.

Pete believes every word.

I want to say that none of it's true and launch into my theory of horizontal gene transfer, but they won't understand. I doubt any of them knows what a gene is. Pete can't even read. Besides, I don't have any proof. It's an untested hypothesis.

If I stay here I will never get to test it. I might be able to gather more data but what will I do with it?

I can't stay.

I can't stick around till I run out of pills. Till my body is no longer my own.

It doesn't matter what I promised Pete.

I don't care if I have to hitchhike back, or ride a freight train, or walk. I'm going back to the city.

AFTER

But I don't have anywhere to go.

No home, no money, no nothing.

My parents don't want me. They cut and ran without looking back. If my own parents don't want me, who in the city does?

Tayshawn?

I have to laugh. His parents are as broke as mine. Tayshawn's on a full scholarship. There's no way his parents could afford anyone else in the house. Especially not someone who eats as much as I do.

Sarah?

Well, she's rich. Or at least her parents are. But no. I embarrass her. What happened between us embarrasses her. Having me in the house, giving up one of her rooms? Not likely. And if she said yes? I wouldn't be comfortable in a place like that. I'd be afraid of breaking something, doing things the wrong way, saying the wrong thing. I'd never belong there.

Besides, what would I tell them? My parents threw me out because . . . because they don't want a wolf in the house anymore. Oh, yeah, that's right, I'm a wolf. You didn't know? Well, it's like this . . .

I don't think so.

How I could prove it to them? The only convincing proof I have no one wants to see.

My DNA test. The one I never opened. What if there's something there?

But that won't mean a whole lot to Sarah or Tayshawn or their parents.

Then I realize who it would mean something to:

Yayeko Shoji. My biology teacher.

FAMILY HISTORY

My parents stopped loving me long before they dumped me at the Greats'.

Their love was already tempered by the fur I was born with, by the way I run, because those were both signs of what I was going to become.

Then, after my first change at the age of twelve, their love was gone completely.

That was the year Jordan died.

My parents still said they loved me, still kissed me good night, still let me live in their home and eat their food, but it was pretend: they were waiting for the right time to get rid of me.

For five years I lived a shadow life with shadow parents and never knew the difference.

Except that I did.

I just couldn't admit it to myself.

But they never admitted it either. They abandoned me.

Who's the bigger liar?

Me or them?

Isn't lying about love the worst lie? Isn't that worse than anything I've ever done?

HISTORY OF ME

I've told you all the important moments between me and Zach. All the memories I go over again and again and again.

I fear I will wear them out. Break them by thinking of them too long and too often. But maybe doing so is what keeps them fresh and alive.

That first day in the park when he came up and kissed me out of nowhere . . . Me, who he'd never looked at before. Why did he choose me? How'd he know we'd be good together?

Did he know?

Or did he kiss all the girls? Like the princess kissing all those frogs. I was the frog. He made me into a real girl. A human girl.

When I was with him I wasn't a frog, wasn't a wolf. I was me. Micah.

I worry that I will forget Zach. Forget his face. Forget the feel of his lips against mine. His hands on my skin. The feel of us naked and wrapped around each other.

Forget what it was like running by his side, matching strides, breaths, heartbeats.

I'm alive.

He's dead.

He'll always be dead.

I think about joining him.

But I can't.

The wolf inside won't let me. It wants to live. Even without him.

———

AFTER

Lurking outside the school waiting for Yayeko Shoji to leave is not as great a plan as I thought. There's not much cover and I don't want anyone but Yayeko to see me.

I narrowly avoid Brandon spotting me. He slouches out of school with a backpack over one shoulder. Alone, of course. The scowl on his face has spread to the rest of his body. He looks up, and for a moment I think he sees me, across the street, crouched behind a car. Why didn't Pete kill Brandon instead of Zach? But then Brandon turns his gaze back to his feet where it belongs.

I should have disguised myself. Gotten a wig or something. Mom has one. I should have grabbed it along with my DNA result.

I finally opened it. The proof I need. It says the blood I sent in isn't human. Yayeko watched us take blood samples, seal them, and she sent them. She'll understand what the test means: I'm not human.

If I knew where Yayeko lived, I wouldn't have to wait outside school. But she's not listed.

I watch Tayshawn come down the steps, basketball in his hands. He's heading for the court down the block, Will at his heels. I am tempted to join them. Tayshawn wouldn't mind and Will does what Tayshawn says. But I don't, because, well, what would I say?

By four o'clock no more students drift down the front steps, just teachers. A bit before five Yayeko Shoji, lugging a shopping bag overloaded with papers and a heavy backpack, takes the steps. I wonder if the papers are the ones we did on plant systems. I handed mine in last Friday.

I follow her from across the street until she turns onto West Broadway, then I scamper over.

"Yayeko," I say.

She turns and almost drops the shopping bag in her surprise.

"Micah!"

"It's me," I say.

"But your leg. Your face. You're alright!" She puts the bag down.

"Why wouldn't I be?"

"Your parents said there'd been an accident. They said your leg was broken in ten places, your face a mess. I tried to find out which hospital, but they didn't get back to me."

"They won't." I can imagine Dad going into details about the accident, easy for him to imagine since that's what he *wishes* had happened. I wonder if he mustered a tear, let his voice break to be more convincing.

My eyes sting. I am not going to cry in front of Yayeko. "There wasn't any accident. My parents threw me out."

"Threw you out?" Yayeko says. The shock widens her eyes. "But your parents seem so nice."

"Yes. No. It's a long story. Can I tell it to you?" I say, trying not to sound as desperate as I feel. "Do you have time now, I mean?"

"Where are you staying?" Yayeko asks.

"Nowhere. They threw me out. There's nowhere else for me to stay." I realize how pathetic this sounds. I don't want to beg, but that's what I'm doing. "I don't have any money."

"They didn't give you any?"

I shake my head. They hadn't. I searched the suitcase thoroughly, but there was nothing.

Yayeko looks at me closely. She's weighing her options. I'm realizing just what a big deal it is I'm asking for. I have always been her favorite student, but is that enough for her to let me into her life? It could be nothing but trouble. It will be. I concentrate on not crying.

"Yes," she says at last. "But only until we can find somewhere better. Okay?"

I nod, pick up her shopping bag. I try to say *thank you*

even though those words are nowhere near as strong as I need them to be. I'm quiet for a while. I have to wait until the tears stop threatening to leak out. When I can speak, my *thank you* is so quiet Yayeko doesn't hear.

———

AFTER

Yayeko Shoji's apartment is a six-story walk-up in Queens. Like mine, or, rather, like my parents'. But her apartment is bigger, nicer, too. More rooms, and the kitchen/living room is big enough for a couch and two comfy chairs and a big table with no bicycles suspended above it. Yayeko lives with her daughter and her mother, neither of whom are home. Her daughter plays basketball and is at practice. Her mother is a lawyer who works late.

I'm relieved. I don't want to meet new people. I am nervous and wound up enough as it is.

"Would you like some tea?" Yayeko asks, after she's taken off her shoes and put her bags away. She offers me a seat in the kitchen. I sit down. There are trees out the window. They're still mostly green.

"Yes," I say. "No, not really. Do you have coffee? No, that's not a good idea." I stand up, walk around the kitchen. "Maybe water?"

"Water then. Are you okay, Micah? I'm sorry. Of course you're not. Are you ready to tell me what's going on?"

"Yes. But it's hard, Yayeko. I don't know where to start and there are so many questions you'll ask. I think I should just show you." I pull the test results out of my pocket, unfold it, and hand it to her.

"Your DNA test?"

I nod.

She opens it, pulls the report out, reads, flips pages.

"You see?" I say.

Yayeko looks at me. "Your test was invalid. The blood you sent in wasn't human."

"The blood *I* sent in? You were there when we all took the test. You sent our tests off. That was *my* blood. It says my blood is animal. That's what it proves." I'm pacing.

"Invalid results are common. What are you trying to prove, Micah?"

"I'm a wolf."

Yayeko doesn't say anything. She doesn't bow down before my scientific proof. This is not going as I planned.

"Not all the time," I say. "Obviously. When I get my period, I change into a wolf. Only I don't since I started taking the pill all the time, like you said to. But it's not really because of how bad my period is. It's to stop me changing. Whatever triggers the change—it has to do with hormones because birth control pills stop it."

"You're taking hormones continuously and there's nothing wrong with your menstrual cycle?" Yayeko's voice gets louder. "You're only seventeen!"

"I'm not—"

"You lied to me. I can't believe . . ." She pauses. She's not looking at me anymore.

"I didn't! There *is* something wrong with my periods! I turn into a wolf!" Now I'm shouting.

Yayeko puts her hand up. "There's nothing wrong with being a girl, Micah."

"What?" I'm spluttering. I sit down. "Of course there isn't. I didn't say there was."

"I remember when you pretended to be a boy, Micah."

Yayeko keeps saying my name. She doesn't usually.

"Micah, I know things have been hard for you, but you don't have to take it out on your own body. You have to stop suppressing the girl parts of yourself. Is that why you keep your hair so short, Micah? Why you never wear skirts or dresses? Why you don't have any girl-friends?"

"No!" I scream. Yayeko moves back in her chair. "Sorry," I say quickly. "My hair's short because it's easier—I'm *not* trying to be a boy. I'm a wolf."

"And what's more masculine than a wolf?"

I groan. She's never going to believe me. "I don't know. Lots of things! Half of all wolves are female!"

"Micah," she says, "you're not a wolf. Rejecting your own body isn't the answer."

"I'm not!" I jump up, knocking my chair over. It clatters loud on the tiled floor. Yayeko winces. "Sorry," I say, righting the chair. "I'm not rejecting my body or being a girl or anything like that. I'm trying to tell you the truth."

As soon as I say it I know I shouldn't have. Yayeko looks at me with such sadness I know there's no hope for me here. I'm a liar, even when I tell the truth.

"Micah, taking a pill every day is not going to turn you into a boy. It's not going to make you into someone you're not. You're seventeen years old. Who knows what all those hormones are doing to you? Elevating your risk of stroke, of some cancers. When I talked to your mother I thought you had a problem with your body, but now you're telling me this is in your mind . . ."

My *mind*? She's saying that I'm crazy.

"It's not good for you, Micah. It's not helping. You're overwrought," she says softly, like she's soothing a small child.

I'm calm.

"I think maybe you should lie down."

I nod, realizing how hopeless this is. The cotton curtains at the window move slightly in the breeze. Light floods in, golden fall light. The plates and glasses drying by the sink glisten. It's a beautiful, sunny, normal kitchen. My life doesn't seem real in this kitchen. It makes me feel as if I'm lying.

"I'm a wolf," I say again. I can't help myself. I've finally told the truth and gotten . . . this.

"I'm a scientist, Micah."

"I can prove it. Send my blood to another lab—"

"You believe you're a werewolf." Yayeko's voice is flat. She thinks she understands why my parents threw me out. I have to convince her otherwise.

"I am a wolf, Yayeko. Go ask my parents to let you into my bedroom. There's a cage. A big metal cage with a cloth over it so it looks like a desk. It's the biggest thing in my room."

"A cage? Micah, what are you talking about?"

I don't even try. Mom and Dad would never let her in, never show her.

"Is this because Zach was killed by dogs?" Yayeko asks.

"No!"

"Do you think you did it? This is guilt about your boyfriend's death, isn't it?"

"He wasn't my boyfriend," I say automatically. "I didn't kill him. This is not about Zach. This is about who I am. What I am. I know it sounds . . . I know how it sounds. That's why I've never told anyone. But I can prove it to you."

Yayeko looks at me. I think she's scared, but not because I'm a wolf.

———

HISTORY OF ME

Telling the truth gives you strength.

Telling Yayeko gave me strength. Even though she didn't believe me it made me feel more real, more like someone.

I used to think I was nothing: not black, not white; not a girl, not a boy; not human, not a wolf. Not dangerous, but not exactly safe. Not crazy, but not entirely sane.

I felt like nothing at all.

I thought that half of everything added up to nothing. I was a nonperson who belonged nowhere. Not in the city, not with the Greats.

I have never known what I was. If I'm not completely any one thing, then what am I? Who am I? Something in between?

Or nothing?

I don't think that now: half of everything is something, not nothing.

Lots of somethings.

AFTER

This is what I thought would happen. This is what could have happened. This is what *did* happen.

We go to a track at the local middle school where Yayeko's daughter is a member of the girls' basketball team. Yayeko talks to the track team's coach. He's thin and lean-muscled like a marathon runner. A silver whistle bounces at his chest when he moves. I don't know what she says but he agrees to let me race with his sprinters. A hundred-meter sprint.

They line up, putting their feet in the blocks. They are all smaller than me. Except for one boy who is muscle-heavy and tall for a fourteen-year-old.

I have never raced before. Never put my feet in blocks. I glance at them, copy what they do. Place my hands precisely on the line just as they do. The muscly boy notices and grins. He thinks he's about to blast me. I know better.

When their coach blows his whistle I stumble, but then I find my balance, lift my knees high, pump my elbows. I do everything Zach taught me. The track is springy, the give helps propel me along. I run faster than I ever have before. I pass the other sprinters. Easy. There's a hum of air past my ears. I turn with the track. The world blurs. It feels so good that I'm long past the finish line before I stop.

I jog up to Yayeko and the coach. They're staring at me.

"Holy shit, girl," the muscly boy says. He's staring at me, too. So are all the runners. Their mouths are open. All set to catch flies, Grandmother would say.

The coach looks at his stopwatch, then at me, then at the stopwatch again. The whistle around his neck bounces with every twitch. "Just over eight and a half seconds," he says at last. "I must have made a mistake."

I have beaten the men's world record. Crushed it. I grin at Yayeko. She is ashen.

"We need to do it again," the coach says.

I laugh. "Wanna see me run a mile?"

HISTORY OF ME

Maybe it was ten seconds?

I'm dizzy.

So many lies.

I thought I'd done better than this.

What number lie is this? Eight? Nine? Ten? I can't even figure out how to count them anymore.

The fabric of my life unravels. Is anything I've said true?

It's cold in here. Dark, too. No windows.

My grip slips. The cogs grind. Do I know anything that's true?

Actual real genuine true truth.

Is there anything at all?

I'm a wolf.

A wolf. All the way down to the marrow of my bones. Every cell. Every fiber.

Wolf=me.

That's all I've got.

————

AFTER

I do know what's real and what's not.

I did run on that track. I did prove what I am. But not the way I said.

Here's how it really happened.

Yayeko does not believe me. Though she pretends she does. Or at least she lets me stay. She introduces me to her daughter, who is fourteen years old and wary. Megan holds a basketball behind her back and stays in the doorway, her hair falling over her eyes. She's short. Shorter than Yayeko. Point guard.

"Wanna shoot some outside?" I ask. I noticed a netless hoop on the side of the apartment building on our way here.

The girl's still looking down.

"Answer her, Megan."

Megan mumbles.

Yayeko's mother arrives, pulling a briefcase on wheels through the door, dressed in a suit, tiny and elegant and frostily polite. I smile. She smiles. She makes me feel oversized and badly designed. We eat Lebanese delivery. After, I wash. Yayeko's mother dries. As soon as the dishes are done she disappears into her room, as Megan has long since disappeared into her own.

From Yayeko's room I hear phone calls. First she calls Mom and Dad. Her side of the conversation is sparse. She must be talking to Dad. He doesn't want to hear what she has to say. I hear Yayeko straining not to raise her voice. Then the call's over. I wonder what Dad said. "Keep that monster away from me!" Or worse.

The next call isn't short. Nor the one after. No one wants to take me in.

Yayeko comes back into the kitchen, blinks at me, sits at the table opposite.

I can't imagine this working.

She talks about making the couch into a bed, wonders about whether I should go back to school. I'm all paid up, after all. She prattles on like this and I nod and grunt and think about whether I should go back to the farm.

Then her tone changes. "There's nothing wrong with being a girl, Micah. There really isn't."

"This again," I think, but I don't say it.

"You need to accept who you are."

She's right, but not the way she thinks she is.

"I don't want to be a boy," I tell her. "Honest."

I don't know what Yayeko is thinking, not till later. But I can tell you now: while she talks about my denying my femininity, she's thinking about substituting sugar pills for my real ones, which she does.

On the third day in her home, I change.

AFTER

It's 5:00 a.m. and I wake out of a dream of forest and deer. I'm flushed and sweating and I know.

I've thrown off the blanket. There's spotting on the sheets.

I'm itchy, I'm worse than itchy, it's like my skin is trying to tear itself from my flesh. Coarse hair has sprouted across my arms, my back, my everywhere. My head throbs, my eyes. Everything blurs. My muscles ache, my bones. My teeth shift, get bigger, move. My jaw is breaking.

I roll off the couch, land heavily on the floor. The shudder goes through the apartment.

I hear stirring. Yayeko, her daughter, Megan, her mother. Their breathing hurts my ears. My hands and feet slip on the floor because they're not hands and feet anymore: paws, claws.

I'm crouching, my backbone ripples, lengthens. There's howling. I think it's me.

Smells flood me. Human smells: salt, sweat, meat, blood, fear.

I smell prey.

Lots of it.

I'm always hungry after the change.

HISTORY OF ME

My first memory is of looking into the eyes of a wolf. They were gigantic and blue. I was small enough that when the wolf looked at me, sniffed at me, and then licked me, it was all I could see. I stared up into those wolf eyes.

Except it wasn't a wolf, it was a husky. Owned by the old couple who used to live next door.

I remember that I liked its smell. I remember that it smelled like home to me. I couldn't have been more than a baby. Later I asked. My parents told me that the old couple and their dog moved away before Jordan was born. Before I was two. "So cruel," Mom said. "Keeping such a big dog in so small a space."

I wonder if the wolf in that dog could see the wolf in me?

It accepted me without question. Let me pull its tail, lean against its belly, and fall asleep.

Wolves don't lie. Nor do their dog relations. We recognize each other.

I didn't feel that at home again until I met Zach.

But there was no wolf in him.

————

AFTER

I smell blood moving in the veins of the tallest one. I smell it in the other two, hiding behind salt, water, and fear. Their fear smells delicious. It's the prey smell.

I move toward them, growling. I am hungry; saliva drips over my teeth, down my jaw. The smaller one backs away. The old one moves with her. Their movements are slow and awkward. Even without kin here, this is an easy hunt. But I wish Hilliard could see me corralling them.

The tallest one takes a step toward me. She does not smell like fear.

The young one moves again.

I leap.

But the tall one moves between me and my prey. I land on her, pushing her to the floor, my teeth bared.

The small one and the old one yelp and whine. I swipe a paw and knock the old one over. She lands hard and is quiet. I smell urine. The young one caterwauls as if I've already gutted her. I tense to leap again.

But the tall one is looking up at me, low sounds vibrating in her throat.

I know those sounds.

I turn back to the little one. I'm hungry and she's whining at me to eat her.

The tallest one reaches up and touches the fur around my neck, she digs her fingers in, pulls my gaze back to her. My saliva drips on her face.

Her low sounds continue, unwavering and steady and sure. "Micah," she is saying. Over and over again.

My name.

"Micah," Yayeko says.

I'm hungry. I'm a wolf.

"Micah, Micah, Micah, Micah, Micah, Micah, Micah."

"Micah's a wolf," I want to tell her. But wolves can't talk.

Megan is leaning over her grandmother, crying.

"Micah," Yayeko says again and again. "Micah."

Her words are making me sleepier than I am hungry.

I rest my snout on my paws, remembering what it's like to have fingers.

———

AFTER

Yayeko believes me now.

She wants to talk to people at the Center for Genomics and Systems Biology at NYU. She studied there and a friend of hers works there. She has another friend in the sports science lab at Fordham. They could chart just how far outside the limits of human I am.

I'm not sure.

Wolfishness isn't my secret. It's the whole family's. Grandmother and Great-Aunt would eat anyone who tried to take their blood. They don't believe in science.

Or civilization.

They don't hold with outsiders. They don't want anyone to know what they are. Hell, *they* don't want to know what they are, or how werewolfism works.

But I want to know.

If I do more tests and they prove what we know they will, Yayeko thinks they'll get funding to study me. It could pay my college fees. I'd be someone's research project, a paid lab rat.

If I let them test me.

If I show them what I am.

But what kind of life will that be? I'll be a bigger freak than ever.

There are scholarships for running. Zach once asked me about it. The only thing stopping me was Dad telling me to hide my wolfishness. But I can tone it down: I can run fast enough for a scholarship, but not so fast I scare them.

I have choices.

This one is easy: I can't betray my family, my *real* family—the Greats, everyone up on the farm. I don't want Pete to lose his new home.

I'll go to school. A good school with a strong track program and a good biology department. I'll find out what I am.

LIE NUMBER TEN

This one's more of an omission than a lie. I don't know how to count it: is it just one omission or many? How many omissions add up to a lie?

I didn't mention all the reporters. I didn't mention what it was like going to school past a throng of press, questions screamed, cameras in my face. My photo in the paper. Tayshawn's. Sarah's.

And Zach's, of course. Almost every day. His parents started getting love letters from strangers. Truckloads of them. Love letters to a dead boy from people who never knew him. That's much sicker than anything I did, isn't it?

Reporters followed me to and from school.

People I didn't know pointed at me and whispered.

My parents had to get rid of their landline. It's another reason they were so determined to send me upstate. The reporters never found the farm. No one ever found it.

And the trial.

The trial was worst of all.

You're wondering why I didn't tell you about that?

It was a distraction. Doesn't add to the real story. Which is me and Zach and my wolfishness.

Yayeko Shoji understood—*understands*, I mean.

That's why she visits me so often.

———

THE TRUTH OF ME

The apartment is small. One tiny room. The kitchen is along one wall, the bed along another, and a desk and a bookshelf along the third. There's a view of a park, and no cage disguised as a desk.

I'm not in the city anymore, but it's a good school in a good town, and I have a full ride.

Running, just like Zach said. I never run top speed. Not when anyone's looking. I don't have to.

The hormones I use are more precise than my pills ever were. I inject them once every three months. No more fear of forgetting to take my pill. I visit the Greats, even when everyone is changed, without the faintest itching of my palms. I told Grandmother and Great-Aunt Dorothy about my research. They say they're proud of me, especially Grandmother, but they wish I would stay on the farm.

The white boy, Pete, is always pleased to see me. He's learned how to smile.

He's changed. Taller, healthier, there's flesh over his bones, not just skin.

I haven't talked to my parents since the day they abandoned me. My mom writes me letters via the Greats. I don't write back.

I refuse their visits. That's a power left to me.

I saw Dad once, watching me run. I didn't show that I

saw. He looked older, more gray, and his face more gaunt. I wonder if I did that to him.

I'm not ready for my parents. I don't know when I will be. Maybe never.

Tayshawn and me stay in touch. He made it into MIT. He wants to make robots. Sarah went to Harvard. I haven't seen her since graduation. She doesn't write.

I have friends here. Other runners and a few from my classes. But they don't know who or what I am.

So, yeah, I'm still lying, but never to Yayeko, not to the Greats, and not to Pete.

It's a start.

___

PROMISE FULFILLED

So I did it. I told you the truth, the whole truth, and nothing but the truth. Like I said I would. Are you proud of me?

You should be.

Though I suspect you're not.

I suspect you're muttering to yourself, "Werewolves? Really? She expects me to believe in *werewolves*?"

You think my happy ending is too much. Too

unlikely. A girl who runs so fast she breaks world records—*men's* world records? Without any training. You don't believe that either, do you?

You're insulted I think you're so gullible that you'll believe such outrageous lies. You were never fooled. You can read between the lines, pull away the werewolf bullshit, and see what's left.

You don't think it's the pretty picture Micah the liar painted.

You think you know what really happened, who I really am, what I *really* did.

You think I did it *twice*. Maybe more. Five times?

You don't believe in my teeth and claws. You believe in my hands, in my knife. You don't think I wrote this from a cozy little apartment—you think it was composed from a cold, padded cell.

But you're wrong.

I didn't. Not Jordan. Not Zach. And certainly not Yayeko and her daughter and her mom. Yayeko saved me. Why would I kill her?

Besides I told you often enough: werewolves don't kill people. You should *listen* to what I say.

Everything I told you is true: high school, the farm, the Greats, the wolves, the white boy, my scholarship—everything.

Most especially Zach.

I loved him so much. Every fiber, every tooth, every

bone. I could never hurt him. Every minute of every day I ache for him.

That is my life. The beginning and end of it.

Would I lie to you?

ACKNOWLEDGMENTS

Jill Grinberg believed in this book even when it was a tiny kernel of an idea that I was too scared to write because I didn't think I was good enough. She thought I was, and pushed when I most needed pushing. *Liar* was much easier to write knowing I was in such excellent hands. Thanks to everyone at Jill's agency, Grinberg Literary: Cheryl Pientka, Laura Ross, and Kirsten Wolf. You're all worth your weight in gold.

My Australian and U.S. publishers are the best in the universe. Love and thanks to everyone at Allen & Unwin and Bloomsbury, especially my fabulous editors, Melanie Cecka (Bloomsbury) and Jodie Webster (Allen & Unwin). This book would not have found its way into your hands without the hard work of the following people: Caroline Abbey, Jackie Aitken, Liz Bray, Beth Eller, Katie Fee, Luke Frost, Anne Hellman, Bruno Herfst,

Julia Imogen, Margaret Miller, Kevin Peters, Hilary Reynolds, Deb Shapiro, Chris Sims, Sarah Tran, Erica Wagner, Melissa Weisberg, and too many others to name. Thank you!

Liar had many first readers: Holly Black, Gwenda Bond, Coe Booth, Libba Bray, Cassandra Clare, Alaya Johnson, Maureen Johnson, Jan Larbalestier, Karen Meisner, Maude Perez-Simon, Diana Peterfreund, Carrie Ryan, Robin Wasserman, Scott Westerfeld, Lili Wilkinson, and Doselle Young. Thank you so much for all your comments and continued advice throughout the writing process. You're all amazing. Thanks, too, for catching so many of the Australianisms!

Extra big thanks to Karen Joy Fowler for showing me how to fix Part Three.

This book was written using Scrivener, a brilliant and indispensable piece of writing software by Keith Blount, which allowed me to write *Liar* as though it were a jigsaw puzzle. Without Scrivener, this book would most likely not exist.

I had a great deal of help with the research for this book. Any mistakes, of course, are mine. Guarina Lopez's assistance with research across many areas was indispensable, and I made frequent use of her reference photos. Lisa Herb and Peter Zahler helped enormously with my descriptions of the flora and fauna of upstate New York. The language Micah uses to describe her favorite bird calls was influenced by Peter's. Coe Booth and Alaya Johnson were my hair advisors. Maud and Luis Pérez-Simon helped me with Micah's mum's French. Marvin Ward taught me about running techniques. Rebecca Skloot helped me understand DNA testing. I am aware that cheek swab saliva testing is the most common method these days, but blood is more dramatic. Plus, Micah's a liar, remember? It probably was a cheek swab saliva test. I mean, if she did the test at all.

There were many inspirations for this book. The song "Why Do I Lie?" by Luscious Jackson was particularly important. I listened to it many, many times during the writing. So, too, was a long conversation I had with John Green on the subject of lying, which you can find here: http://justinelarbalestier.com/blog/2006/09/21/john-green-and-the-art-of-lying/. Conversations with Chantal Bourgault over the years about her doctoral research also had a huge impact on this book.

Charles Ardai and Sarah Weinman very kindly gave me a great deal of advice about how the mystery book world works.

Thanks also to Melissa A. Calderone for giving me secret information.

I am a writer who does not thrive on being alone. In addition to everyone already mentioned, conversations with the following wonderful people had an impact on this book: John Bern, Niki Bern, Deborah Biancotti,

Tempest Bradford, Kate Crawford, Margaret Crocker, Bo Daley, Sarah Dollard, Adrian Hobbs, Emily Jenkins, Ellen Kushner, Yanni Kuznia, Margo Lanagan, Jennifer Laughran, Stephanie Leary, Lauren McLaughlin, Jeannie Messer, Jaclyn Moriarty, Garth Nix, Olivia Rousset, Sarah Rees-Brennan, Ben Rosenbaum, John Scalzi, Delia Sherman, Cat Sparks, Micole Sudberg, and Edwina Throsby.

Lastly and always, thank you to my wonderful family, John Bern, Niki Bern, Jan Larbalestier, and Scott Westerfeld.